THE KITTEN TRAP

ANNETTE MORI

Also by Annette Mori

Single Books
The Love Demand
Compound Interest
Georgetown Glen
Artist Free Zone
Disconnected
The Others
Sculpting Her Heart
One Shot at Love
The Panty Thief
Pleasure Workers TWC2
A Window to Love
The Book Witch
The Book Addict
The Dream Catcher
Unconventional Lovers
Captivated
The Termination
The Review
The Thanksgiving Baby Caper
The Ultimate Betrayal
Locked Inside
Out of This World
Asset Management
The Incredibly True Adventure of Two Elves in Love
(Affinity 2014 Christmas Collection)

Love Forever, Live Forever
The True Story of Valentine's Day
Vampire Pussy...Cat
Nicky's Christmas Miracle X3
(It's in Her Kiss, Affinity's Charity Anthology)
Donner Junior Saves the Day

Series
San Diego Series
Undercover Love
Politics of Love
Love Bonds

The Next Generation Series
The Next Generation Book 1
Love Hacks Book 2
Love Sins Book 3

Co-authored
The Organization with Erin O'Reilly

Co-authored with Ali Spooner

Humbug
Heart Strings Attached- TWC3
Free to Love
Trouble in Paradise -TWC4

THE KITTEN TRAP

ANNETTE MORI

Affinity
Rainbow Publications

2025

The Kitten Trap
© 2025 by Annette Mori

Affinity E-Book Press NZ LTD.
Canterbury, New Zealand

Edition First

ISBN: 978-1-991357-04-5 (paperback)

Editor: A Koenig
Proof Editor: S Lee
Cover Design: Irish Dragon Designs
Production Design: Affinity Publication Services

ACKNOWLEDGMENTS

A huge thank you to Ali Spooner, who is my only beta reader at this time. I would also like to express my gratitude to Affinity Rainbow Publications—JM Dragon and Nancy Kaufman—who continue to provide feedback to tighten up manuscripts that need help and publish my unconventional work. I am eternally grateful for the opportunities they give me to let my stories see the light of day. Thanks to Angie for her magic as the final editor to further tighten the story. She is a delight to work with. Inevitably, those pesky errors slip through, and I am thankful that the final proof editor, Sue Lee, caught those before the book went to print. Thanks to Nancy Kaufman for the final cover. A huge thanks to all the other readers and fellow writers who have sent personal emails, written reviews, and posted nice things on Facebook (you know who you are). The Affinity authors are an incredibly supportive group and often share posts or send words of encouragement. Finally, my wife, Jody, continues her support even when it interferes with our time.

DEDICATION

For all the animal lovers, especially cat owners, who adopt or care for feral cats that need our love.

TABLE OF CONTENTS

PROLOGUE

Midnight heard the murmurs well before she laid eyes on the two women who'd entered the crowded room. "Lesbians." The whispers traveled to their cage at the end faster than a freight train barreling down the tracks. Everyone knew that the gold standard for adoption was lesbians. The older cats talked about it all the time. If there was an adoption pecking order, it went something like, lesbians, single women, gay men, young couples, families without other pets, and finally, as a last resort, families with young children.

The large room with the bleak white walls that had seen better days, housed rows of large cages. To Midnight, this wasn't the worst place to live, but perhaps not the best either. At least they separated the noisy dogs from the cats. They stacked cages on top of one another, and when the cats weren't napping, which admittedly was often, it could get very noisy. The overworked staff tried to keep up with cleaning out the litter boxes, but with that many cats and kittens, frankly, the place smelled. Midnight licked her paw, the kitten version of trying to remove that distasteful aroma. She'd had to use that nasty box two minutes ago.

Still, if Midnight and her twin sister, Onyx, weren't adopted soon, they'd undoubtedly dump more kittens into their cage, making it overcrowded and unpleasant. Her littermates, Ginger, Tux, and Sebastian, had taunted her and Onyx, reminding them that black cats never got adopted. All three had already gone to their forever homes. Midnight didn't care because she'd spied the tail-pulling toddler and turned away, dragging Onyx to the back of the cage. No way did she want to live with some snotty little demon.

The food dish was empty again, compliments of Onyx. The tiny, rotund kitten loved her food. Midnight didn't care. In fact, she understood. When the good Samaritan had scooped up the motherless litter of five, they'd all been well past the point of starvation. It was a miracle the emaciated kittens had all survived. Food deprivation had a way of shaping a less confident kitten's psyche. Midnight didn't fall into that trap because, once the nice woman had rescued them, Midnight knew they wouldn't starve. On the other hand, if Onyx did not stop hogging the food, that might be a distinct possibility. She'd have to have a kitten-to-kitten talk with her sister.

Midnight rushed to her sister, who was sleeping peacefully in the corner on the fleece blanket the staff had provided. She smacked her on the head with her paw and whispered, "Get up, hurry. Lesbians are on the prowl. Fluff your coat and get your furry butt to the edge of the cage."

Onyx yawned, blinked her green eyes, and said, "What?"

"Use your cute chirping meow and get their attention. I'll stick my paw out through the cage. People love that. How do I look? Is my fur shiny?" Midnight asked.

"You're beautiful," Onyx said.

"You only say that because we're twins. Here they come, do the chirping thing. You're better at that than me."

"Meow brmmp," Onyx called out in her practiced voice.

"Oh, Mac, look at these two. They are absolutely precious. So fluffy. They're going to grow into beautiful cats. I had a black cat growing up. They're the best," the woman with flowing, raven-colored hair said.

"Won't long-haired cats get tangled fur, especially when they go outside and hunt for mice on the farm?" the woman with short blonde locks replied. "Remember, the primary reason to get a cat is to reduce the mouse population on the farm. Yes, we'll spoil them too, but—"

"We'll brush them every day. I'll brush them every day," she amended.

Midnight wiggled her paw, reaching for Mac, who she figured might be the harder sell.

"He *is* awfully cute. It's like he's waving at me," Mac said with a smile.

Hmmf, why do people always think black cats are males?

Mac turned to the tired-looking guy who cleaned their cages. "Can we pick them up?"

He shrugged. "Sure, but Midnight and Onyx are females. So, if you want males, we have other kittens you can look at."

"Chirp again," Midnight directed.

"Meow brmmp."

"Aw, that's the cutest little meow I think I've ever heard," the dark-haired woman said. "I'll pick her up and see if we're a fit. I want cuddlers. Mousers are great, but cats who cuddle are the best."

Midnight shifted her eyes to her sister, who apparently didn't need further instruction, as she started purring loud enough to rouse any of the older cats who hadn't bothered to wake from their afternoon naps. When the skinny dude opened the cage and the woman picked her up, Onyx settled against her neck, purring loudly and giving a tiny lick for good measure.

Not to be outdone, as soon as Mac brought Midnight out of the cage, she snuggled against the woman's neck and rubbed her furry face against her skin. While her purr was softer than Onyx, it was still a respectable volume for the women to notice.

"Oh, Mac, I think these are the ones for us. I even like the names the shelter gave them. What do you think?"

Mac kissed the top of Midnight's head. "All right, Carmen. I'm definitely sold. It would be cruel to break them up, right? It's a good thing that one is bigger than the other, or we might not be able to tell them apart. Yours is a chunky little gal. Still adorable though."

Carmen covered Onyx's little ears. "Don't tease her about her weight. She might get a complex. It could have been hard on them if they had to fend for themselves. I'd want to eat all the food placed in front of my face too if I had to fight for every morsel."

Exactly, Midnight thought.

Mac chuckled. "Presumably, they both had the same experience, and Midnight doesn't have a little pot belly. Just saying. I think mine is the athlete in the family. Like me," she added with a wink.

"Whatever. We'll both love them equally."

"Yes, we will," Mac agreed. "I just hope they're both good mousers."

Midnight would remember this day as a pivotal moment in their young lives. Still, another momentous occasion was on the horizon, and only the sisters' careful planning would set everything on the right track again.

CHAPTER ONE

Mackenzie Sullivan held her hands out for the carrier that had been on Carmen's lap for the relatively long drive back to the farm. Carmen continued sticking her fingers inside the plastic cage, cooing at the new kittens. Whenever Mac glanced at her girlfriend, she was playing with the little balls of fluff. The curious creatures kept nosing her fingers, offering gentle licks every chance they got. Occasionally, they would bat at her hand when Carmen wiggled her fingers, offering a perfect target for their playful attacks.

Taking the carrier from Carmen, Mac gently admonished, "You know, Carmen, you shouldn't teach them that hands are a toy to play with. It won't be so cute when they start to bite your fingers. We need to emphasize that hands are for petting, not playthings for their private amusement."

"Their little nibbles don't hurt," Carmen responded.

Mac chuckled. "Just wait until they get more confident. Trust me, kittens in full play mode can definitely cause pain. They may be small, but their little teeth and claws are sharp. Besides, we need them using their skills on mice."

Opening the side door leading to the farmhouse's large kitchen, Mac called out, "Pops? Are you here?"

Sean Sullivan shuffled into the kitchen and smiled at his daughter. "You don't need to yell. I'm not deaf yet. Oh, what do we have here? New mousers? Why are you bringing them into the house?"

Mac felt the flush rise to her face. She hadn't figured out how to tell her father that the new kittens would be pets. After the brief conversation with Carmen, who was horrified to learn that farm cats were supposed to stay in the barn, she'd capitulated to Carmen's pleas that the new kittens should be proper members of the family. And that meant living in a warm house, not a dirty barn.

Carmen had only moved to the farm two months ago, and already she was making changes to Mac's routine. It was a good thing her pops loved Mac's girlfriend and encouraged the move; otherwise, the changes might have been his undoing. It didn't hurt that Carmen was a gentle and kind nurse who doted on her father. Whenever his arthritis flared up, Carmen was right there, rubbing ointment into his joints and basically pampering him like Mac's mother used to do. Her pops had pulled her aside one night and, through teary eyes, gruffly said, "You got a good one, Mac, don't screw it up."

"Um, they're going to stay inside the house. We bought a litter box for them…" Mac replied.

"What's wrong with the barn?"

Carmen offered Sean her winning smile. "Sean, it's too cold in the barn. They'll be indoor/outdoor cats. The best of both worlds. The litter box is just for those occasions when it's snowing a lot and nippy outside. I suspect they'll do their business outside most of the time."

"We don't get a lot of snow." Sean shook his head and mumbled, "Just like Deidre. She used to let the cats inside too. She thought she was being all sneaky, but I always knew."

Mac tried not to look too sheepish when she responded. "You knew?"

"Course I did. Your mother wasn't very good at hiding anything."

"She did that for me because I begged her," Mac answered.

"Meow brmmp. Meow." The cats had chimed in on the conversation.

Sean chuckled. "Oh, don't be so sure about that. She loved those cats as much as you. Fine. Let them out of their little cage. They might as well explore their new home."

Carmen winked at Mac as she set down the carrier and opened the front latch. Mac stroked Carmen's beautiful hair, leaned in to kiss her cheek, and whispered, "Nice job. You have my pops wrapped around your little finger, just like me."

At first, the kittens slowly emerged. As they gained confidence, they raced around the house, chasing one another, then flopped on the hardwood floor and looked up at the two women as if to say, "Okay, we're done; it's cuddle time."

"I'm going to run to the truck and get the supplies," Mac announced. "First lesson, how to use a litter box. After they get settled in the house, we need to introduce them to the rest of the farm. Hopefully, they'll want to go outside and explore."

Carmen nodded and scooped both kittens into her arms. "I'll just snuggle with them for a bit until you return."

Sean shook his head and smiled. "I got a few chores left to do before dinner. Need to move the goats to the south enclosure."

"I can do that, Pops. Just let me settle the kittens, and I'll take care of it."

Sean waved his hand in the air. "No need. I'm having a good day. The joints aren't acting up too much. Doc put me on a new medicine, and it seems to work well."

†

While it was still new to Carmen, making the move to live with Sean and Mac was almost seamless. Working the day shift at the hospital made it easy for her to prepare dinner for the hard-working farmers. If she stayed on the medical-surgical unit versus transferring to critical care, she could continue to get off at 3:30. The critical care unit only offered twelve-hour shifts. She'd make more money as a critical care nurse, but the schedule didn't fit as well.

While Mac made the goat cheese and cared for the animals, Carmen tried various recipes on Mac, Sean, and Evan, their farm hand. She loved living on the farm with its abundant fresh vegetables, herbs, free-range chickens, pigs, and grass-fed and grass-finished beef; it was the best food she'd ever worked with to create her culinary masterpieces. Cooking was a hobby she'd honed over the years, and having three very appreciative recipients of her creations made her feel like she contributed to the farm.

Of course, Carmen could not muster the courage to slaughter any of the animals they consumed. If she had thought too long about what she was eating, she'd have turned into a vegetarian years ago. Ironically, Mac, who'd grown up on the farm, couldn't do it either. They both left that task to Sean or the slaughterhouse for the larger animals. Carmen could gather the eggs and vegetables, but that was the extent of what she could stomach. She tried very hard not to get too close to the cows, pigs or chickens lest she begin to think of them as pets. The goats were a whole other story. Since the goats were only on the farm to produce milk for the cheese, she could play with them all she wanted, knowing none of her friends would make it to the dinner table.

Swaying to the music, Carmen was preparing a new chicken dish when Mac snuck up behind her and placed her arms around Carmen's waist, kissing her neck.

"Have I told you how much I love having you at the farm with us?"

Carmen turned around and accepted a kiss from Mac. "Mmhm, many times and in many ways. You know, we've kind of done everything ass-backward," she teased.

Mac furrowed her brow. "What do you mean?"

"Well, we've only been living together for a few months and already have children. Outside of wedlock," Carmen exclaimed in an exaggerated fashion.

"Huh? Have I missed something?" Mac asked. "Even if it was possible to have finger or tongue babies, your being pregnant is a precursor to kids. Are you trying to tell me something?"

"I meant Midnight and Onyx. They're a pretty big deal. A commitment."

Mac laughed. "Funny. You had me worried for a minute. Don't you think when you moved into the farmhouse, that was a big enough symbol of commitment?"

"Not necessarily. Lesbians move in together all the time after a short period but never progress to the next level," Carmen reasoned.

Mac smiled. "Are you asking me to marry you?"

"Would that be crazy?"

Mac stepped back and cocked her head to the side. "Kind of, yes. I mean, don't get me wrong, I definitely see that in our future, but we've only been living together for a few months," Mac quickly amended. "I want to make sure life on the farm isn't going to chase you away. It isn't always an easy life. And you know I won't leave the farm. Pops can't handle everything on his own. Even with Evan living on the property and helping us, it's just too difficult with only three people. He'd lose the place, and that would break him."

"Four people," Carmen corrected.

Mac gently brushed aside a lock of hair. "Yeah, you've been a godsend to us, but you know that isn't why I asked you to move in with me."

"Yes, of course I know that. It might break you as well, if you lost the farm. I know you love it here. I do too. Have I ever suggested this life was too hard for me? It's not like you expect me to play an integral role in keeping the farm going. I have my job at the hospital. Cooking for you is the least I can do. Besides, I love to cook. You know that."

Mac grinned. "Let's get through the winter in this drafty old house before we have further conversations about marriage. If you still enjoy living here after enduring the bitter cold with subpar heating, then by all means, you won't have to drag me down the aisle. I'll be the one leading the way. I love you. I can't see myself growing old with anyone else. Besides, Pops said he would kick my ass if I ever did anything stupid enough to drive you away. He loves you too. You're like a second daughter to him."

Carmen's eyes glistened. "I know. I love him too. Maybe more than you," she teased. "Memories of the time spent with my father are waning, and with Mom being so far away…it's just…hard. I didn't know how much I missed being near a parental unit."

"How long has it been since you visited your mom?"

"Too long. I get the sense that something is going on with Mom because she's been particularly cagey lately. When I first moved to Washington, she ended up in the hospital with pneumonia and never told me. I only learned about it after the fact because my brother went begging for money and discovered she wasn't home. I'm going to pin down that irresponsible waste of life and get him to pay her a visit. He better get the scoop for me. He takes enough from her, showing no regard for her health and well-being. The least he can do is check up on her every now and again."

Mac sighed. "One of these days, I'll feel confident enough to leave the farm for a few days, maybe even long enough for a vacation, and I can finally meet your mom. I just really feel the need to increase production to have enough for critical repairs. If you think the house is drafty, wait until you experience our leaky roof. Next on my wish list for the farm is a new roof and better insulation. A new heating system isn't a bad idea either. All of those items cost more than we can afford right now."

"I'd love that. I wish you would let me help. You know we aren't finished with the conversation about living expenses. I'm not even contributing anything to rent. How is that fair? I make a good living as a nurse and have nowhere to spend the money. If you really want me to settle into farm living, you'll let me tackle those projects to make the house more comfortable in the winter. At least one of them. New roof?" Carmen suggested.

"I'll think about it," Mac answered.

Carmen frowned. "That means no. Stubborn mule," she muttered good-naturedly.

They'd been having the same conversation ever since Carmen had moved in two months earlier. Sometimes, Mac had too much pride for her own good. She had insisted that since she was the one to ask Carmen to move in and see how she took to farm life, Carmen paying rent was out of the question. Carmen desperately wanted to wake up every day with Mac, so she'd capitulated, biding her time for the right moment to renegotiate the deal. Carmen felt confident that, one day, she'd wear Mac down and make the perfect argument. Perhaps that would come when she convinced Mac she wasn't going anywhere and farm life suited her just fine. Hopefully, that would come along with marriage.

Because if there was one thing Carmen was sure of, it was that she wanted to marry Mackenzie Sullivan. Despite Mac's stubborn streak, Carmen had fallen head over heels in love with the strong, compassionate woman. She couldn't wait to introduce Mac to her mother. She was sure her mom would love Mac as much as she did.

CHAPTER TWO

Mac crawled from the warmth of the bed where Carmen remained fast asleep. Although her shift at the hospital started at seven, Carmen usually waited until the very last moment to wake and ready herself for the longer drive since moving to the farm. Onyx, her shadow, remained curled against her body. *Lucky girl.* Onyx liked her creature comforts; one of those was snuggling under the covers with her favorite human. Carmen was such a softie. The fact that Carmen did not do a thing to discourage this nightly ritual warmed Mac's heart, although the kitten's presence definitely interrupted their sexy times at night. Eventually, Onyx learned to climb into her soft bed with her sister until the two women succumbed to sleep, and she could safely crawl under the covers with Carmen. Midnight had learned the signs early on, and if it wasn't such a ridiculous notion, Mac could have sworn the insistent meows from Midnight to Onyx were Midnight's way of teaching Onyx about human sexy time.

Midnight was Mac's shadow. The moment she felt or heard Mac stir, she bounded off the foot of the bed where she usually slept. At just before five in the morning, the little kitten was always raring to go. She'd follow Mac around as she did her morning chores. Both kittens were extremely good-natured, except when Evan arrived. For whatever reason, neither kitten took a liking to Evan. Maybe it was the delighted squeal from Evan when Mac first introduced the farm's only employee. Perhaps their sensitive ears took an immediate dislike to the noise and decided to snub her for all eternity. Mac shrugged. At least the mornings were their time to hang before Evan arrived, and Midnight hissed until Evan went off to do her own chores.

Carmen had joked that both kittens saw Evan's blatant attempt at flirting and didn't at all care for the disrespect to their mommy. Mac had laughed at that, but it didn't escape her notice how Evan often found herself in the same general vicinity as Mac while working the farm. Sometimes, it was necessary for both women to accomplish specific tasks, but for the most part, they had separate duties.

On the days that Carmen had off, she'd have a big breakfast ready for Mac, Evan, and Sean after they returned from their morning chores. Mac thought this was especially sweet since Carmen had no reason to wake up so early. Carmen would shrug and argue that getting up early was a habit after working the day shift for the past two years. The least she could do was make herself useful. However, on days when Carmen worked at the hospital, Mac, Sean and Evan were on their own.

Mac grabbed her heavy coat, slipped into the sleeves, and put on her gloves. Fall was here and would soon ease into winter. Mornings were particularly nippy, but for whatever reason, that didn't keep Midnight from following her to the large enclosure where the goats slept. Soon, she wouldn't have to milk them and could concentrate on other parts of the farm. Giving the goats a break before the next kid season was essential for optimal lactation. Her father had taught her that. Leasing part of their land helped keep them afloat financially, but the addition of Evan allowed Mac to focus on their hottest-selling products. Lately, people had clamored for organic, sustainable food, free-range chicken and grass-fed beef. Mac prided herself on supplying the specialty markets with the highest quality, and as a result, their farm had made a name for itself. The markets let her know about the increased demand, placing pressure on Mac to expand.

"Ready to visit the goats?" Mac asked.

Midnight responded with a *meow* and continued to walk beside Mac.

"Pretty soon, it'll be too cold to milk the goats. Then what will we do?" Mac continued to converse with her shadow. "I don't suppose you'll want to join me when I start my winter chores, like fixing the fences and other minor repairs that need to be done after the craziness during the spring, summer, and fall."

"Meow."

"Oh, so you really think you'll want to brave the wind and cold, do you?"

"Meow."

Mac finished milking the goats and took the milk to her cheese shed to store. Today, she'd start a new batch of cheese. Although Mac called it her cheese shed, it was the most state-of-the-art building on the farm. The first few times Midnight had followed her around the farm, she cried outside the building for what seemed like hours to Mac, until she finally realized that Mac couldn't let her inside. The health department would never allow it. Eventually, Midnight understood. Mac supposed the small house she set right outside the door with the comfortable bed helped. Midnight would crawl into the house and take a nap while Mac made cheese in the strange building that neither of the cats were allowed to enter.

"I'm making cheese later today, Midnight, so you'll need to return to the house or settle in your spot for a long nap.

But I'm only storing the milk, so wait out here. After I'm done, we can go to the chicken coop to collect eggs. I won't be long."

"Meow."

"You're the best helper I've ever had."

"Hiss."

Mac glanced at Midnight, then looked up and saw Evan approach, chuckling but remaining a respectable distance from Midnight. She'd learned her lesson when Midnight hadn't stopped at a warning hiss and took a swipe at Evan's ankle.

"Midnight, be good," Mac admonished.

"Midnight's the best helper, huh? What about me?" Evan asked as she glared at the kitten. "You should have renamed her Satan. Is there anything I can do to help in the cheese shed?"

Mac decided to let the "Satan" comment slide. "No. I'm just dropping off the milk. Will you move the cattle again? We'll need to set out the hay pretty soon for them."

"Okay, boss. Want me to collect some eggs and make you breakfast? Remember, I make a mean omelet," Evan offered. "Carmen has a shift at the hospital today, right?"

Mac knew that Evan offering to collect the eggs was a huge gesture since she still hadn't figured out how to accomplish the chore without getting pecked. But Mac wasn't about to encourage Evan's crush and give Carmen more fodder to tease her.

"I'm afraid Carmen has me so spoiled lately that I can't even think about eating someone else's omelets. Sorry, my friend, yours were good, but Carmen's are amazing. I'm planning on grabbing something quick after I finish collecting the eggs. But you can feel free to make Pops an omelet. I'm sure he would appreciate the gesture. I assume you haven't eaten yet. His joints are really acting up lately. I told him to sleep in this morning." Mac glanced at Evan right before she rearranged her face. The sour look caused Mac to cringe internally. *Shit, I've offended Evan.*

Evan turned away and said, "Sure, I can do that after I move the cattle."

Mac walked up to Evan and touched her shoulder. "Hey, I'm sorry. I didn't mean it like it came out. You've been a lifesaver to me and Pops. I know I don't tell you how much I appreciate you, but I do. I'm sure you could get a much better paying job at one of the bigger farms…"

Evan beamed. "No. No way. I love it here. I can't imagine working alongside anyone else but you. You're the best boss and friend I've ever had. You'll never get rid of me. Carmen is such a lucky woman. I wish I could find someone like you to share my life with."

"Hiss."

Before Midnight could take another swipe at Evan's ankle, Evan stepped away.

"Whew, that's good to hear. See you later. I'm going to gather the eggs now. I'll leave several out for you to make

21

your omelets." Mac turned and offered a small wave as she marched to the chicken coop, her trusty shadow following close behind. Mac glanced toward the house just in time to see Carmen set a course to intercept her.

†

Onyx was a little princess. When the weather turned cold, she refused to go outside. By now, she knew Carmen's routine. If Carmen jumped in the shower as soon as the alarm woke her, that meant that Carmen wouldn't be making breakfast for Mac. This also told Onyx that she wouldn't get the tiny treats Carmen would drop on the floor for her— accidentally on purpose, of course. Onyx was an intelligent kitten. She'd picked up on the game immediately. Carmen loved that little fluff ball. She loved Midnight too, but Onyx seemed to gravitate to Carmen, while Midnight barely left Mac's side.

Carmen had woken earlier today before her alarm had even gone off. She felt the missing spot where Mac slept and knew that Mac had probably been up for at least thirty minutes because the place was cold to the touch. Although she didn't have enough time to make an extravagant breakfast, like on her days off, she'd at least be able to cook something quick and leave it in the oven for Mac. It would probably cause Onyx confusion, but Mac deserved to be spoiled. If she hurried in the shower and didn't blow dry her long hair, she'd have enough time to make French toast.

As usual, Onyx followed Carmen into the bathroom and jumped on the counter while Carmen brushed her teeth. After her shower, Carmen hurried to the kitchen to make the French toast. Onyx tilted her head and meowed as if to ask, "What's up, Mommy?" As Carmen prepared the French toast and fried the bacon in a separate pan, Onyx began her cute *meow brmmp.* Carmen promptly set aside one piece of bacon, letting it cool.

After putting the French toast and bacon in the oven, Carmen broke the bacon into smaller morsels, dropped it on the floor, and exclaimed, "Oops! I guess you'll have to eat that, Onyx."

"Meow brmmp." Onyx gobbled the treat and looked up at her mommy.

"No, no more. It's not healthy for you to eat too much people food." Carmen scooped the chunky kitten into her arms and kissed the top of her head. "You be good today." She glanced at her watch, then set the kitten on the floor. "Time to go, or Mommy's going to be late."

Carmen rushed out the door and narrowed her eyes when she saw Mac touch Evan's arm. It looked like Mac was reassuring Evan in some way. She wondered what that was all about. She held back her laughter when she heard Midnight hiss. *Good girl, Midnight.*

Carmen wasn't exactly the jealous type, but something about Evan didn't sit right with her. Whenever Mac was around, Evan was nice as pie to her, but when it was just the two of them, Carmen had the distinct impression that Evan wished Carmen would disappear. Carmen shook her negative thoughts from her head and hurried to Mac to let her know breakfast was warming in the oven.

"Hey you." Mac smiled. "Off to work?" She touched Carmen's hair. "Running late, I see. Your hair is still wet."

"Nope. Wrong, smarty pants. I woke early, missing my beautiful lover, so I made breakfast. It's in the oven. There's plenty for all three of you. But I'll be late if I don't head out soon. Something the matter with Evan? She seemed, oh, I don't know...upset?" Carmen searched for the right word to describe Evan's facial expression.

Mac leaned in to kiss Carmen. "I don't deserve you. You're way too good to me. Not that I wouldn't love to stay kissing and talking with you, but you need to get in your car and crank up the heat. Being out in this cold weather with wet hair is not good. You'll catch your death of cold."

Carmen laughed, then kissed Mac again, noting how Mac avoided answering her question about Evan but figured it wasn't worth pursuing. "Don't tell me you believe all those old wives' tales? I'm a nurse. It might feel uncomfortable, but viruses are only transmitted through bodily fluids. I have a better chance of catching a cold by kissing you when you're sick."

Mac pounded her chest. "I never get ill. Excellent constitution. Kiss away. You've nothing to fear from me," Mac teased. "But you will be late unless you leave soon."

Carmen pouted, bent to pat Midnight's head, then grabbed one last kiss before heading to her car. She waved to Mac, Midnight, and Onyx, who peered at her through a window in the farmhouse.

CHAPTER THREE

Mac stood at the electric fence, scratching her head. Her largest steer kept stomping his feet, and Mac knew what that probably meant. The unusually cool temperatures at night were the likely culprit. She often had to pay attention when her steers started chomping on the grass like it might be their last meal. During cool weather, the grass grown at lower temperatures was initially digested more rapidly, leading to bloat. *Fuck.* Mac couldn't afford to lose even one steer because her margins were so slim on the farm. Each steer that died could amount to a four-to-five-thousand-dollar loss. She'd have to call Olivia and ask her opinion. Although her friend's clinic mostly cared for small animals, Olivia was a talented vet and had been known to make house calls upon special request.

Olivia and Deb were good friends. Mac had actually met Carmen one night when Deb played matchmaker. Deb and her sister, Kathleen, were nurses who worked at the local hospital. When Carmen started working there, Deb befriended the single lesbian and talked her wife into inviting Mac for dinner the night she'd asked Carmen to come. To say they had instant chemistry would have been an understatement. It didn't hurt that Carmen brought the most delicious home-baked pie she'd ever had in her entire life. Mac had a serious sweet tooth, and Carmen's baking skills were the most expedient way to her heart. Her beauty, both inside and out, didn't hurt either.

Midnight and Onyx had an appointment with Olivia for spaying, but Mac didn't think the steer could wait. She hoped Olivia's day wasn't too packed and she could sneak in a visit to the farm. Maybe it was time to invite them over for dinner anyway.

On her way to the house to call, Evan rushed to catch up with her. "Hey, Mac. What's up? It looks like your ass just caught fire. Something wrong? Can I help?"

Mac frowned. She didn't have time for a chat with Evan. *Why the hell didn't she notice?* Mac took in a deep breath and tried to be patient. Evan wasn't new to farming, but she was new to raising cattle. Not that Mac was an expert either, since ranching and raising cattle was not their primary business. With a scant number of cattle, she often considered the small herd a hastily planned afterthought. Initially, Mac had only intended to supply grass-fed beef to her family and friends. But due to market demand, the business had expanded to cater to the local organic markets. Mac needed to give the young woman a break. If it weren't for Evan, she would never have been able to expand the farm operations.

Midnight hissed at Evan, and Mac scooped her up. "Midnight, be nice." She turned her attention to Evan and pointed to the large steer. "See how big boy keeps stomping his feet and trying to kick his belly?"

Evan turned to look into the field where the cattle were grazing. "Uh, yeah, he started doing that yesterday. I just figured he was reacting to the colder-than-normal temperatures. You know, like how people sometimes jump up and down to get warm."

Mac sighed. "No, they can handle the cold, but those are signs of bloat, and if we don't jump on it right away, we chance losing him and maybe some others in the herd. I need to call Olivia." She continued walking and talked as she went. "I thought maybe I'd invite Olivia and Deb for dinner. Two birds. We haven't seen them in a while, and I thought Carmen would appreciate a fun evening. It's not like I want to take advantage of Olivia's expertise. I'll pay her, of course, besides offering dinner. Hopefully, Carmen won't mind cooking for two more."

"Saint Carmen, doubtful," Evan joked, but Mac detected a bite to her voice. "I haven't seen Olivia and Deb in months. I'd love to catch up with them too," she hinted.

"No hot date tonight?" Mac joked.

"Nah, but maybe Deb knows another single attractive nurse she would introduce me to since it worked out so well for you."

"How about if I make that call and plant the seed? You know you're always invited to join us whenever you don't have plans." Mac felt terrible for Evan. She seemed so lost sometimes, like a puppy that just wanted someone to play with her. She wasn't a bad sort—always eager to please. And Evan was certainly attractive enough. She'd been a lifesaver to their farm. There weren't many young women who would work as hard for what Mac could afford to pay. The least Mac could do was ask Olivia if Deb knew any single lesbians.

Evan's smile grew. "Really? I won't be crashing the party?"

"Of course not. You're family. Most nights you join us for dinner. But if I'm going to make the arrangements, I have to get in there to make the calls right now."

"Right, right. I'll check out the herd and see if I notice others exhibiting the same behavior."

"That would be helpful. Thanks, Evan." Mac turned and hurried into the house with a squirming Midnight still in her arms.

†

Carmen was sitting at the nurses' station charting a few notes when her friend Deb bounded up to her with a massive grin on her face. "So, what gourmet meal can we expect tonight?"

Carmen looked up. "What?"

"Your girlfriend invited Olivia and me to dinner at your house tonight," Deb answered.

Carmen furrowed her brow. "She did? I wonder why she didn't tell me. Not that I care. I miss you guys. It's funny because I was just thinking about talking to Mac and asking her if we could invite you two for dinner. Mac must have ESP or something. You're going to love the seasonal crops ready for harvest. The raw ingredients I have to work with are amazing. But it isn't like her not to call and let me know." Carmen plucked her phone from her pocket, noticed the missed call and smiled. She shook the phone in her hand. "Looks like I need to listen to my messages."

"I didn't get Mac in trouble, did I?" Deb asked.

"No, of course not. I love cooking for people. So, do you have any special requests for tonight?"

"Nope. Whatever you make, I know it will be fabulous. In case you didn't know, we're arriving around 6:00, but Olivia told me she has to look at your cows or something. I also invited Marcia. Olivia said something about Evan

30

wanting to meet other single lesbians. It sounded like Mac wanted me to find someone to join the party so that Evan doesn't feel like a fifth wheel."

Carmen's face scrunched in confusion. "Mac never worries about Evan feeling out of place at dinner. I better listen to the message. If something is happening with the cattle, it can't be good for Mac to call Olivia."

Deb shrugged. "I wouldn't worry. Olivia is the best vet in town. She'll figure it out." Deb glanced up and noticed one of the call lights. "Hey, gotta go. Mr. Forbes probably needs help going to the bathroom. The last time I didn't get there ten seconds after the call, he tried to get up and almost fell. Poor guy hates feeling like he's an invalid. His words, not mine. But there is no way I want him to break a hip and have to be in the hospital any longer than necessary. Safety first."

Carmen waved her hand and smiled. "Go, go."

After Deb left, she shifted her focus to the unit secretary. "Hey, Rosie, I need to take a quick break during this momentary lull. Mac called, and I should listen to the message."

"No worries, Carmen, it's not like you ever take breaks, even though you should. The other nurses on shift can cover for you for a change."

Peeking into the break room, Carmen noticed it was empty, so she pressed the button to listen to Mac's message. "Hey, beautiful, I hope it's okay that I asked Olivia and Deb to dinner tonight. I know you have this weekend off, so I thought it would be a good night to have company. But the real reason I wanted Olivia to come over is that I think at least one of the herd has bloat, and if we don't nip it in the bud, we could lose a lot of money, especially if others have it too. I don't mean to put the burden on you to cook everything tonight, so just tell me what you need me to do. It won't be as good as you, but I can make the dinner."

Carmen burst out laughing and looked around lest she appear to be a crazy woman. Mac cooking dinner was a recipe for disaster. She could handle grilling steaks or other simple meals, but that was the extent of her cooking prowess. Carmen pushed the button to return Mac's call.

"Hey you," Mac answered. "You must have gotten my message. Sorry to disturb you at work."

"It's fine. Deb already told me the plans. But don't even think about entering my domain. I'll prepare dinner tonight. All I need you to do is take a rib roast out of the freezer, and I'll do the rest."

"Have I told you lately how much I love you? Oh, and Evan doesn't have plans tonight either. So, she'll be joining us," Mac noted.

Carmen chuckled. "Yeah, I know. Deb already told me about the guest list, and she took it upon herself to invite Marcia for Evan. Gotta love that woman. Maybe they'll be as good a match as us. I feel bad for Evan. She has a crush on you, you know. She follows you like a little puppy."

Mac laughed. "Well, I'm taken. No chance of her winning my heart. It already belongs to you."

"Smooth talker. I'll see you tonight. I should be home by fourish and will start on our meal. So, no disturbing the chef while she prepares her masterpiece. Dinner should be ready by 7:30. That should give you and Olivia enough time with the cattle."

"Yes, ma'am," Mac answered.

†

Mac guessed what vegetables her girlfriend would want to pair with the beef. She decided to make things easier on Carmen by harvesting the spinach and digging up the potatoes and other fall vegetables she thought might go well with the meal. Whatever Carmen decided not to use, Mac would place in the refrigerator for the weekend. Selecting her favorite goat cheese, she added that to the pile of food from the farm.

Grinning, she came face-to-face with Carmen, who'd entered the kitchen and caught her putting away the cheese. Onyx and Midnight trotted over and wove in and out of Carmen's legs.

Dutifully, Carmen bent to pet both kittens, before she propped her hands on her hips and smirked. "So, you think you figured out what I would cook besides the beef, did you?"

Mac nodded and pulled Carmen into a searing kiss. "Yup. And whatever you decide not to use won't go to waste. We have the entire weekend to enjoy this bounty. Besides checking on the cattle, I plan on taking most of the weekend off. Of course, I have to milk the goats and gather the eggs, but everything else can wait. Anything I can help with now?"

After the kiss ended, Carmen playfully pushed Mac away. "Go do whatever farming thing you need to and leave me to the cooking. I have a tight timeframe to get everything prepared before 7:30. You'll simply be a distraction with your breathtaking kisses. Take Midnight with you." Scooping Onyx in her arms, she deposited her on the fluffy bed perched on the cat tree with a bird's-eye view of the backyard through the window. "You need to watch the birds while Mommy prepares dinner. There's a special treat for you later if you don't get in the way."

Mac chuckled. "First, do you really believe that Onyx understands a word you say? And second, cats own us, not the other way around. They're notorious for not listening to a word we say. If you wanted an obedient pet, we should have adopted a dog or two."

"I refuse to believe any of that. Onyx is very bright. She knows exactly what I'm saying, and bribery most definitely works for my little black ball of puff. Besides, if we got dogs, you'd make them working dogs, and then I wouldn't have anyone to keep me company. It's bad enough that Midnight follows you around like a puppy. I know we got them to be mousers, but Onyx just isn't cut out for that. Midnight does a good enough job, right?"

Mac laughed again. "Yeah, Midnight is an excellent mouser. Kind of unbelievable, really, because she's still so small."

"Small but feisty. Is she still giving Evan fits?" Carmen asked.

Mac nodded. "Unfortunately, yes. Can you have a heart-to-heart with her and straighten that out, please, since you're so good at making deals with the kittens?"

"I don't think Midnight is as food-motivated as Onyx. You'll need to think of something else to bribe her with," Carmen teased. "Now go." Carmen made a shooing motion.

Before Mac returned to finish a few tasks that would allow her the free time to spend with her girlfriend over the weekend, she glanced at the bed and saw Onyx blink at her. Her green eyes taunted Mac as if to say, *yes, I'd do anything for Carmen.* Mac thought she would too. Carmen had them both wrapped around her pinky. She shook her head and pushed open the door, heading to the south field.

Evan smirked at her as she approached.

"Wifey kicked you out of the house, didn't she?" Evan taunted.

"Yup. Help me with the south-side fence?"

"Only if you keep the panther from biting my ankle or taking a swipe at my face," Evan answered.

Mac crouched in front of Midnight and decided to give Carmen's suggestion of talking to Midnight a try. It couldn't hurt. "Hey, my favorite shadow. I need you to lay off Evan while we work on the fence. I'll bring out the laser and play with you tonight if you're a good girl and can do that for me."

Evan roared with laughter. "Seriously, Mac. She's a cat. They don't listen."

"Onyx does. Carmen trained her. I swear she follows Carmen's direction. It's the damnedest thing. I've never seen anything like it."

"Whatever. Let's go." Evan began the trek to the south-side field as Mac and Midnight trailed behind.

"I'll grab some wire and meet you there."

Mac and Evan had just finished the south-side fence when Mac saw a car pull into the long gravel driveway to the main farmhouse. Mac noted that the woman with Deb and Olivia seemed fit, almost as tall as herself. She hoped Marcia would hit it off with Evan. Working with Evan and attempting to place boundaries around their relationship was becoming increasingly uncomfortable. Mac didn't want to be the kind of boss who wasn't friends with their employees. It didn't work so well on a farm when you had to depend on that person to work hard and have your back. Paying Evan so little was bad enough. She appreciated how Carmen took in stride the unspoken invitation for Evan to join them for dinner almost every night. Mac supposed that was a perk that wasn't offered to most farm hands, even those that lived on the properties. Since Carmen was such a fabulous cook, maybe free meals made up for the lower pay.

Mac squinted at Marcia, trying to make out her features. She gestured at Evan with a quick shift of her head in the direction of their guests. "Why don't you clean up while Olivia and I discuss the situation with the steer? You don't want Deb's friend to think you're some uncouth backwater farmer," she joked.

Evan bobbed her head. "Yeah. Do I have time for a shower?"

"Duh. I would definitely recommend one." She sniffed the air. "We're both a little ripe."

Deb and Marcia veered toward the house while Olivia strode purposefully in their direction. Always prepared, she carried a large bag over her shoulder that she'd retrieved from the back of the car. Mac supposed they'd taken Deb's car instead of Olivia's big red truck because of the extra passenger.

Evan shifted her attention to Marcia. "I can't tell if she's cute."

Mac lightly shoved her. "Go. Looks aren't the most important thing."

"Says the woman with a goddess for a girlfriend. Who could ever compete with that?" Evan mumbled as she strolled toward the small cottage on the property.

"Hey, thanks for coming," Mac greeted her old friend.

Midnight swirled around Olivia's legs, then stretched her paws against Olivia's pants. She set down her bag and crouched to pet the friendly kitten.

"Of course. I would never miss the chance to have one of Carmen's famous creations. Besides, I wanted to see how much the kittens have grown. They're both going to be beauties. They're very friendly. I guess this little girl doesn't remember her first visit to the clinic. That's good."

"Unfortunately, Midnight seems to have taken a dislike to Evan. I have no idea why. Carmen is making a rib roast, but I know she'll have some spectacular vegetarian dishes just for you. I harvested a bunch of vegetables, so she'd have her pick of something to use."

Olivia stood and pointed to the steer that was stomping in the field. "That the one you're talking about?"

"Mmhm. I haven't noticed any others yet, but I'm concerned."

"You're probably spot on," Olivia responded. "You can help me pass the stomach tube. It isn't going to be pleasant doing this in the field, but it's the easiest way for me to confirm bloat."

"Should I learn how to do this and have Evan help me if others start showing symptoms?"

Olivia smiled. "That, or I could come out again and snag another sumptuous meal. You know we love spending time with you guys."

"I'm paying you for this trip." Mac held up her hand. "No arguments."

"I'll take some of your chickens in exchange for the house call." Olivia held up two fingers. "Two should be plenty. They're better than gold, you know. Deb is extra nice to me whenever I bring home chickens from your farm." She winked. "I brought a large bloat needle with me in case we needed it. It'll save you from having to spend the evening wrangling him into a place where he can't graze and then walking him."

"Yeah, that doesn't sound like an entertaining evening." Mac chuckled.

"Let's get this done so we can relax, have a few beers and catch up." Olivia lifted the bag and placed it over her shoulder.

"Midnight, you need to stay here. I don't want the steer to step on you and cause Olivia to perform emergency surgery right here in the middle of the field." Mac pointed to the round smashed-down grass, a favorite spot for Midnight to take her afternoon nap.

Olivia chuckled as she followed Mac through the gate. "If you ever need a job, come see me. We could use a cat whisperer."

CHAPTER FOUR

Carmen almost had everything ready and was worried Mac and Olivia would be late, when the two women shuffled inside. Both smelled like cow shit and those general farm smells most people found offensive. Marcia wrinkled her nose, but the rest of the group either didn't notice or were accustomed to the smell.

Midnight rushed to where Onyx lay curled on her bed and pounced on her, waking her for a short play session as they tussled with one another.

Carmen wouldn't normally say anything because Mac always did a good enough job of washing up before dinner. But when she caught Mac's eyes, and they had traveled to

Marcia, she suggested, "Dinner will be ready in about twenty minutes if either of you want to shower."

Deb gestured to Olivia with a quick jerk of her head.

"Uh, sure. I did bring a change of clothes, just in case. Thanks." Olivia lifted the small bag she had carried into the house.

"You can use my shower," Pops offered.

"Thanks, Pops. Down the hall and to the right?" Olivia asked.

Pops nodded.

"I think both of us can shower at the same time. At least I hope these old pipes can handle it," Mac teased. "I won't be long. I promise." She walked over to Carmen and kissed her cheek. "Everything smells delicious. I can't wait to sink my teeth into that roast." She trotted up the stairs.

While Carmen continued to put the finishing touches on her meal, paying careful attention to the homemade béarnaise sauce she had prepared using goat butter, she juggled her host duties by politely asking Marcia a question. "Are you still liking Moses Lake?"

"I enjoy the smaller setting, but I suppose that makes it harder to find eligible women to date. It isn't exactly a gay mecca like Seattle, but I don't really enjoy living in large cities. Besides, Seattle is way too expensive," Marcia answered. She turned her focus to Evan. "Have you lived here long?"

Evan blushed. "Born and raised in this area. My family owns a large potato farm, but we don't get along, so I'm trying to learn more about organic farming, pasture-raised animals and sustainable food. Things like that. Mac is a brilliant teacher."

"I think that's important. I wish more farmers offered healthier food. It's kind of expensive though," Marcia noted. "I mean, don't get me wrong, I understand why it's more expensive, and I can afford to buy local, but it seems like a lot of people who live in Moses Lake can't afford the higher quality food."

"It's a conundrum," Carmen inserted. "I know Mac worries about that and wishes she could sell her products for less. Fortunately, she found her niche market, and the folks who buy our products have no problem affording them. It's what allows us to keep the farm going." Carmen smiled to herself as she recognized how easily "our products" and "us" slipped into her vocabulary when talking about the farm. She knew she saw herself living at the farm and being the kind of partner that contributed more to Mac's pride and joy. Mac's goat cheese was gaining recognition beyond the state. Carmen didn't know if that was a good or bad thing.

"However, that doesn't stop her from donating as much as she can to the food bank. They love seeing her truck pull up to the donation station," Carmen added.

"Yeah, Mac's a good egg," Evan said.

"You must be too, if you left your large potato farm. I hear the potato farms around here supply all the McDonald's restaurants, and that's big money," Marcia noted.

"Yeah, my family's not hurting for money," Evan answered bitterly. "They could use a few lessons in humanity though. Rabid supporters of the former president."

"Oh..." Marcia shifted in her seat.

"No politics tonight," Carmen warned. "How's Bri and Sierra doing? Is their dog grooming business still going well? Can they groom cats?"

Carmen had met Bri and Sierra, the young Down Syndrome couple, early in her friendship with Deb. Although her boss, Kathleen, was proud of her daughter Sierra, Deb had confided in Carmen about Kathleen's hesitancy with her daughter developing a friendship and subsequent relationship with Bri. Kathleen believed that was a recipe for disaster. Fortunately, Kathleen had come around. Carmen respected Deb and Olivia for always being in their corner. In her humble opinion, she'd never met a more delightful couple than Bri and Sierra. It was clear how much Olivia and Deb adored their nieces, and Carmen could easily see why, because she'd never met more loving individuals in her life.

Deb's eyes lit up. "Yes, some people take their cats to groomers, especially long-haired cats prone to mats in their fur. They are doing great. Olivia and I are so proud of them and all they've accomplished. Starting a new business isn't easy, and they did it almost completely on their own with little help from Olivia."

"Maybe when Midnight and Onyx are older, we can take them to Bri and Sierra," Carmen said as she looked over to the bed where both kittens curled against one another.

Onyx raised her head and declared, "Meow brmmp."

"Yes, we're talking about you, my sweet little girl."

Both kittens began licking their paws and meticulously cleaning their fur.

"So adorable," Marcia said. "I think it's time for me to go to the shelter and pick out a kitten."

"I can go with you," Evan offered. "I've been meaning to get one myself. Onyx and Midnight are only tolerant of Carmen and Mac's attention. Besides, another mouser on the farm might not be a bad idea since Onyx doesn't seem interested in going outside."

"That would be great," Marcia answered.

Deb caught Carmen's eyes, and she waggled her eyebrows, grinning. Carmen suspected Deb believed she'd made another perfect match. She certainly wished that was the case. Anything to change the direction of Evan's focus.

†

Mac bounded down the stairs, hair still wet, giving her a slight chill inside the drafty kitchen. She hadn't wanted to be late to dinner, and drying her thick blonde hair would have taken too long. Carmen had worked hard to prepare a scrumptious meal. The least Mac could do was make an effort to smell nice and be on time. Dressed in her usual outfit of blue jeans, a tight tank top and flannel shirt, she knew her attire wouldn't catch the attention of most women, but for whatever reason, she'd caught Carmen's eye eighteen months ago, and for that, she was eternally grateful. Mac supposed it hadn't hurt how much Deb had sung her praises.

When she'd shown up on Olivia and Deb's doorstep, the last thing she expected was to fall in love. However, it was practically love at first sight for both of them. Mac was coming off a particularly painful break-up. Her previous girlfriend had tried unsuccessfully to change nearly everything about Mac, from how she dressed to her chosen profession. Despite growing up on the farm and thoroughly enjoying that life, Mac had gone to school to obtain a law degree, hoping to assist with the complicated aspects of agribusiness. She'd seen firsthand how farmers were often taken advantage of when they depended on the expertise of shifty lawyers. Mac vowed not to let that happen to her pops. When it became evident her beloved father could not handle the farm on his own with only one additional laborer, who, in Mac's humble opinion, was a worthless piece of shit, she stepped in to take over. Her ex didn't see herself as a farm wife, and that was the end of that. A prestigious lawyer with a growing practice was acceptable; a farmer was not.

Carmen grabbed her by her soft flannel shirt and pulled her in for a kiss. "Goddess, you look good enough to eat. I love this shirt on you."

Mac shivered, and she wasn't sure if it resulted from her damp hair that had soaked through her shirt or the kiss that she felt all the way to her tippy toes. "Y'all haven't been waiting for me, have you?"

Carmen grabbed the ends of Mac's hair and frowned. "Why didn't you dry your hair?"

Mac shrugged. "It would have taken too long, and the smells wafting from the kitchen were far too enticing."

Olivia strolled into the kitchen, adding to Mac's declaration. "I second that sentiment. No way was I going to take the time to completely dry this mop." She lifted her ponytail, then let it flop onto her back.

Mac lifted her fist to Olivia, who took the cue and offered an enthusiastic fist bump. "Priorities. Am I right?" Mac had already noted Olivia's hair was also damp, but Olivia had been smart enough to pull on a beanie. Olivia was used to the old farmhouse, and Mac knew she didn't care one whit if she looked odd wearing a hat inside. Mac still heard the voice of her ex taunting her whenever she dressed in a manner inconsistent with a young, successful professional. And that had often extended to inside her own home.

Olivia chuckled. "Unlike my rugged friend here, I did a thorough towel-dry and put on my beanie."

Pops grinned and chimed in, "Mac used to run outside with her hair wet all the time. Her mama was constantly chasing after her to dress properly."

Carmen shook her head. "Go dry your hair and put on a hat, please. We can wait five minutes. That will give me time to set the table."

Mac pouted. "All right, but I feel bad about not helping. It's my job to set the table."

Carmen gave her a playful push toward the stairs. "I think you and Olivia had enough to worry about getting the cattle all squared away. I believe I can give you a pass." She shot Mac that special smile she reserved only for her. The one that made Mac's heart beat rapidly.

At that moment, Mac knew she was the luckiest woman in the world. She was going to make Carmen her wife—sooner rather than later.

†

After all the guests left, Mac and Carmen settled into their large bed with the soft, downy comforter providing enough warmth to keep out the chill in the air. Midnight jumped onto the bed to join her sister, who had burrowed under the covers and snuggled beside Carmen. Propped against the headboard, Carmen asked, "Did you notice the looks shared between Evan and Marcia?"

Mac smiled. "Sure did. Deb is a miracle worker. Two for two, huh?"

Carmen frowned. "Maybe. I hope so. Evan needs to find someone to spend her free time with. It isn't healthy for her to pine over someone who isn't available."

Mac chuckled. "Is it bad that Evan joins us for dinner almost every evening? I just thought it would be rude not to extend the invitation, then it evolved to a nightly affair. I suppose I should have asked you about that rather than assuming you didn't mind cooking for one more person. I don't pay Evan that much, so I kind of thought it made the job more attractive—a perk for working at a farm that pays a little less than the big farms."

"Nah, if you need to do that to keep her, I don't have any concerns. Cooking for four is just as easy as preparing a meal for three. I know she's a hard worker, and you'd be in a world of hurt without her." Carmen smiled.

"It's an innocent crush. She's still young."

"Not that young. I'm not that much older than Evan. I'm just not sure that Marcia is a match made in heaven for Evan. Deb might have overshot this one. Marcia's nice and all, but I don't think she's quite settled into Moses Lake. From what I hear, she's moved around quite a bit, and it's not like she graduated from nursing school that long ago. She might be telling the truth about wanting to live in a smaller city, but I get the sense that the east side of the mountains isn't exactly her cup of tea. A lot of younger nurses chase the opportunities to make more money relative to their living expenses, with a chance to gain skills before moving on to where they'd really like to live. She probably wants to move to a more progressive place, like Bellingham. It happens all the time. That's why Moses Lake has such a high turnover."

Mac's heart started beating rapidly. She was on the verge of a full-blown panic attack. Maybe Carmen was trying to tell her something. "Do you enjoy living here? Or would you rather be in a more progressive city? Does it bother you it's so conservative on the east side of the state?"

"Well, in a perfect world, Moses Lake would be a mecca for progressive politics, but you're here, and this is home for me now. I admit, initially, I took the job in Moses Lake because I wanted to hone my critical care skills and maybe eventually work my way into obstetrics. I would have been stuck on the night shift medical-surgical unit for years had they not offered me this opportunity. However, my career goals became a distant consideration the night I met you. I don't need to work in some world-renowned hospital to do the work I love. I'm happy here."

"Are you sure?" Mac asked. "I'd never want to hold you back."

"Positive." Carmen nudged Mac. "You better not be serious about that because I expect you to fight tooth and nail for me if I even hint at looking for bluer skies. Not that I ever would," Carmen quickly amended. "But I don't want someone who would give up so easily." Carmen turned to

Mac, her face a mask of seriousness. "Mac, we're going to have challenges we'll have to overcome. That's what commitment is all about. Working through them. Compromising. Doing what's best for both of us. Together. Not making decisions that are good for one but not the other. Understood?"

Mac nodded. "Message received. Loud and clear. Yes, I will fight for you because there is no question in my mind that you are the love of my life. That will never change."

CHAPTER FIVE

There was no reason to believe Mac's life would upend in a few scant hours. She hadn't expected it. Blind-sided wasn't enough of a descriptor for the events that transpired, sending her world into a pile of steaming shit. The day had gone so well until that life-changing phone call. If she knew now what she'd come to learn, she would have handled things so differently.

No more signs of bloat in the cattle put Mac in a good mood. Add to that the recent change in Evan. She was beyond excited about her upcoming date with Marcia. Sure, it had affected her work. She wasn't working as fast or efficiently as usual, but at least she wasn't stepping on the

51

back of Mac's heels, following her around like a lost puppy anymore.

Pops had his monthly card game with the old farmers he palled around with, and Evan had her big date, so it was just Mac and Carmen for dinner. Mac had offered to take Carmen out since it'd been a while, but Carmen was having none of that. She wanted to cook something extra special and spend the night tangled in Mac's embrace. They could be as loud as they wanted, with no one to hear them scream. Mac smiled at the phrase normally associated with some cheesy horror flick. In this instance, it was a guaranteed epic evening of lovemaking.

She had plenty of time to shower, dry her hair, and wash the stink from her body after working most of the day wrangling animals and stepping in various piles of shit. Knowing how much Carmen liked it when she put on her tight jeans and one of her loose flannel shirts, she quickly dressed, eager to make her way downstairs and set the table. The mouth-watering smells sent a direct message to her stomach.

Carmen hummed while she put the finishing touches on the meal. Setting the beautifully plated meal on the table with the soft flickering candlelight glowing against her flawless face, Mac didn't believe there was a more beautiful woman in the entire world. She poured the wine and grinned.

"I literally cannot wait to sink my teeth into this meal. And later," Mac waggled her eyebrows, "I can't wait to sink my tongue into something else. I'll let you know later which is more delectable. But I can say with a fair amount of certainty it will be a close call."

"Hmm, I don't know which will be a bigger compliment," Carmen answered.

Mac had barely taken two bites, gushing appropriately over the exquisiteness of the meal, before Carmen's cell phone rang. Carmen frowned.

"Let it go to voice mail," Mac mumbled around a mouthful of food. "Don't let any of your work buddies guilt you into coming into work. They know you're a soft touch. You always say yes, but how often do we have the house to ourselves? I'm not letting any of them con you into it. That includes Kathleen. I don't care if she is your boss and Deb's sister. She can't use Deb's best friend status to get you to agree to work an extra shift."

Carmen chuckled. "I promise. I won't accept an extra shift tonight, but can I at least see who it is? I've been trying to get my mother or brother to call me back. Both have been curiously silent lately. I don't trust my brother. He's between jobs again, and that means mooching off Mom."

Mac nodded. "Of course, we have all evening. I can share your company for a few minutes."

"Thanks. You're far too good to me. I know this is rude to do during the middle of dinner." Carmen grabbed the phone, but before she could answer, it stopped ringing. Her face morphed into surprise. "Well, it looks like hell has frozen over. The douche finally returned my call. Do you mind if I call him back? I'm worried. I don't particularly enjoy talking to him, so it'll be a quick call. I just need to find out what's going on with Mom."

"Babe, it's totally fine. I'd do the same if I was worried about Pops."

Mac tried not to listen, but she became increasingly concerned as she heard the one-sided conversation. Something was very wrong.

†

"Well, well, well, miracles do still exist. Nice of you to return my calls. Yes, plural, Daryl. I left at least six messages over the last two days," Carmen seethed.

"Temper, temper, Little Sis. So, here's the thing. I got offered a really good job, but it's two states away. I can't take care of Mom any longer, and she's running out of money because I had to hire a home health nurse. Oh, and she's in the hospital right now. Pneumonia again."

"What!?" Carmen nearly screamed as she tried to control her temper. "When have you ever cared for Mom?"

"Don't take that tone with me. I've been the dutiful child living with her for the past three months," Daryl answered. "She can barely go anywhere without getting winded."

"You better tell me right now what exactly has been going on for the past three months. I can believe you were living with Mom because someone undoubtedly evicted you from whatever rathole you lived in, but I doubt you lifted a finger to help her out."

"I did too. Whenever I ordered takeout, I made sure to get enough for Mom. She hasn't been eating a lot, but still," he defended. "I also took her to a few appointments. Mom wasn't too crazy about using an Uber."

"You selfish prick. Living with Mom and having her pay for every single thing. How does that make you a dutiful child? What's wrong with Mom?"

Carmen could almost hear her brother shrug on the other end of the line. "I don't know all that medical mumbo jumbo. That's your expertise. Pulmonary something or other and lupus."

"Pulmonary embolism?" Carmen asked.

"Yeah, that's it. Makes her super tired. I don't think getting pneumonia helped."

"What hospital?"

"Sherman. So, can you get here in the next day or two? I told the nurse you'd call and make all the arrangements. They're kind of worried Mom won't have anyone at home to care for her, and besides needing to kick the pneumonia, they won't discharge her from the hospital until we make the arrangements. You know Mom, she hates the hospital and can't wait to leave."

"Fuck. Yes. I'll be on the next plane to Chicago. I don't suppose you can pick me up from O'Hare?"

"Uh, sorry, Sis, no can do. Heading out tomorrow for my new job," Daryl said. "But once you get to the house, you can use Mom's car to get around. It still runs great. I'm not taking that," he said as if that was a major sacrifice.

"You better not, or I'll be sure to send the police after you, and they can arrest your sorry ass for car theft."

"Mom gave me money to buy a new car. She knew I would need it," he defended.

"Of course she did," Carmen sniped. "Thanks for nothing, Daryl."

"Don't be like that, Carmen. I did the best I could. You weren't here. Uh, you should be prepared for how Mom looks right now. She lost a bit of weight. It might be shocking for you to see her looking so fragile. Just forewarning you."

"I gotta go. I need to make the arrangements and call my boss to take a leave of absence. I don't suppose there is any chance Mom will agree to move to Washington?" Carmen asked hopefully.

"Not a chance in hell. She's more stubborn than you," he answered. "Talk to you later, Sis. Let me know how she's doing, okay? You're not the only one who loves Mom." The dial tone was the punctuation of the disastrous call with her brother.

Carmen returned to the dinner table and slumped in her chair. She caught Mac's concerned gaze while a single tear traveled down her cheek.

"Mom is in the hospital, and from what little my brother told me, I'll be needed there for a little while. I'm going to call the hospital and get the real scoop. But it sounds like I'll have to take Family Medical Leave to care for her until I do my damnedest to get her to sell the house and move to Washington."

"I know living in the farmhouse isn't the best situation for someone prone to pneumonia. I have a small amount set aside in savings for emergency repairs. I think this constitutes an emergency. I'll call for estimates tomorrow. If we have to, we'll redo the whole damn insulation and install a brand-new heating system. I promise I can make this comfortable for your mom. We can remodel the guest room. Get new furniture. Whatever she needs," Mac offered.

Carmen swiped her eyes. "Oh, Mac, that's why I love you so much. Unfortunately, it's not that simple. If it were just a matter of money, I would be delighted to cover the costs. Mom is extremely stubborn. It won't be easy to convince her to move. But I can't leave her all alone to fend for herself while my asshole brother does whatever is best for him." Carmen sighed and reached over to stroke Mac's face. "I have to go home. Do you understand?"

†

Mac wanted to scream. This wasn't fair. She'd just found the love of her life. Of course she would never keep Carmen from doing what was right. She'd do the same. She had done just that four years ago when she left her thriving practice and took over the farm to help her beloved pops. Mac stood, pulling Carmen into her arms, wrapping her in the most loving hug she could manage, to give her the support she needed. "Of course I do. What do you need me to do?"

"Can you see if you can find a flight to O'Hare? The sooner, the better. I need to call the hospital and talk to the charge nurse. That'll give me a better idea of what I'm up against. Then I should call Kathleen and tell her I need to take a leave."

"How long do you think you'll be?" Mac asked.

"I don't know. If my stupid brother got even half of what he shared correct, at least three months. Pulmonary embolisms take months, sometimes years to go away. And that's without other complications. Apparently, Mom has also been diagnosed with lupus."

"Onyx will be heartbroken. Midnight too," Mac added.

"Not you?" Carmen teased.

"I think you know the answer to that. I'm going to miss you like crazy. We'll find a way to make it work. I have a friend whose wife had to move for two years before she retired from the Navy, and they made it work. Granted, they could fly back and forth, visiting one another, which won't be easy for us, but remember, I've already declared my willingness to fight for you. Why don't you take Onyx with you? At least you'll have someone to cuddle with during those cold winter nights. It gets colder in Chicago than here. Besides, I'd rather you snuggle with one of our fur babies than a leggy blonde."

Carmen playfully shoved Mac. "As if. But that's not a bad idea. First task is calling the hospital to get an update on Mom's status. Daryl might have under-reported her condition, and that worries me more than I'm willing to admit."

"I'll find you a flight," Mac assured.

"Use my credit card. You are not paying for this," Carmen stated, leaving no room for negotiation.

"Okay," Mac acquiesced. She knew better than to argue and add undue stress. Carmen had enough to deal with. Debating who would pay was insignificant in the big scheme. Mac could find other ways to show her support—like driving her to the airport, even if it meant taking the whole day off. There was no way she would have Carmen take the bus and not be able to take the next flight out. With only one bus to Seattle every day, flights rarely worked out without the person having to stay overnight in Seattle or take an ugly flight that required twenty hours in a cramped plane. Evan could cover milking the goats, especially since their milk production had drastically reduced over the last month.

Even though she hated that task, Evan could also handle gathering the eggs. The hens constantly pecked at her. Mac tried to tell her they sensed her fear. She needed to be more confident and establish herself as the boss.

With Carmen's glorious meal left practically untouched except for the few bites that Mac had snagged before the call had interrupted their evening, Mac walked to her office to find the next flight out. Mac figured they had just enough time to pack up Onyx and pull together enough clothes to get Carmen through the next few weeks. The rest of the logistics could wait. She climbed the stairs to their bedroom, thinking she might get her packing started. While Carmen made her calls, Mac scratched her head. She wasn't even sure she had a suitcase. Maybe Carmen had one. She hadn't paid much attention to everything Carmen brought to the house when she moved in. The farmhouse may have been old, but it had plenty of storage. She'd need to wait until Carmen finished with her calls because, even if she found a suitcase, she didn't have the foggiest idea what to pack. Mac slumped on the bed. The reality of their situation was starting to sink in.

†

Things were worse than Carmen thought. Her mom was not doing well at all. The sooner she arrived in Chicago, the better. At least Kathleen had been more than understanding and told her not to worry about a thing. Kathleen would contact HR first thing in the morning and get the ball rolling with the paperwork necessary to place Carmen on Family Medical Leave. Kathleen was sure they could handle everything via email. She'd heard Mac climb the stairs and wondered what she was doing as she looked at the beautifully set table and noticed most of their meal untouched. She couldn't worry about that now. That was the least of her concerns.

Carmen found Mac sitting on the edge of the bed, looking more lost than Carmen thought she'd ever seen in the confident woman. Mac's eyes lifted to meet Carmen's.

"There's a 6:05 flight out tomorrow morning. I'll take you to the airport. I don't have a suitcase…" Her words trailed off.

Carmen offered Mac a weak smile. "I have a large rolling case that I stuck in the guest room closet when I moved in. I suppose I only need to worry about winter clothes for now, and I don't need anything fancy. It's not like I'll be out clubbing every night." Carmen attempted to lighten the mood.

"How can I help?"

"Maybe you could gather four to five of my sweaters. It doesn't matter which ones. And all my hoodies," Carmen answered.

"Okay. I should be the one to grab your undies too. There's no way I'm sending you to Chicago with a single pair of sexy panties. And I'm going to select your bras. Fat chance I'll let any of your racy matching sets find their way inside that suitcase. Those are for my eyes only," Mac teased.

But Carmen could tell the joke was forced. Mac's lips formed a straight line versus how they usually curved at the corners, and her eyes weren't twinkling with mirth.

Carmen attempted a weak chuckle. "I don't have any racy matching sets of underwear. Just pretty ones that I hoped would get your motor running."

"Oh, my motor needs no additional assistance to run smoothly," Mac responded. "Right, then." Mac clapped her hands and stood. "I have my tasks."

Carmen could see how brave Mac was trying to be, but if the glistening in her eyes was any indication, Mac was on the verge of unshed tears. Her stoic nature would not allow Mac to ugly cry in front of Carmen. Carmen was sure that would come later, perhaps on the shoulder of her beloved Pops. *It better not be on Evan's shoulder.* The thought snuck in before she had a chance to edit it. Regardless of who supported Mac, she was glad Mac had someone while they were forced apart, for hopefully not more than three months. But Carmen had her doubts. Pulmonary embolisms could take years to resolve, and if her mother refused to move, Carmen didn't know what she would do. At least there was Deb and Olivia to lend a shoulder.

Midnight and Onyx watched from their perch on the cat tree next to the bedroom window as the two women packed in silence. Midnight, the braver of the two, jumped on the bed and began playing with one of Carmen's bra straps. Carmen was thankful for the lighter moment and genuinely laughed at Midnight's antics. Eventually, Onyx joined her sister and plopped into the middle of the suitcase to settle into a small ball. Carmen's favorite sweater, while not cashmere, was just as soft, and Carmen supposed Onyx, always seeking the most comfortable place, had decided this was now her spot.

"There's no need for you to claim a place inside the suitcase, Onyx. You're coming with me. I would never put you in the cold luggage area of the plane. Nope, you're going to settle underneath the seat in front of me. I promise it won't be as traumatic as you think. I'll be loaded with your favorite treats," Carmen comforted.

Onyx lifted her head when Carmen uttered her name and offered a sweet, *meow brmmp.*

Carmen felt Mac step behind her and rub her back. "Midnight is going to be so distraught without her sister. She's going to miss her so much."

Carmen turned to look at Mac and saw the pain in her eyes. "Do you think it's the wrong thing to do?"

"No. Just stating a fact."

"Goddess. I hate everything about this. I am so mad at the universe right now. Would it have been so bad to let us have our happiness? Why does she have to fuck with us?" The tears now fell freely down her face as Mac gathered Carmen in her arms.

"It's going to be okay. Just a hiccup. Whatever doesn't break us makes us stronger. Right?"

Carmen nodded. "Stupid fucking saying. Only someone with enough strength to endure life's shit sandwich would say that."

Mac chuckled. "What a potty mouth you have when you're upset. First, you call your brother a selfish prick, and now the f-word keeps flying out. Do you kiss your mother with that mouth?" she teased.

"Oh, don't get me started. I know enough swear words to make a sailor cringe. Besides, I do believe that particular word has slipped from your mouth."

Mac kissed her lips. "Goddess, I love you."

"We're going to make it because I love you too. More than I've ever loved anyone else. We're meant to be together," Carmen stated with authority.

"Yes, we are. I'm not sure about many things in life, but I'm damn sure of that."

CHAPTER SIX

The wailing of Midnight and Onyx when Carmen placed Onyx in her carrier could still be heard throughout the house. Pops shuffled into the kitchen, presumably wondering why Midnight was crying. They needed to leave soon if Carmen was going to make it to the airport in time. When Pops had returned from his poker game, Mac had let him know what was going on, and he'd asked them to wake him up before they left for the airport.

"What in the blue blazes is Midnight hollering about?" Pops asked.

"Midnight is upset because Onyx is in the carrier without her. She's smart enough to sense something big is happening," Mac answered.

"Why didn't you wake me up? I wanted to be here to say goodbye to Carmen. I'd go with you two to the airport, but I'm going to milk the goats and gather the eggs. It's the least I can do since you've been practically taking care of the farm all by yourself for the past year and a half. No arguments, Mac." Pops held up his hand to stave off any further debate.

"Pops, Evan can do that. I was going to call on my way back from the airport. I didn't want to disturb her date tonight. And I haven't run the farm all by myself. Evan is a hard worker, and you help when you can."

"My joints have been real good lately, ever since Carmen suggested that acupuncturist. One day of milking won't kill me. It's not like they're all producing right now. It shouldn't take me long." Pops got a mischievous twinkle in his eye. "As soon as Evan starts on her chores, I'll let her gather the eggs. Don't you worry about a thing. Just get your girl to the airport on time, and I'll fill Evan in on everything." Pops opened his arms. "Now bring it in and give me a hug. Give your best to your mother. I know you'll do your darnedest to get back to us as soon as you work things out with your mother. You know we have plenty of room for her. It isn't the fanciest place, but having someone my age to talk with in the evenings would be nice. If she's anything like you, she'll be nice to look at too." Pops winked.

Carmen folded herself into his arms. "Oh, boy, I'm afraid with the legendary Sullivan charms, there will be another Torre that falls madly in love with an Irish charmer."

"Doubtful. It's a good thing that Mac here got her mother's good looks." Pops kissed her on the forehead. "Be safe. Love you like one of my own."

"Love you too, Pops." Carmen wiped the tear from the corner of her eye. "I'm ready."

With the suitcase and carry-on already in the truck, Mac lifted the cat carrier. Both kittens continued to cry. "It's going to be a long drive to the airport. Pops, will you let Midnight sleep with you? Hopefully, you can console her while I'm gone."

Pops scooped up the kitten and held her close while she squirmed in his arms. "I'll do the best I can. Hurry, go while I still have her with me."

Carmen kissed the top of Midnight's head and whispered, "You take care of your other mama and give her kisses and snuggles every night while I'm gone."

Carmen ran out of the house with Mac following closely behind and Onyx wailing her tiny little head off.

†

Once Carmen and Mac made it on the road, Carmen let Onyx out of the carrier, and she seemed to calm down. At least she wasn't wailing anymore. As she stroked her silky fur, Carmen comforted the little feline with soothing talk. Mac glanced at the two, and the touching sight filled her with love again. Carmen was a kitten whisperer, a bona fide lifesaver since she'd developed a nasty headache, compliments of no sleep, and two very upset kittens, not to mention their mamas.

They'd discussed the possibility of calling Olivia for her advice on how to calm Onyx during the long car ride and flight. Mac had suggested that she might need some kitty Xanax, but Carmen had assured Mac she didn't want to put something inside a kitten that might do more harm than good. That tracked with Carmen's philosophy on the overuse of drugs. She often railed against the pharmaceutical industry, which, in her opinion, pushed unnecessary medication on gullible people. Carmen was insistent the same probably held true for animals, even though she trusted Olivia.

Mac eased her truck into a parking space in the garage intended for larger vehicles. But who was she kidding? It was a damn tight spot, and she feared scraping her beat-up old truck against one of those newer fancy SUVs. With Onyx safely tucked inside her carrier, she'd allowed plenty of room for Carmen to crawl from the passenger seat. Unfortunately, that left little room for Mac, who had to perform an act of contortion to avoid hitting the behemoth of a vehicle next to her. Opening the tailgate of her enclosed truck, Mac pulled the heavy suitcase from the back along with the smaller carry-on.

"I've got these. You just make sure the little princess is calm," Mac said as she yanked hard enough to extend the telescoping handle on the larger bag. She set the carry-on atop the handle and rolled the bags through the parking lot.

Carmen chuckled. "Always the gentlewoman. My shero. You know, you could have dropped me off outside. They have places right there on the curb to check baggage. At least, I think they do. It's been years since I flew anywhere."

"No way. I'm taking you as far as possible to see you and Onyx off. I don't care if the whole airport witnesses our teary goodbye. It's Seattle, not Moses Lake. I don't think anyone will even blink an eye."

Taking the escalator to the fourth floor, where the breezeway leading to ticketing was located, they made their way to baggage check. There was barely a line as Carmen strolled to the front when a dour man waved them forward. Mac thought she might be less than perky at four in the morning too, so she gave the man a pass. At least he was efficient, and they were on their way to find the security checkpoint.

SeaTac, or Seattle Tacoma International Airport, was oddly quiet for such a busy place. But what did Mac know? It wasn't like she was some sort of jet setter, flying all over the world. Hell, Mac hadn't even traveled much in the United States. She supposed it was like this in any airport at a quarter to four in the morning. They'd left after midnight, and with the snow on Snoqualmie Pass, it had taken them that long to get to the airport.

Nothing was open yet, which was a shame since they'd packed up their barely eaten dinner the previous evening, and Mac's stomach growled. Working on the farm took a lot of energy, and she was used to eating three square meals a day.

Carmen glanced over at Mac. "I'm so sorry. I thought to bring treats and food for Onyx, plus a few snacks, but I didn't even think about breakfast for you. Will you please stop on the way back and get something to eat? Maybe you should check into a hotel, get some food and rest, then head back early tomorrow. I worry about you driving over the pass today."

"I'll be fine. Hotels are ridiculously expensive here. I'll stop for coffee. Seattle is like the coffee capital of the world. There's bound to be something open. I'll grab a pastry or something else not entirely healthy." Mac grinned. "It looks pretty empty. Should we hang out here for a bit since I can't sneak through security with you?"

Carmen nodded, sat on a bench, and set Onyx's carrier on the floor. Thankfully, the kitten had worn herself out and was napping peacefully inside. "Yeah, I'd like that, but not for too long. I really want you on the road and safely home before I land in Chicago if you aren't going to stay in Seattle today. I'll call the minute I touch the ground. Unless you'd rather I wait because you'll be sleeping?"

Mac turned and grabbed both of Carmen's hands, using her thumbs to stroke the tops. "No, I'd prefer for you to wake me. I'll worry until I get a call from you. Promise me you'll call whenever you need to talk. If phone calls and FaceTime are all we have for the next several months, I want them to be frequent enough to soften the blow of not having you sleep beside me every night."

"I promise. I won't be able to survive without daily calls." And with that simple statement, the floodgates opened. Carmen openly cried as Mac tried her best to comfort her while her own heart broke into a thousand jagged pieces.

"We're going to make this work, no matter what it takes," Mac assured her.

Carmen angrily brushed aside her tears. "I'll hold you to that."

The two women stayed close together, not saying anything more until Mac felt Carmen shift and look at her watch. It was time. She brushed her lips against Carmen before watching her approach the TSA checkpoint, where she showed them her boarding pass and continued through to the rest of security by setting her bag and empty carrier on the conveyor. Carmen and Onyx walked through the metal detector, and Mac couldn't see her anymore. Finally, she could let her tears fall as she made it to the parking garage and the long, lonely drive back to the farm.

CHAPTER SEVEN

Traveling solo was a bitch. O'Hare was as busy as Carmen remembered. She struggled with her giant suitcase, carry-on and Onyx's carrier, but finally reached the location where she'd pick up her rideshare. Goddess knew how much it would cost to go from O'Hare to Elgin. An Uber was undoubtedly less expensive than a cab. Wanting to get the ride situated first, she had waited to call Mac. She'd have a long enough drive to her childhood home with nothing better to do, so she decided it was preferable to delay the call. Maybe it would give Mac more time to sleep. Although, by her calculations, she doubted Mac had been asleep for more than a few hours.

Her Uber driver didn't speak perfect English, nor was he a chatty sort. That didn't matter to Carmen. She actually preferred his silence while she dug out her phone and made the call.

A groggy Mac answered on the third ring. "Hello, gorgeous."

"I woke you up."

"It's fine. I can easily go back to sleep."

Carmen could hear Mac yawn. "I won't keep you awake long, so you won't have trouble returning to sleep. I just wanted to let you know I'm heading to Mom's. I also needed to hear your voice to ensure you got home okay. How's Midnight?"

"She's good. Finally snuggled against me after following me around until I jumped into bed. She doesn't understand why the routine has changed. She's confused about not seeing you and Onyx in bed with me. I'll have a long talk with her after getting more sleep."

"You sound like you're exhausted. I'm going to let you go back to sleep. Call me when you wake up. I should have an update on Mom by then. I love you."

"I love you too. Give your mom a hug for me. I'll talk to you later."

Carmen settled in the back of the car, and when Onyx meowed to be let out of her carrier, Carmen obliged and set the kitten on her lap, stroking and calming her for the long ride to the house. Although Carmen really needed to get to the hospital pronto and talk with the nurses and physicians caring for her mom, she didn't dare leave Onyx in a strange house without toys, a litter box and soft bed. She'd need to find her mother's car keys and make a quick trip to the pet store to get Onyx settled. Hopefully, the kitten would understand if she patiently explained everything to her.

Fortunately, time seemed to go quickly, and before Carmen knew it, the car had stopped on Century Oaks Drive in front of her childhood home. The established neighborhood hadn't changed a whole lot. Not that she had expected it to. The same towering oak trees, lilac and rose bushes that had been her father's pride and joy, surrounded the large brick home. Although he wasn't the one who had to mow around the trees or rake the leaves, he left that task to her and her brother, which ultimately meant Carmen was the one who completed the chores.

Carmen hadn't even had to ask her brother to make sure he left a key for her because there was always one in the pot by the front door. After the Uber driver was nice enough to help her unload her luggage, she dragged the cases up the long driveway and set everything on the ground before trekking to the front door to retrieve the key. No one ever entered the house through the front door, but Carmen didn't have a remote control to operate the garage door. Onyx began wailing again the minute Carmen started toward the front door. Turning her head, she tried to explain to the distraught kitten. "Onyx, shh, Mommy is not abandoning you. I will come get you as soon as I open the garage door. Then we'll go shopping."

As soon as Onyx heard her voice, she quieted some, but tiny meows still escaped, as if she wanted to ensure that Carmen knew she was still trapped inside the carrier.

The house key was practically sitting on top of the dirt, screaming, "Come one, come all, it's a fire sale for all levels of burglars. Everything is free without the possibility of jail time." Carmen shook her head and pushed the key into the lock, needing to jiggle it around before the key turned. Carmen wasn't as mechanically inclined as Mac, but she could spray some WD-40 to make it easier to open the front door. Then she laughed at how ridiculous that thought was. Since her family didn't use this door, that would simply make it easier for someone to break in, especially if her mother continued to place the key on top of the soil, shining like a beacon to criminals.

Carmen hurried through the house, noticing how dirty it was, until she reached the door to the garage and pressed the button to open it. As she hurried to collect Onyx and bring her inside, she mumbled to herself, "If I knew where that little bastard was, I'd personally wrap my hands around his neck and strangle him." *Of course, he wouldn't care one bit about keeping the house neat and tidy, despite knowing how much dirt would upset Mom.*

Even Onyx found it disgusting. After being let out of her carrier and sniffing around, she promptly returned to the safety of her protective plastic house and scrambled inside.

"I know, my sweet baby." Carmen wrinkled her nose and forced her gag reflex back. She had a dilemma on her hands. Should she spend the time cleaning the house before going to the pet store and visiting her mom, or grab Onyx and worry about the house after she returned? One thing she knew for sure: there was no way she would bring her mother home to this disgusting mess.

Caked-on dishes were piled high in the sink. Empty carry-out containers littered the counters, and it looked as though the carpets and floors had not been touched for weeks. Carmen almost didn't want to venture into the bathrooms. The disgusting pig had probably peed all over the floors, missing the toilet either in the middle of the night or after an evening of drinking.

Later. The germs aren't going anywhere, even if I wish they would. Decision made. Carmen rooted in the drawers until she found her mother's car keys, then she closed Onyx's carrier and grabbed it on her way out the door. She set the carrier on the passenger seat, quickly retrieved her luggage from the driveway, and brought both bags inside the house before returning to the car.

Prior to turning the key, she sent a small prayer to the universe. With her luck, her asshole brother had abused the car, and the damn thing wouldn't start. When the engine turned over, she shouted, "Hallelujah!" Her eyes traveled to the dashboard, and she noticed the blinking light indicating she was almost out of gas.

"Fucking hell. I really am going to track him down and kill that lazy son of a bitch."

With an unknown amount of gas in the tank, she couldn't dilly-dally and wait until the car warmed. Carmen practically slammed out of the driveway, pushing the garage remote as she backed out, and headed for the closest gas station. Things were fuzzy, but everything was coming back, and she knew the gas station was less than two miles away. She remembered riding her bike to the mini mart to get a slushie on one of those hot summer days that were so typical in the Midwest. At least if she ran out of gas, she could walk there. Suddenly, she felt exhausted. All Carmen wanted to do was fold herself inside Mac's solid arms and block out the world with its vast problems and challenges. But rest would have to come later, after she'd taken care of the most critical items.

†

Try as she might, Mac could not return to sleep after the brief call with Carmen. If she didn't believe it would make her seem pathetic, she would have called Carmen back less than an hour later. Instead, Mac gave up on trying to recapture sleep and crawled from the bed. After a quick shower, she decided to head outside and check on the animals. Not that she didn't trust everything essential had been taken care of by Pops and Evan, but she needed something else to focus on besides her fractured heart.

She found Evan cleaning the goat enclosure and greeted her assistant. "Hey."

"You're up. Pops filled me in. I'm so sorry, Mac. It must have been hard to say goodbye. Do you think she'll ever come back?"

"We didn't break up, Evan!" Mac exclaimed with a fair amount of irritation.

"Oh, I know, but it sounds like she'll be there for a long time. Carmen's a catch, so I'm sure she'll have plenty of offers. Doesn't she have friends or something in Illinois? I mean, she grew up there and spent the better part of her life in the Midwest. She's only been out here for a few years. Maybe being back home will remind her of what she's missing. It's not like living in Moses Lake is that great for lesbians. I heard Chicago is a good place to be queer. Lots of opportunities to meet other queer women."

Mac didn't want Evan's words to take root, but a tiny part of her had wondered the same thing. Carmen was beautiful, kind and intelligent, and Moses Lake wasn't exactly the most exciting place to live. Mac shook her head as if she could loosen those thoughts and let them fly right out of her skull and onto the ground, where she would stomp them into oblivion.

"Don't be daft. Carmen loves it here, and she loves me. She's coming back as soon as she can either get her mother situated and stable, or convince her to move here," Mac declared with less conviction than she should have. "I'm going to check the chicken coop." Mac stomped out of the enclosure, muttering to herself and feeling an acute desire to call Carmen to settle her nagging uneasiness. *Later, I'll call later. She doesn't need an insecure version of me to deal with right now.*

She nearly ran into her pops on her way to the chicken coop. Mac wasn't even sure if she'd been muttering to herself or just had those thoughts.

"Whoa. Where's the fire?" Pops asked. "You look like when you used to almost get the fish all the way to the shore before it would wriggle off the hook and swim away."

Mac tried to offer a smile. "Yeah, I hated that. I never could understand how that didn't happen to you. It's not like you weren't the one to teach me to fish. Did you leave out some important trick, you old codger—just so you would have bragging rights about who caught the biggest fish?"

"Still haven't told me what's got you so upset. It isn't the fact that Carmen is thousands of miles away because that look is a whole lot different from this one. More sadness, less irritation."

Mac sighed. "Evan insinuated Carmen might hook up with one of her old friends in Chicago. And when I say hook up, I don't mean have a glass of wine and talk about old times."

"Evan is a little shit that would like nothing better than for you and Carmen to split. I like the kid, but she's a child in a woman's body. Evan is a hard worker, and I don't mean to suggest you can her or anything, but the kid has the hots for you," Pops explained. "Didn't she have a date or something last night?"

Mac pinched the bridge of her nose. "Crap. I was so wrapped up in wallowing inside my pit of despair over my empty bed I forgot to ask." Mac pivoted and started to head in the opposite direction to talk to Evan.

"I'm proud of you, Mac." Pops clapped her on the back. "You consistently take the high road. You'll always be the bigger person. And that's what will bring Carmen back to you. Look, I'm not going to lie. Carmen is a catch, but so are you. The two of you are meant to be together."

"Thanks, Pops." Mac continued walking to the goat enclosure. Once inside, she interrupted Evan, who was removing more straw with a pitchfork. "Hey, Evan, I'm sorry for being short with you earlier. You didn't deserve that. How was your date last night?"

Evan turned and smiled brightly. "No need to apologize. I know it's tough for you right now. I should have been more sensitive. If you ever need someone to talk to or just, you know, vent, cry, whatever, I'm here for you. The date went well. Too early to tell if something will come of it, but we're going out again. At least we're compatible in bed. She's kind of a dark horse in that respect. Who knew she'd be that wild?" Evan chuckled.

"Wow! You don't mess around. You two already slept together? On a first date? It took Carmen and I two months to reach that point. I nearly died from all the pent-up sexual chemistry."

"Old school, huh?" Evan teased. "Yeah, I don't have the patience for that. My philosophy is that you have to make things happen. No one else is going to do it for you. Take the bull by the horns, you know?"

"Good things come to those that wait," Mac countered. "Well, I'm glad your date went well, and you're going to see one another again. We're coming into the slow season, so that should give you plenty of time to woo the girl. She seems nice. Attractive too. Just let me know if you need to take any time off for a long weekend or something."

"Will do. You're the best boss ever," Evan gushed. "And a good friend."

CHAPTER EIGHT

Carmen hadn't wanted to abandon Onyx alone in the pigsty that Daryl left for her to deal with, but leaving the kitten in the car was not an option, and Carmen didn't know how long she would be at the hospital. She found a moderately clean guest bedroom and set the litter box, toys, scratching post and cat bed in the room, then opened the carrier door for Onyx to explore her new surroundings.

After Carmen felt she'd settled Onyx enough to be alone for a couple of hours, she scooped up the kitten and whispered, "You be a good girl for Mommy, and I'll be back in a few hours. I know this is stressful for you, so I promise to shower you with love and treats when I return."

"Meow brmmp."

"Thank you for understanding. Mom is going to love you. Maybe having something soft to pet will help with her recovery. You and she are going to become best buddies."

†

Checking in at the hospital's information desk, Carmen was startled to hear someone call her name.

"Carmen?"

"Allison! Oh, my goddess, you haven't changed a bit. Do you work here?" Carmen asked.

The joy in Allison's expression suddenly turned somber. "I do. Heard about your mom. She's actually on my unit right now. Let me escort you there."

"Are you her nurse?"

Allison shook her head. "No, but Trina is good. Your mom is getting the best care here. I made sure of that, but Carmen, you need to be prepared for what you'll see. She's not been doing well lately. This is the third time in three months that she's been here. The other two times, she was on the medical-surgical unit, but because of the deterioration in her condition, we put her in critical care as a precaution," Allison explained.

Carmen was almost afraid to ask but barreled on anyway. "Is she on a vent?"

"No, but her care team seriously considered it at one point. I think she's turned a corner, but your brother did not do her any favors by waiting so long to call the ambulance."

"Thanks, I appreciate it. I'm guessing you were the one to get Mom admitted to your unit. I owe you."

"Let's get together and have dinner. I'd love to catch up with you." Allison touched Carmen on the arm and gently guided her to the elevators.

"I'd like that, but maybe after I feel like I can leave Mom at home alone," Carmen answered.

Allison pushed the button for the elevator. "Hey, you know caregivers need breaks. I have the names of some superb home health aides who could give you a breather. I highly recommend that, not only for your health and welfare but also for your mom's. I remember how independent she was. The woman will probably fuss if you hover over her twenty-four-seven."

The two women stepped into the elevator, and Allison pressed the button for the sixth floor.

Carmen chuckled. "Yeah. That's an understatement. Okay. Don't forget to give me your contact information."

After the women stepped off the elevator, Allison led Carmen to the private room. "Don't worry. I'll make sure to get that before you leave. I'll grab Trina; she can give you all the details about your mother's condition. It's so great to see you, Carmen. How about a hug?"

Carmen stepped into Allison's arms and melted into her good friend's embrace. "Thank you." Her voice threatened to break as she choked back tears.

Carmen sucked in her breath and prepared herself as she stepped into the room. She couldn't suppress the gasp when she saw her mother. She'd lost a lot of weight. The woman lying in the bed looked nothing like her vibrant mother. This person was as frail-looking as a ninety-year-old woman.

Her mother's eyes slowly opened, and she croaked, "Carmen."

"Oh, Mom. Why didn't you call? I would have been on the first plane to Chicago."

"You have your own life to live, Carmen. You don't need to drop everything to care for your mother."

"Why did you let *Daryl* take care of you?" Carmen couldn't help the hurt that crept into her voice.

"I didn't *let* Daryl take care of me. I allowed him to live in the house because he had nowhere else to go. He'd been evicted from his last residence."

"That little fucker. Why do you let Daryl take advantage of you?" Carmen asked, exasperation dripping from every syllable.

"Carmen," her mom started patiently, "your brother doesn't have the same gifts that you do. He's had a hard life. Can you imagine what it's like to constantly stay in the shadow of a younger sibling? All the ribbons you won for nearly everything you touched. He couldn't compete with that. Pain sometimes causes people to gravitate to things that are not good for them. At least he's clean now. Can you imagine if he was living on the streets? I didn't want him to go back to the drugs and alcohol."

"How do you know he hasn't?" Carmen asked.

"I know when he's using. Give me some credit."

"Fine. I don't want to talk about Daryl. Here's how things are going to go. I'm staying until I'm one hundred percent convinced you are strong enough to live on your own and thrive. Unless you want to move to Washington and live with Mac, Pops, and me at the farm. I know this is your home, Mom, but rambling around in that big house without Dad can't be what you really want to do."

"All my bingo buddies are here. I don't want to move."

"We have bingo in Washington too, you know. We also have great casinos. If you sell the house, you'll have plenty of money to gamble and play bingo to your heart's content. Mac and Pops won't take a penny in rent, and the farm supplies nearly everything we need. Plus, it's much healthier than all that hormone-injected meat you get at the store."

"Can we talk about this later?"

A middle-aged woman entered the room. "Hi, I'm Trina, your mother's nurse. Allison told me you're her daughter. I'm happy to answer any questions you may have. I've already checked. Your mother gave you medical power of attorney. Mrs. Torre, I assume it's okay with you if I discuss your medical condition with your daughter. I just need your authorization to do that."

Rose Torre lifted her shaking, feeble hand and answered, "Yes, of course. If I don't give her permission to root around in my medical records, she'll harangue me until I do," she teased. "Plus, she can play interpreter for me because, honestly, I don't understand half of what the doctors and nurses tell me."

"You just made my job a whole lot easier." Trina winked at Rose. "Not that we don't enjoy having Mrs. Torre stay with us, but she's been a frequent flyer lately, and I can't imagine the flights have been all that pleasant. We think we've got a handle on her pneumonia and could have probably moved her to the medical unit, but we're still watching the pulmonary embolism. Her autoimmune disease hasn't helped, with her susceptibility to bacterial infections. We also noticed a dramatic weight loss. Whatever you can do to strengthen her body will help."

Carmen continued to talk with Trina while Rose remained quiet. She would summarize everything for her mother in layman's terms as soon as they discharged her mother and released her from the hospital, which wouldn't be for at least another day or two. Carmen thought that was fine since she wanted to make the house presentable with a thorough top-to-bottom cleaning. Carmen also needed to arrange a mold inspection to ensure she wasn't dealing with that nasty situation before her mother settled back into her home. If there was black mold, that could be a contributing factor to her mother's discomfort on top of all the other medical challenges she faced. All these thoughts rumbled around in her head, and she made a mental checklist of everything to do over the next twenty-four hours. Sleep was overrated. She could rest when she'd made all the necessary arrangements.

†

It wasn't like Mac ever excluded Evan from joining them for dinner. Even before Carmen came to live with Mac, Evan had eaten with Mac and her pops nearly every night. After all, Evan lived and worked on the farm. It just made sense to include her most evenings unless she had plans. But today seemed different. Wrong. With Carmen missing, Mac almost felt like she was cheating to have another woman at the dinner table with her and Pops.

Mac was no chef, but she could pull together a basic meal. It helped that there were plenty of leftovers from the night before. Adding a couple of pork chops and grilled zucchini, she set the food on the table before Evan emerged from the downstairs bath after washing up. Pops had already shuffled into the kitchen, favoring his right leg. Either he'd been lying about his joints feeling good after seeing the acupuncturist, or the cold, wet day had caused him a round of fresh pain.

"I saw you limp into the kitchen, Pops. How much time did you spend outside today while I was sleeping?" Mac asked.

"Don't start coddling me now. I'm still the parent here," he responded gruffly but with affection. "You got enough to worry about without me sloughing off the minuscule duties you still let me do on *my* farm."

Evan kept looking between Pops and Mac but wisely kept her mouth shut as she piled her plate high.

"Oh, so it's *your* farm now? Eat before it gets cold," Mac ordered. "I know it won't nearly be as good as what Carmen makes for us, but we'll just have to suffer together."

Pops shook his head. "Now, you know I didn't mean it that way. Of course, it's your farm too. Always has been. I just hate being put out to pasture before my time."

"No one's putting you out to pasture, Pops. I still need your expertise in running the farm. But that help has much less to do with the manual labor than the business end of things."

"I'm old, Mac, but I'm not stupid. With your fancy law degree, you know a lot more than me about the business end of things. Don't think I haven't noticed how you've expanded the farm and increased our profit margins. I haven't taught you diddly squat. It's more like you've schooled me on more than one occasion." Pops cut off a piece of pork and shoved it into his mouth. "Not bad," he mumbled around his mouth full of food.

Evan had already started shoveling the leftovers in her mouth and remarked, "Yeah, it's actually fantastic."

Mac laughed. "That's because you're chowing down on what Carmen made for us last night. You'll recognize the difference in our skill sets as soon as you eat a bite of pork or zucchini. You better savor the goodness now. There's a pie for dessert, but from now on, we'll need to skip dessert or run to the bakery for something that won't be nearly as good."

"I could try to bake a pie," Evan offered. "Seems wasteful not to use the apples, peaches, blackberries, and blueberries we harvested."

"Have at it. I won't turn down freshly baked desserts." Mac cut a small piece of pork and popped it into her mouth, chewing slowly. "Well, it isn't like Carmen's, but it's edible, I suppose."

Mac glanced at her watch and noted the time. It was after five in Washington, which meant it was after seven in Elgin. Mac remembered she was supposed to call when she woke, and that had been hours ago. She almost excused herself from the table to make the call but remembered her manners and decided if something critical had occurred, surely Carmen would have phoned. Carmen was probably busy taking care of things.

The three farmers ate in silence until Evan, who was the first to finish, pushed her plate away. "Great meal, Mac. I'll do the dishes. I think I need to let this settle before cutting a slice of that pie sitting on the counter. Do you want to grab a beer at Sporty's tonight?"

Mac must have looked at Evan like she had three heads because Evan quickly looked away. *Do I look like I'm in the mood for a beer?* Instead of spitting out her less-than-friendly response, she provided an answer that was considerably more polite. "I'm still a little tired from the drive to the airport. I'll pass, but thanks for asking."

"Sure, sure. I just thought you might need something to take your mind off of…uh, things." Evan grabbed the empty plates and began clearing the table.

"I'll help with the dishes, and then I need to call Carmen." Mac grabbed her plate and took it to the sink. There weren't many leftovers to pack up, so cleaning the kitchen took no time. Mac cut into the pie and took a large piece to bring to her office. She wanted privacy while she talked with Carmen. "I'll see both of you tomorrow. After talking with Carmen, I'm going to read a little and then head to bed."

"Okay, boss. See you tomorrow," Evan answered as she waved her hand in the air and exited the kitchen with a large slice of pie on a paper napkin.

Midnight, her constant shadow, dutifully followed Mac to her office and curled her body inside her bed. As soon as

Mac settled into her worn leather chair, she pressed the number for Carmen and waited until she answered.

Carmen sounded winded after answering on the fourth ring. "Oh, Mac, I'm so glad you called. I just noticed the time, and I know you haven't been sleeping this whole time. Everything okay?"

"I should be asking you that question. Why do you sound like you just ran a marathon?"

"Ugh, I was upstairs finishing cleaning my brother's room. Needless to say, it was an absolute disaster. I might have to get an exterminator to fumigate the damn room. His room was the last one I needed to tackle. I wanted to put on a respirator while working on it."

"You sound exhausted," Mac replied sympathetically.

"Yeah, it might be hitting me now just how little sleep I've gotten in the last thirty-six hours," Carmen admitted. "After I left the hospital, I got a second wind and wanted to take advantage of that extra energy. Besides, there was no way I could leave the house the way it looked while I slept. Poor Onyx does not know what to make of things."

"I wish I could have been there with you to help. How's your mom doing?"

Carmen sighed loudly. "Not great, but I think I can help her turn a corner. Unfortunately, it's going to take time. Her appearance shocked me. She's been in and out of the hospital with pneumonia these last few months. I'm concerned about her pulmonary embolism, but an even larger issue is her weakened immune system. Lupus is not helping. We also need to work on her weight. She's a bag of bones right now, and that isn't helping either."

"Did you float the idea of your mom coming to live with us in Washington?" Mac asked, hopeful that Carmen had received a positive reaction.

"I did. It's a no-go for right now, but I haven't given up."

"How long do you think you'll have to stay in Elgin?" Mac had to ask the question, even though she knew she probably wouldn't like the answer.

"Oh, babe, it'll be at least three months, and if the pulmonary embolism is still there, or goddess forbid, has grown, I can't leave Mom. We also need to manage her lupus, which might take a while. I'll know more in the next couple of months after taking her to the specialist and seeing how she responds to different treatments."

"I understand. Maybe I can find a way to travel there and stay for a week or two. Winter is our slow season. Even if I have to hire a temporary farm hand to help Evan, I feel like I need to do this to show my support."

"That's so sweet of you. I love you. The one bright spot in this whole mess is that I ran into an old friend. She's a critical care nurse at the hospital, and I'm convinced she's been pulling strings to ensure Mom has received the best care possible. Allison and I went to school together. She'll be a tremendous support. Plus, Allison knows people I can hire to help me care for Mom. She warned me about caretaker fatigue. She's right. For me to do a good job caring for Mom, I have to be physically and emotionally healthy."

Mac wasn't sure how she felt about hearing this. She wanted to be the one to support Carmen, but she supposed if she couldn't be there by her side, at least Carmen had someone she could lean on. In the final analysis, this was about Carmen and not Mac's nagging insecurity. If Allison could be there for Carmen, Mac was all for it.

"That's wonderful news, Carmen. I'm glad you have a friend to lean on. I wish I could be the only person you need, but that's selfish and unrealistic," Mac said with more conviction than she actually felt. "So, I added to the leftovers and made some pork chops and grilled zucchini. It wasn't a Carmen masterpiece, but it was edible. More than half the pie is already gone. Evan offered to use our fruit stores to bake pies versus buying them from the bakery."

"Evan? A baker? You'll have to let me know how that goes." Carmen chuckled. "I'm surprised Pops didn't offer to take over that task. He's watched me make pies before. I'll bet he could do it."

"Pops is too smart to offer his nonexistent baking skills, even if he watched you. I'm sure he only sat there to keep you company, not to learn how to bake pies."

"Maybe, but I always explained what I was doing and offered tricks and tips. No doubt something snuck inside that cunning brain of his," Carmen argued.

"Cunning is the operative word," Mac answered. "No way would he admit his knowledge after Evan offered to take on that task." Mac chuckled. "I saw a few marks on Evan's hands tonight. The chickens did a bit of pecking because Pops made Evan gather the eggs."

"That's mean. Your pops knows how to gather those eggs without getting pecked."

"It's Pop's way of teaching humility. He did that to me as well. I might have swaggered about as a youngster, thinking I knew more than I did. Well, Pops nipped that in the bud. He let me get pecked a few times before showing me a trick or two," Mac explained. "I should probably let you go so you can get a decent night's sleep. Please take care of yourself. I'll call tomorrow, or you can phone me when you have a free moment. I'll take my cell with me to avoid missing your call. I love you."

"Love you too. Talk to you tomorrow."

After the call ended, Mac took a large bite of her pie and moaned in delight. There were so many things she would miss. Having Carmen by her side had spoiled Mac—doing all the little things she undoubtedly took for granted. Mac vowed to express her appreciation for Carmen as soon as she returned. Three months was a long time. Mac didn't know how she would survive if their separation lasted much longer than that. It had been less than twenty-four hours, and she was already miserable.

"Ready to snuggle with your mama?" Mac asked.

Midnight's tiny ears perked up, and when Mac slowly lifted her body from the chair, she stretched and yawned, jumping off the bed to follow Mac as she made her way to the bedroom. When Mac crawled under the covers and grabbed the tablet on her nightstand, Midnight paced the bedroom, meowing loudly, until Mac patted the spot beside her.

"Remember, I told you that Carmen and Onyx are going to be away for a little bit. But they'll come back. I promise."

Midnight tilted her tiny head, and Mac chuckled when she heard the almost human-like huff push out of her mouth.

CHAPTER NINE

Midnight knew perfectly well what was happening, but that didn't mean she had to like it. It was bad enough they'd separated her from her sister, but now her favorite human was equally sad and miserable. It wasn't like she didn't miss Carmen too. Carmen always snuck her a few treats under the table. Perhaps not as many as Onyx got throughout the day, if you could go by her ever-increasing belly, but Onyx didn't get to explore like Midnight, and that was preferable to the treats. Besides, Midnight had developed a taste for fresh meat after catching her first mouse. She'd tried to offer the treat to Mac, but Mac had told her to keep it.

There was no sense in punishing Mac for something clearly out of her control. When Mac patted the spot on the bed that Carmen usually occupied, Midnight jumped up and settled next to her. But she was a cat, and cats expressed their displeasure, so the huff spilled from her mouth as a sort of warning. *No more surprises.* Midnight wanted to clarify that she wasn't in the mood to accept anyone else in Mac's bed except Carmen and Onyx.

Evan wasn't getting her message. Midnight thought she'd made her feelings loud and clear. If Evan didn't watch out, Midnight was going to take a major chunk out of whatever exposed area of skin she could sink her teeth into. Mac had been oblivious to Evan's overtures. Sure, they were subtle, and Evan had made a big deal about her date, but Midnight saw right through the ruse. Suggesting that Carmen would find someone new. *Preposterous.* Midnight could tell that Evan had landed a direct hit. She'd heard the slight hesitation in Mac's voice. Plus, it was never a good sign when Mac muttered to herself.

Midnight started purring as she settled on top of the comforter. She never understood how Onyx would burrow under the covers. That was far too restrictive for Midnight. Not that she didn't trust Mac, but an escape route was first and foremost on her mind. Midnight was easily overstimulated, but she never wanted to remind her mama to stop petting her with a tiny bite that might get misconstrued. Because if there was one thing she wanted Mac to feel confident about, it was that Midnight adored her. She would never leave her side.

"Guess it's just you and me for a while. You'll keep me company, won't you Midnight?"

"Meow."

†

Carmen had crashed hard the previous night after cleaning the house from top to bottom. The following day, she woke to Onyx kneading her chest. Glancing at the clock on the nightstand, she was shocked to learn how late it was.

"Oh, my poor baby. You want your morning treat, don't you?"

"Meow brmmp."

"Oh, goddess, not only have I ripped you from the only home you've ever known, but now I'm late with your treat. I know you won't starve because I put out the dry food last night, but that isn't as tasty as chicken or fish, is it? I haven't had the chance to stock the refrigerator yet to cook something for you. Will a can of wet food suffice for now?"

"Meow brmmp."

"I'll take that as a yes until you turn your nose up." Carmen laughed and pushed aside the covers. It was still early but not by Onyx's standards when she expected her morning treat.

Carmen shuffled into the bathroom to relieve herself before heading straight to the kitchen, where she'd stashed the cat food. She'd settle Onyx first before showering and heading to the grocery store. If all went smoothly, she could be back to put away the groceries and still make it to the hospital, right as visiting hours began.

The prior day had been difficult because Carmen didn't want to leave her mother's side. Unfortunately, she had so many competing demands on her time. Knowing the house was an absolute disaster, she'd left Onyx alone, creating warring emotions. Her mother had finally ordered her to leave and get some rest. She'd insisted she couldn't get any rest with Carmen hovering over her, and that tiny spark that was her mother had shown through. Feeling encouraged by how her mother had perked up, and with Allison's assurance that she would call if there were any changes in her mother's condition, Carmen made the decision to go home and tackle the house.

Having a clean kitchen was such a relief. Carmen started a pot of coffee, opened a can of food, dumped the contents on a plate and then searched for her phone. She set the wet food on the floor and punched the number for Mac. Onyx did not seem impressed with the morning treat on offer as an irritated *meow* erupted from her mouth. The adorable chirp was missing.

"Meooooow."

"Hey, I was just thinking about you but wanted to wait to call in case you slept in. Was that Onyx meowing like someone was pulling her fur?" Mac asked.

Carmen chuckled. "She isn't happy with her morning treat. I haven't had the chance to stock the refrigerator yet. I wonder if she'll like Atlantic salmon as much as Pacific? I haven't called too early, have I? I wanted to catch you before you got into the swing of things."

"No, not too early at all. I've been up for a while. It's hard to sleep in the big old bed without you. Midnight's a great companion, but there are limitations to how much comfort she can provide," Mac answered.

"I won't keep you. I just needed to hear your voice and to tell you I love you."

"Aw, I love you too, and of course, you already know this, but I miss you like crazy. So, what's on your agenda for today besides grocery shopping and visiting your mom?"

"That's about it. I might contact those home health aides that Allison suggested and interview them for a short or potentially long-term position. I have enough savings to cover things for a while but may have to consider picking up some per diem shifts to supplement. I don't have nearly enough paid time off for the next three months. That will run out in about a month and a half, and then my leave will be unpaid." Carmen sighed.

"I have some savings I could give you," Mac offered. "It'll just mean a delay in those repairs on the house. And if you do manage to convince your mom to come live with us, one of those repairs was redoing the insulation and making the entire house more energy efficient so it's a lot less drafty."

"That's incredibly sweet of you to offer, but no way will I take your money. Do the repairs. In fact, I should contribute half the costs to those repairs since I live there too. And I hope to convince Mom to come with me. Actually, I should foot the bill for the entire cost of making the farmhouse more efficient since I suspect you're only doing that for me."

"I could get into a cozier house. I'm sure Pops wouldn't hate it either. It'd be a lot easier on his joints. So, no, I wasn't planning on doing this just for you. Although I admit, I'm interested in pushing up the timeline because I want to make the place enticing for you and your mom."

"I'd still like to contribute," Carmen insisted. "Will you please let me? That would make me feel more like it's our home and not just yours."

Mac chuckled. "Damn, you're good. Using the emotional argument, you know I can't resist. I like hearing you talk about the farmhouse as our home. I'll think about it. That's the best I can do right now."

"Call me tonight?"

"Absolutely. I'll call after dinner. Will you be home around nine?"

"Probably, but I can still take your call if I'm at the hospital. I'll just step out of Mom's room."

"Okay. I love you. Give my best to your mom. Maybe when she's feeling better, we can FaceTime, and she can get to know me a little better. I can be very persuasive and charming. Perhaps stereo pleas for her to come live with us will work."

"Oh, I know how charming you can be. Unfortunately, Mom is very stubborn. Love you too. Talk to you later tonight."

"Bye, love."

Carmen ended her call, looked at the untouched plate of wet food and sighed. Onyx sat patiently, looking up at her.

"Okay, fine, I'm heading to the shower now. Give me a little more time, and I'll bring back something yummy from the store for you."

"Meow brmmp."

Onyx brushed against Carmen's ankles, then stretched her paws onto Carmen's legs. She scooped the little furball into her arms and headed to the bathroom for a quick shower.

†

Mac whistled as she headed to the chicken coop to collect her eggs. She was in a good mood. As good as she could manage with the distance between Carmen and herself. Of course she needed to wait until Carmen returned to Washington, but hearing Carmen talk about the farmhouse like she already considered it their home, suggested permanence. Not that Carmen had given any indication otherwise. She had been deliberate in her decision to move in, meaning she also believed they'd make it official one day.

After filling her egg cartons, Mac left the henhouse, dreaming about a simple wedding ceremony with their closest friends and family. She must have been entirely in her head because she didn't hear Evan greet her until she was almost on top of the woman.

"You must be thinking of something awfully sinful," Evan joked. "I've been calling you, and that smile on your face is electrifying. Better watch out, or I'll tattle to Carmen. When the cat's away…"

"If you must know, I was dreaming of our wedding. And I would greatly appreciate it if you didn't say anything to Carmen. I plan to ask her to marry me as soon as she returns."

Evan frowned. "Carmen's great, and I know you love her, but what if she stays in Chicago for years? Don't you think that it would be unfair to her if she has to build a new life there? You had to do that when you returned to the farm. You, of all people, should understand family obligations. Sometimes, we have to give up our dreams for the ones we love."

Midnight charged Evan and swiped at her ankle, hissing. While Mac knew she had to chastise Midnight for attacking Evan, secretly she applauded her.

"Fucking hell. She has sharp claws. The little beast drew blood. I don't understand why she hates me so much."

"Midnight, stop that. Come here." Mac patted her leg, and Midnight pranced over. Mac could swear she saw the kitten smirk. Clearly, Midnight had no remorse for her actions. "If I thought for one second it would be years, I would ask Carmen what she wants. But I don't believe it will come to that. Besides, I know Carmen loves living here. Why would she leave the Midwest in the first place if she didn't want to be in the Pacific Northwest? I'm pretty sure Carmen hated living in Illinois. Unlike me, she left the state for a reason. I might have abandoned my law practice and returned to the farm, but I never left Washington. The two situations are totally different."

Evan shrugged. "If you say so."

"Hey, listen, I was hoping you might consider a kind of promotion. I'd like you to become a lead of sorts, like when I have to go out of town. I could hire a part-time worker to help. You know, like the hospital has per diem workers."

"Since when do you go out of town? I've worked here for nearly a year, and you've never gone anywhere."

"Well, I thought that I might visit Carmen. Help her out with her mom. Perhaps take a week here or there, especially during our slow time," Mac explained.

"Well, you know I'd do anything for you, and I sure wouldn't turn down more money. Now that I'm dating

Marcia, taking her someplace better than a ratty old bar would be nice. But can you afford to do that?"

Mac scratched her head, considering the pros and cons of leasing another sizable chunk of their land. She'd been approached by an interested party several months ago, and his offer was more than generous. Unfortunately, she suspected he planned to plant something she wasn't too crazy about. And she was sure he'd use pesticides that might find their way to her crops and livestock. It wasn't like she could try him out for a year, and if it didn't work out, they'd part ways. He had insisted on a multi-year agreement, which was fair because most farmers needed the flexibility for planned crop rotation. Since this was potato country and he could plant quickly without fumigation, Mac suspected the higher offer wasn't because of that high-income cash crop since Carson had insisted on a five-year lease to start.

"Carson offered me a top price to lease those fifty acres we haven't touched for years."

"I thought you had plans to expand operations. Won't you need that land?" Evan asked.

"Yeah, well, Carmen is more important. I can think about that in five years after the lease runs out. Besides, I can still expand some operations with the remaining land."

Evan shook her head. "Sounds risky. Carson is kind of a bastard. You know that, right? He doesn't give two shits about organic farming. He'll use whatever harmful pesticides or anything else that will bring higher dollars with less effort."

"Maybe I can write something into the lease agreement to protect our business."

Evan grinned. "Our business? I knew I was your right-hand woman, but to hear you call it our business...well, I can't explain how much that means to me. I never wanted to overstep or make assumptions, but I hoped we could be partners one day."

Shit. Mac had really stepped into it now. She had no intention of taking on a partner, but she needed Evan. She'd have to finesse this without making any promises.

"Evan, you're still way too young to take on that kind of stress. I absolutely don't want to put that kind of pressure on you. You've been invaluable to the farm's success, and I certainly don't want to lose you as my right-hand woman. A partnership is a whole other level. If, after working here for a few more years, you see that in your future, maybe we can talk more about it. Plus, it isn't just my decision. Pops and Carmen would need to weigh in on that."

Evan's face distorted in anger or disappointment. Mac wasn't sure which one. "You seem convinced that Carmen is coming back."

"I am. I suppose you're right about Carson. I'll need to consider that more carefully. But if I can find a way to hire a temporary worker, could you run the place for maybe a week? I'm sure I could find the money to hire a temp for that short period and offer you a lead stipend."

"Uh, sure. Whatever you need."

CHAPTER TEN

Before the end of her shift, Allison had stopped by her mother's room and asked Carmen if she wanted to grab some dinner. Declining was on the tip of her tongue, until Allison suggested it might be good for her mother to have another decent night's rest. Rose had vastly improved from yesterday. She remembered how the doctor had hinted that if her recovery continued progressing, he'd consider discharging Rose tomorrow. She had agreed as long as they went for dinner a little later in the evening. Allison had smiled and suggested seven. Carmen was almost looking forward to catching up with her old friend. She was dying to get the scoop since Allison intimated she had so much to share with Carmen.

"I thought you were happy and in love with Mac," Rose said after Allison left.

Carmen scrunched her brow in confusion. "I am. What are you suggesting? It's not a date, Mom."

"I don't believe that young woman got that memo."

Carmen laughed. "Don't be ridiculous. First, Allison is straight. And second, we're good friends. That's all."

"Don't say I didn't warn you," Rose teased.

"Well, you certainly are getting back to your old self— giving me relationship advice. I can't say I'm displeased by that. At least you now have your old spark back. Although, I don't believe I need relationship advice from you anymore."

"I've never given you relationship advice," Rose huffed. "I've only ever been that shoulder to cry on and offered a different perspective on past loves. Sometimes, you're a little blind to certain realities. You've always jumped in with both feet and fallen hard. Mac seems a little different from your previous girlfriends. I hope to meet her someday."

"Oh, you will. Don't worry about that. Mac suggested we have a FaceTime call so you can at least look her in the eye and maybe get to know her. It's hard for her to get away from the farm and all her responsibilities there. She also mentioned trying to find a way to visit for a short time during her slow season, which is now. I really want you to meet her. I know I've had previous relationships where I believed that was it for me, but I'd marry Mac tomorrow if she asked. She's the one, Mom."

"Why does she need to be the one to ask? I don't understand how lesbian relationships work. Is this some kind of butch-femme thing? I read about that. She doesn't look like a man, does she?"

Carmen had to control her laughter. "No. This isn't a butch-femme thing. Mac is all woman. She might fall more on the androgynous side because I can't imagine her willingly wearing a slinky dress, but Mac is gorgeous." Carmen shrugged. "I don't know. I guess I want to be the one to receive the proposal versus stepping on that ledge and doing the asking."

Rose shook her head. "Still don't understand. If I was a lesbian all those years ago, I would have been the one to ask. I suppose I still could have asked your father to marry me, but it seemed so important to him to be the one to propose. Goodness knows that was the last time he had much control over the relationship." Rose laughed. "He always said I was the one who wore the pants in the family. Pretty sure he liked it that way. Not that I'm glad he went first, but I'm not sure how he would have handled my health challenges."

"Oh, Dad was kind of a selfish prick sometimes, but he loved you, and I've no doubt he would have stepped up."

"Yeah, stepped up and called you," Rose joked. "You shouldn't speak ill of the dead," she chastised.

"Why? You just did," Carmen countered.

"At least we did right by you. I'm so happy to know that you grew into such a confident, strong woman. I guess you got that from me."

"Oh, I most certainly got that from you. Daryl takes after the worst parts of Dad. Unfortunately, he didn't get his good traits, because, yes, I recognize he had those as well. He was always a good father. I can admit that."

Rose held out her hand. "Love you, Carmen. I only want you to be happy. I hope Mac is the one for you. I worry that this separation will not be helpful to you and your relationship. Long distance can put quite a strain on a new couple. It's never been my intention to have my children look after me."

"Don't even try to get rid of me, Mom. I'll be here until we get all of your health conditions under control. Remember, I'm just as stubborn as you. Actually, more so, since I have the youth and vitality to win this argument."

"If your visit extends to more than three months, we'll need to revisit this conversation. I won't have you ruining your future happiness. That's something I'd rather not take to my grave."

"Shush." Carmen kissed her mother's forehead.

"Why don't you take off and prepare for your non-date?" Rose grinned. "I'm feeling a little tired right now."

†

Mac rushed through dinner so she could call Carmen before it was too late. Pops and Evan made all the appropriate comments about the dinner being good again, but Mac knew they were both lying. She simply didn't have the same flair as Carmen. Sure, dinner was edible but absent the wow factor.

Mac hoped her surprise would be a good one. Not wanting to throw away money, she'd opted for a flight in a couple of weeks versus the next day like she really wanted. Mac could survive two more weeks. Besides, she thought that should give Carmen time to settle her mother back into her home and start a routine. Mac wasn't a trained health professional, but she could certainly help out while she was there.

Evan had grumbled about handling the farm for two weeks until Pops put an end to her grousing by stating that he'd dealt with the farm for years on his own with limited assistance during the busy times. Surely, a young pup like Evan, who he knew to be a hard worker, could handle bossing around a kid from the local 4-H club who had eagerly agreed to work for the farm before and after school, and on the weekends. The fact that this was the slow season highlighted how ridiculous her trepidation was about possibly letting Mac down. Mac had been thinking the very same thing. She only kept Evan on during the winter to ensure she had a full-time helper throughout the year.

To be fair, Evan was worth every penny. When the farm was in high season, the hours were long, and Evan never complained. It was the least Mac could do to ensure Evan was happy and secure with a year-round job. Other farms only employed seasonal help.

Mac waited patiently while Carmen's cell rang. She wanted to see her face when she shared the good news about visiting, so she FaceTimed Carmen.

Carmen's phone jiggled when she answered. "Hello, love."

"Hi yourself. I needed to see your beautiful face. Where are you?"

"Oh, sorry, I thought taking the call at dinner would be rude, especially since you were FaceTiming me. I'm walking to somewhere more private," Carmen answered.

"Dinner?"

"Yeah, Allison invited me to dinner so we could catch up. Mom nearly pushed me out the door. I think I'm irritating her with my hovering. She doesn't like me being so assertive with her doctors and nurses. But I swear, if you don't advocate for your loved ones, they get put on the bottom of the rung. The quiet patients get the shaft. It's how it works. The squeaky wheel *is* the first to get oiled. The good news is that Mom is getting better. She'll probably be discharged tomorrow. Her recovery still has a long way to go, but the fact that she's been grumbling about me hovering is a testament to her renewed strength."

Mac didn't want to interrupt Carmen's monologue, so she wasn't sure what part of everything she'd said she would respond to. She'd wanted to learn more about the dinner with Allison but thought that was the least essential thing in what Carmen had shared with her.

Opting to be the supportive versus jealous girlfriend, she answered, "That's great news about your mom. I have some good news to share myself, or at least I think you'll believe it's a happy development."

"I'll take all the positives I can get right now to keep the momentum going," Carmen said with a broad smile.

"How would you feel about having a visitor for two weeks?" Mac asked, failing to control the excitement she felt.

"Oh my goddess, really?" Carmen squealed. "When? Are you sure you can get away for that long?"

"Yeah, I hired a kid to help Evan. The only bad news is that I had to make the reservations for two weeks from now. The last-minute cost of the flights was outrageous, so I opted for the later dates," Mac explained.

"I don't care if it's two months from now. The fact that you're coming and getting to spend two weeks here is more than enough for me to shower you with kisses and so much more when you arrive. I'll pick you up from the airport. Just let me know your flight, and I'll be there with bells on my feet. You have no idea how happy that makes me. I want you to meet Mom and get to know her. We can double-team her and maybe convince her to move. Oh my, I just realized you'll be here for Thanksgiving. Despite being apart, I still have a lot to be thankful for this year. I'm going to make the biggest spread possible for Thanksgiving. Nothing says love more than having family around for the holiday. Damn, I wish Pops and Evan could be here too."

Mac smiled. It was just like Carmen to think of Pops and Evan and make lemonade from lemons. She really was the perfect woman. No wonder the kid she'd hired jumped at the opportunity to help on the farm. Less school to work around during the Thanksgiving break.

"I can't believe that didn't register in my tiny pea brain. I'll make sure to call Olivia and Deb so they can invite Pops and Evan over," Mac noted.

"Sounds like a plan. I know Kathleen and Jeremy have a big shindig at their house. Not only do they invite family, but Kathleen invites what she calls the orphans. That's how I spent my first Thanksgiving in Moses Lake. And, of course, I met Olivia and Deb. I think Deb, Olivia, and I became fast friends because of the pies I brought." Carmen laughed.

"Listen, I don't want to keep you from your friend. I'd love to meet her too when I come," Mac suggested.

"Yes, that would be lovely. Allison was about to tell me some big news before your call. It's been years since we connected. I'm so curious about what she's been up to. We used to have a lot of fun when we were in nursing school together. Allison is a riot. I'm sure you two are going to get along famously."

"Tell her I said hello, and I'm thankful she's been there for you since I'm so far away. Love you."

"I love you too. I'll call you tomorrow morning before I go to the hospital."

"Okay, bye, gorgeous. Have fun tonight. You deserve a break from all the stress."

"Bye, love."

†

Carmen nearly skipped to the table she shared with Allison, an enormous smile on her face. Allison looked up and smiled at Carmen.

"Must have been an exceptionally wonderful phone call. Good news? Is it about your mother?" Allison asked.

Carmen was so giddy she imagined she was gushing her response to Allison. "No, not about Mom, although that would have put an equally big smile on my face."

"Well, don't keep me in suspense. What's the big news?" Allison inquired.

"No, no, you first. I already feel bad about interrupting you earlier. Goddess, I'm a terrible friend," Carmen lamented.

"No, you're not. I know you have a lot going on with your mom and all." Allison waved her off. "It's expected that you would need to answer your phone."

"Quit stalling. The suspense is killing me. What's your big news, Allison?"

"Well, apparently, I've joined the rainbow brigade. Oh, Carmen, I had no idea until someone literally smacked me in the face. Or, more accurately, this woman kissed me right out of the blue. I was trying to be a good friend and went to a gay bar with a colleague who needed a wingwoman. Anyway, this attractive woman asked me to dance, and I thought, what the hell, it's just a dance. So, here we are on the dance floor, and I must have been putting off some kind of vibe because she leaned in and kissed me. Suddenly, everything made sense to me. You know, why it never worked with my past boyfriends and how I didn't know what all the fuss was about sex. I honestly thought that maybe I was asexual." Allison laughed. "Turns out I'm a lesbian."

Carmen chuckled. "Welcome to the rainbow family. I'll run out and get you a toaster tomorrow," she joked. "So, are you seeing this woman who laid on the big liplock? Ballsy, or should I say titsy of her."

"No, no, nothing like that. I enjoyed the kiss, is all," Allison shared. "I was seeing someone for about three months, but it didn't work out. I've been honestly obsessing over all my relationships and realized something the other day when we reconnected."

"Oh, what's that?"

Allison's face turned red. "You're going to think it's silly, but I had the biggest crush on you and never realized that was what I was feeling until the kiss. I...don't know if you're seeing anyone, but..."

Carmen tried to mask her reaction, but one glance at her friend, and she knew she hadn't done a stellar job. "Oh..."

"You're not single anymore, are you?"

"Uh, no. In fact, the call I just took that brightened my day was from Mac. She told me she's coming to visit for two weeks. I can't even tell you what a big deal that is. A couple of years ago, she gave up a thriving law practice to take over the family farm. Mac never takes time off. She works from morning to night. It's a major production to even get a weekend to ourselves. Trust me when I say if I wasn't so in love with Mac, I'd jump at the chance to date you. I predict you won't be on the market very long, Allison."

"So, when is this wonder woman coming? I'd love to meet the woman who captured your heart."

"Not for a couple of weeks. I'd love for you two to meet. I told Mac we were having dinner. She said to tell you hello and thank you for supporting me while she's so far away and can't do a proper job of it herself."

"She sounds dreamy. I can't wait to meet her. But, you know, if you two don't work out..." Allison teased, leaving the rest of the sentence unsaid.

"We're solid. Living apart until things settle with Mom is a tiny hiccup. But I'd love to be your wingwoman. My secondary mission will be to find you the perfect woman," Carmen offered.

"That'll be a tall order since the perfect woman seems to be taken already," Allison quipped.

"Mac isn't the jealous sort, but just to be on the safe side, you'll need to tone down the flirting when you meet her." Carmen laughed.

Allison smiled. "Noted."

CHAPTER ELEVEN

Carmen sounded happy over the phone. She had a good friend who could support her during this crisis with her mom. Mac wasn't about to give any oxygen to that slight niggle of jealousy at the back of her brain. Nope, no sense in breathing life into something that could turn into a monster. The guilt she felt for not being the one to be those broad shoulders for Carmen to lean on was quite enough. Unfortunately, she had given a ton of oxygen to that destructive emotion. She couldn't help herself. Mac was used to carrying the load. It nearly killed her that she couldn't be there by Carmen's side.

Shaking her head to rid herself of those maudlin thoughts, Mac brightened. She couldn't wait to spend the holiday with Carmen, even if it meant making alternate arrangements for her beloved Pops and Evan. Pops would understand. Perhaps that's why she'd gotten such a strange reaction from her assistant. Evan had said very little, but her nonverbals told the entire story. No wonder she reacted that way. Being estranged from her family meant that Evan had nowhere to go for the holidays, and now Mac was deserting her. Mac needed to call Olivia and correct this oversight. She wasn't sure if she should apologize to Evan or not. The topic of family and the holidays was a touchy subject. No wonder Evan didn't bring that forward.

She punched the number for Olivia who answered on the second ring.

"Hey, bud. I'm sorry I didn't call earlier. Deb told me what was going on. You know I'm here for you. Whatever you need."

"Thanks. Funny you should mention that. Listen, I'm taking two weeks to visit Carmen in Chicago, but I booked the flight in two weeks, so I'll be there for Thanksgiving."

"Okay. That's great. Isn't it?" Olivia asked. "You'll get to spend the holiday with Carmen, and since it's the slow season, Evan and Pops should be able to handle the farm. Unless you need some help with the farm while you're gone."

"No, I don't need your help with the farm. I hired a 4-H kid. But I'm worried about Pops and Evan. Could you talk to Deb about getting her sister to invite them over? I remember

Carmen saying how Kathleen likes to take in the orphans for the holidays."

Olivia chuckled. "Yes, she does. And we reaped the benefits when Carmen brought her famous pies. I'm surprised you two haven't added that to the farm's growing list of delectable foods. She'd make a killing at the farmers' markets. You two could easily develop a partnership and make some real money. I listen to NPR sometimes, and they have this segment on entrepreneurship. There was a podcast called *Hungry for MO*. They talked about this woman who was a self-taught caterer and achieved national acclaim for her sought-after biscuit recipe. Well, Carmen's pies are that good. She could go national. Your cheeses are next level of deliciousness as well," Olivia praised.

Mac chuckled. "Gotta get the woman to return to Moses Lake first. It would make a lot more sense to partner with Carmen versus Evan."

"You aren't thinking of establishing a business partnership with Evan, are you?"

"Um, I might have sort of hinted at the possibility when I asked Evan to take a lead role," Mac admitted. "I needed her to step up if I was going to be away for chunks of time."

"Look, I don't mean to step on any toes, and you can tell me to mind my own business, but I don't think that's a great idea. Have you talked with Pops about this? Around here, farms stay in the family. I assume you and Carmen will get married someday, which makes her family by extension.

Evan's got her own family, even if they are right-wing asswipes. Besides, that young woman has her sights set on you."

"I know," Mac answered miserably. "I was in a moment of weakness, desperate to visit Carmen."

"Let's go have a beer together soon, and I can help you work through this latest dilemma."

"Sounds good. Talk to you later."

"Don't worry about Thanksgiving. We've got you covered. Bye, Mac."

Mac would apologize to Evan tomorrow for not realizing it was Thanksgiving, and that she was leaving the total responsibility of the farm on her shoulders during the holiday season. Sure, it was slower in the late fall, but Thanksgiving brought significant business in with their late fall harvest of vegetables that people clamored over.

†

The next day was busy for Carmen as she ensured the house was ready and stocked for when they discharged her mother. The doctor was late with the discharge papers, but Carmen could finally take her mother home and settle her.

She'd made arrangements for her mother to meet the home health aides she planned on hiring, but that would happen later in the week. With Allison's assistance, she interviewed with the critical care director, who was delighted to bring Carmen on as a per diem nurse. She'd hinted at the possibility of employing Carmen full-time because she certainly had more than enough shifts to keep Carmen busy for months. Carmen didn't know how she felt about that. Her whole reason for coming to Elgin was to care for her mother. If she worked too much, that would defeat the whole purpose.

Allison stopped by right before the nurse brought in the discharge papers. Smiling, she said, "So, you're breaking her out of this joint, huh?"

"Yes, and not a minute too soon. I've got my work cut out for me to put some meat on Mom's bones. I almost can't blame her for turning her nose up at the hospital offerings," Carmen teased.

"I suppose you're planning to make a big feast for Thanksgiving, huh? I remember what a splendid cook you were."

"I was. With Mac coming for the holidays, even though it's only us three, that won't keep me from pulling out all the stops. It's my favorite holiday," Carmen gushed. A thought suddenly occurred to Carmen. She was aware that Allison's family was several states away and wondered if she'd have anywhere to go. Of course, she needed to make the offer.

"Hey, are you working the holiday?"

Allison smiled. "Nope, not this year. I have to work Christmas. Not that I have any plans, but that's how the

125

holiday rotation goes. I was waiting for one of the nurses to ask me to work for them. Someone always does."

"Well, don't agree to it because you're joining us for Thanksgiving."

"I am, am I?"

"Yup, and I won't take no for an answer," Carmen insisted.

"Yeah, I remember that about you. What a bossy little thing you can be." Allison laughed. "Well, my momma didn't raise no dummies," Allison said in a pitiful Southern accent. "I'm delighted to accept the invitation. No way would I miss a chance to eat your gourmet Thanksgiving dinner. And take home leftovers."

Carmen clapped her hands together. "Great, then it's settled. Are there other nurses or staff at the hospital with nowhere to go for Thanksgiving dinner?"

Allison furrowed her brow. "I don't really know, but I could ask around."

"Would you do that for me? My boss in Washington always invites what she calls the orphans from our hospital. I'd like to do the same thing. It's just as easy to cook for twenty as it is for four."

"You are an angel, Carmen. Mac is a lucky woman."

CHAPTER TWELVE

Although Mac attempted to keep busy during the two weeks before she would fly to Chicago, the time seemed to move at a glacial pace. At least she'd made sure to have plenty of vegetables to sell and more cheese than she thought Evan could possibly convince the specialty markets to buy. But Evan had assured her that everything would sell like hotcakes. Artisan salads with spinach or arugula and goat cheese were all the rage at Thanksgiving. Mac had her doubts. The people in her small town were traditionalists and meat-and-potatoes folks. Fancy didn't exactly impress most people.

Mac kept tossing in, then pulling out, various clothes, unsure what to take to the windy city. She didn't want Rose to think she was some backwater hick without a single nice outfit. Unfortunately, Mac had given up almost all her nice suits when she'd returned to the farm. The only one she'd retained she was saving for a truly special occasion. Besides, work outfits didn't equate to something nice to wear when going out for an evening. Except her one fancy outfit, she had precisely one nice pair of trousers that were a little dated and a couple of button-down shirts. Those remained in the duffel. It was the other clothing that caused her to pause.

Frowning, she looked at her sweaters that had definitely seen better days. The cuffs were frayed, and the repeated wear had caused all of them to have a misshapen appearance. Laying each one on the bed, she picked the two that were in the best shape. Mac sighed. She really needed to do some major clothes shopping. Perhaps she could find a few deals while in Chicago, but undoubtedly, it would be more expensive than buying something in Moses Lake. Too late now.

Mac chuckled to herself when she looked at her inventory of jeans. Wasn't it all the rage now to purchase worn jeans with ripped holes in them? Or was that the fashion of several years ago? She couldn't remember. Fashion had never been her thing. She shrugged and tossed in two pairs, one with a few rips and the other worn but free of holes or stains.

Now for deciding which flannel shirts to take. Sure, that would mark her as a big old country dyke she supposed, but Carmen loved her in flannel. So there was that. At least she had a few newer hoodies and fleece pullovers. Mac could never resist purchasing the soft top layer that was her go-to wardrobe choice in the winter. She had one in practically every color, including a few almost radical patterns that she'd thought were fun.

Midnight pounced on the bag after she added socks, underwear and sports bras. She looked up at Mac as if to ask, "Where are we going?"

"Meow."

Although Midnight had calmed down a bit after Carmen took Onyx with her, Mac still saw Midnight pace around the house, looking for her sister. Mac suspected Midnight clearly remembered when they had packed Carmen's suitcase and then placed Onyx in the carrier.

"Sorry, little buddy. You can't come with me. But I'll be back before you know it. Unfortunately, I won't be returning with Carmen and Onyx just yet..."

Upon hearing her sister's name, Midnight meowed loudly.

"Meow. Meow. Meooooow."

"I know you miss your sister. We just have to be patient. Easier said than done, huh? Evan and Pops will care for you while I'm gone."

The minute Mac mentioned Evan, Midnight growled.

"Stop that," Mac chastised, then stroked the top of her head. "All right, you spoiled little thing, I'll give Pops explicit instructions to keep you far from Evan. He'll be the one to tend to your every need."

Mac lifted Midnight off her duffel and zipped the large bag. Carrying the bag in one hand, she temporarily set it on the kitchen floor while retrieving the small cooler filled with cheese and vegetables she planned to take as her second carry-on that she would shove under the seat. She hoped that would be a good enough offering. *What did a person bring to meet the mother of the woman she loved?* She supposed she could also pick up a box of Chukar Cherries and a nice bottle of Washington wine. But Mac didn't know if Carmen's mother even drank wine, especially in her current condition. She nodded to herself. *Yeah, it's better to have more gifts to offer than not enough.*

Pops shuffled into the kitchen and asked, "All set?"

"I think so. Um, I hate to put this on you, but maybe you should keep Evan and Midnight separated. And give Midnight some extra treats. She's going to be extraordinarily stressed with me leaving too."

Pops chuckled. "Don't worry about a thing. I know to keep the little furball away from Evan. Not sure who would win in an all-out war, but my money's on Midnight. And I need Evan while you're gone."

"You're sure this isn't too much for you?" Mac asked.

"Too late for that now." He smiled. "I'm kidding. With that kid you hired and Evan, there's more than enough help. Evan will probably only ask me to gather the eggs. She and the young thing won't have a problem with everything else. Actually, I think hiring the kid was unnecessary. You've already done most of the work needed to get by for the next two weeks."

"Yeah, well, I didn't want to take advantage of Evan. Like you said, we need her. She offered to take me to the Conoco so I can take the Flexbus rather than pay for expensive parking. It's going to be a hellacious trip, but the parking fees alone weren't worth it to drive myself."

"That was nice of her. It would have been nicer if she'd offered to take you to the airport," Pops teased.

"Nah, that would have been way above and beyond the call of duty. I would have turned Evan down if she'd offered that."

Pops opened his arms. "Give me a hug before you leave."

Mac grabbed her pops and squeezed. "Love you."

"Love you too. Be safe."

Two quick knocks preceded Evan as she barreled into the kitchen and asked, "You ready?"

Pops scooped up Midnight, who had already hissed at Evan.

"Yup." Mac kissed Midnight's head, then grabbed her bag and the small cooler. "Be good for Pops." She hurried out the door before World War III broke out.

†

Carmen was so excited to see Mac that she'd driven to the airport two hours before Mac's plane touched down. It could take thirty minutes or, if a person was unlucky, a lot longer than that. It was fine. She'd hang out in the cell phone lot until she got the call from Mac.

In the two weeks prior to Mac's arrival, her mother had a few ups and downs. Even during her good days, she barely managed to walk more than a few hundred feet before becoming extremely tired or winded. It was such a hard thing for Carmen to watch. Most days, she needed help to go to the bathroom. And Carmen definitely could not let her shower or take a bath on her own. The risk of falling was far too great.

At Rose's last doctor's appointment, Carmen had grilled the physician on the medications he had prescribed. They were trying something new for her lupus and carefully observing her response to blood thinners. They had discussed the possibility of trying Thrombolytic therapy, but her mother didn't want another trip to the ICU, so they'd held off on that option. Success at getting her mother to gain at least twenty pounds was proving more difficult than Carmen had imagined. She'd assumed that the food previously offered to her mother was simply not enticing enough. Still, Carmen's best efforts to create all her favorite dishes were insufficient to add pounds to her withering body. She didn't want to force-feed her mother, but she was at her wit's end. Carmen understood. Most days, Rose just felt too shitty to have any desire to eat.

Carmen scrolled through her phone, looking for recipes for homemade smoothies, rich in nutrients and calories to help her mother gain some weight. She was so engrossed in her search that when the phone buzzed in her hand, it startled her.

"You're here already?" Carmen answered.

"Yeah, we just landed and are almost at the gate. I didn't check any bags, so as soon as I'm able to navigate this enormous airport, I can meet you outside of baggage claim. That's the best place, right? Can you tell me what you're driving so I know what kind of car to look for?"

"I'm on my way. I'll make circles until I see you. I'm driving my mom's Honda Civic. It's royal blue. Can't wait to kiss you."

"I can't wait to do much more than kissing," Mac teased. "Please tell me your bedroom is far from your mother's."

"Oh, it is. It's not even on the same floor. Hanging up now so I can make my way to the pickup location."

Carmen had an enormous smile as she eased out of the cell lot to meet her girlfriend. The home health aide was at the house and assured Carmen she had everything handled. Her mother was taking a nap, so hopefully, the aide wouldn't have much to do besides help her to the bathroom if Rose felt unstable. The last day or two, her mother seemed to perk up a little and gained some additional strength—enough to insist she could go to the bathroom alone.

The bright smile on Mac's face certainly matched her own as Carmen recognized Mac's tall form. She gave a little wave, and Carmen eased into the spot where another driver had exited. Jumping from the car, Carmen leaped into Mac's arms. An impatient beep from a car waiting to pick up their own loved ones roused Carmen to action, and she reluctantly stepped out of the hug.

"People are so impatient," Carmen noted. "Let me pop the trunk, and you can put your duffel inside."

Mac grabbed the duffel and tossed it into the trunk. She lifted the cooler. "I'll just hold on to this. I didn't know what to bring as an offering to your mother, so I thought some of my cheese and organic vegetables might work."

Mac sounded so adorably unsure of herself that Carmen couldn't resist pulling her into a kiss. After another beep, they broke apart.

"Goddess, I've missed you," Carmen gushed.

"Me too. But we better get into the car and leave this madhouse before Mr. Impatient pulls out a shotgun."

Carmen laughed as she scrambled to the driver's side while Mac eased her tall form into the passenger seat, ducking her head and setting the cooler between her legs. "Chicago may have been known for gangsters and Tommy guns in the 1920s, but I'd be willing to bet there are more shotguns per capita in Moses Lake than in Chicago."

"You may be right about that. So, tell me what to expect from your mother. Will I be able to charm her or not?"

Carmen frowned. "Mom isn't really much herself these days. That spark and fire she used to have, along with her quick wit, seems almost lost. Occasionally, it peeks out, but that is so rare these days. She feels sick and tired most of the time, and I get the sense she just wants to give up. It's heartbreaking to watch."

"I guess I'm going to need to step up my game. I brought some Chukar Cherries but forgot about the three-ounce liquid rule and didn't want to check my duffel, so no wine. But who doesn't love Chukar Cherries?"

Carmen smiled. "I'll order a shit ton of them if she likes them. Thank you. That was very sweet of you. Mom doesn't drink wine. She very rarely drinks, and with her current health challenges, I doubt alcohol of any kind would be appealing to her. I, on the other hand, would have loved a bottle of Washington wine," Carmen teased. "Chicago isn't exactly known for their wines. I'll bet Allison would have appreciated having a Washington wine for Thanksgiving."

"Oh, she's coming to Thanksgiving?"

Mac sounded strained to Carmen's keen ears, and she looked over to find a somewhat pinched expression.

Carmen chuckled. "Please tell me you aren't jealous. You never get jealous. I've invited all the orphans for Thanksgiving like Kathleen does. I figured it was a good tradition to carry forward to Elgin. She was very appreciative of the offer. I can't stand to hear that anyone is spending the holidays alone."

Mac looked down at her lap, and Carmen could imagine the sheepish expression on Mac's face. "Ugh. I'm an ass. I wouldn't exactly say I'm jealous. It's more like I'm envious that she gets to hang out with you, and I'm thousands of miles away. Does that make sense?"

"It makes perfect sense. Thank you for being honest." Carmen ventured a brief glance at Mac.

"Always." Mac looked up, and there was such love in her eyes that it took Carmen's breath away.

For the rest of the trip, they talked about the farm and Carmen's new routines at the house. Carmen filled in Mac on her shifts at the hospital and the differences between working for a hospital as large as Sherman versus the small rural hospital in Moses Lake. She was excited to learn new skills and almost felt like a brand-new nurse working for a larger institution. The biggest downside was missing the rural hospital's more tight-knit family atmosphere.

CHAPTER THIRTEEN

Mac didn't know what she expected when they rolled up to the large brick house on a corner lot. If she had to guess, she thought the house was set on nearly an acre of land. Although the neighborhood had an older, more established feel, all the homes were well cared for.

"Wow! This is nice. I'll bet you had fun as a kid here."

Carmen pulled into the long driveway, hit the button on the remote, and rolled into the tidy garage. An old riding lawnmower was parked in the space to the right where the driveway split and curved into the garage.

"Yeah, there's a tree in the backyard that was huge when I was a child. It's grown even taller since I've been away. I used to climb it and ignore my brother's *boys only* sign in the treehouse my father built for us. My brother was a douche even as a child. Dad had to remind him the treehouse wasn't only for him." Carmen's wistful expression told the whole story of how she missed her home. "It's actually been nice being back. I almost forgot all the things I loved about living here. Of course, I've also been reminded about why I left. It's still fall, and I hate the cold already. It gets miserable here in the winter."

"You know, Moses Lake isn't significantly different from Elgin. Weather-wise," Mac added before undoing her seat belt and walking to the back of the car as she waited for Carmen to pop the trunk.

"Trust me, it is. Moses Lake is considered the high desert, which means it doesn't have that same bone-chilling feeling. I don't believe we'll ever be snowed in either. And don't get me started on the hot, humid summers. No thanks. I'll take Moses Lake weather over Chicago any day of the week. Plus, the snow hangs around and gets all dirty looking. Not like the little snow we get in Moses Lake that remains pretty until it melts in a day or two." Carmen met Mac at the trunk and offered, "Let me take the cooler."

The house was warm and cozy when they entered the small family room with the large television. The exposed brick was a feature that impressed Mac. It probably made it more difficult to heat the room, but it didn't appear as though the place was cold, unlike their old farmhouse. A young woman sat on the overstuffed sofa with a blanket over her legs. Mac thought she must be used to her drafty old house to not notice the chill of the room.

"Hi, Martha. Everything okay with Mom?"

"Yeah, she's taking a nap. She wanted to have enough energy for dinner with you and your friend."

"Martha, this is my girlfriend, Mac," Carmen introduced.

Mac set down her duffel and extended a hand to the young woman who stood. "It's nice to meet you. Thank you for being a support to Carmen."

Martha accepted Mac's outstretched hand. "Oh, it's been my pleasure. Carmen is a dream to work for. Rose is a breeze too. Not cranky at all, unlike some of the other people I've cared for."

"Thanks, Martha. How's your schedule look for the next two weeks?"

"Mostly free," Martha answered. "I didn't know how much you would need me, so I took a few shifts with Mr. Copeland."

"Can I call you to arrange some time? I thought I would show Mac around and maybe take her to Chicago on the weekend. She's never had Chicago-style deep-dish pizza. I'd love for Mom to come with us, but it might be too much for her."

"Just let me know when. I don't think the weekend will be a problem at all." Martha gathered her bag and offered a small wave before exiting to the garage.

"The kitchen is right through there. I'll put away your gifts and check on Mom. Would you mind hitting the button to close the garage? It's on the left of the door. I'll meet you in the kitchen and set out something to nibble on. Maybe Mom will feel rested enough to join us."

"Why don't you let me put away the food in the cooler? Go and check on your mom."

Carmen kissed Mac's cheek. "Thanks."

†

Carmen tiptoed down the hallway to her mother's bedroom and carefully opened the door. Her mother always was a light sleeper, and although Carmen had been quiet, Rose stirred in the bed and opened her eyes.

Rose smiled at Carmen. "You're back."

"How are you feeling?" Carmen asked. "Are you up for something to eat? I was going to make something for Mac."

"Well, I'd like to get up and meet your girlfriend. I'm not very hungry, but perhaps I'll nibble on what you set out," Rose answered.

"Do you need help getting ready or going to the bathroom?" Carmen asked.

"No, I'd like to walk to the kitchen on my own power. Perhaps I'll make a better first impression other than a broken-down old invalid."

140

"Stop that," Carmen chastised. "You're not a broken-down invalid. Nor are you old. We simply have a few health challenges to resolve. And then you'll be back to the woman who ruled the roost."

Rose pushed the covers aside and sat up. "Give me a few minutes, and I'll make my way to the kitchen."

Carmen grabbed her mother's walker and set it next to the bed. "All right. Call if you need anything."

Carmen knew that giving her mother this small amount of independence was crucial. Rose had lost so much of that over the past six months. It had to be excruciating for her to endure what she deemed was a humiliating situation. The fierce independence that was such a core to who Rose used to be was all but lost with her illnesses.

When Carmen returned to the kitchen, she found Mac awkwardly sitting on a stool at the breakfast nook. She looked so out of place and uncomfortable. Her foot tapped the old linoleum floor in a rapid staccato beat.

"Relax. Have you never met *the parents* before? Or rather, in this case, the parent."

"No, actually, I haven't. My past relationships never reached that stage."

Carmen quirked an eyebrow. "None of them?"

Mac shook her head. "Nope. I was too busy with school, making top grades and establishing my law practice. Ironically, when I took over the farm, I had more time to spend on nurturing or exploring a new relationship because I returned to the farm in the winter, which was our slow time. That's when Pop's joints got really bad, and he admitted defeat. Obviously, that extra time hadn't been as important to my ex as being with a lawyer versus a farmer."

"Her loss is my gain. But if our courtship was anything to go by, I can't imagine how you define having free time to explore relationships. I always felt like I'd won the lottery when we had a night to ourselves."

Mac blushed. "True. I suppose I don't do idle very well."

"How in the world will you survive these two weeks with nothing to do all day long?" Carmen asked.

Mac scanned the kitchen. "Well, I haven't exactly taken an inventory, but I imagine there are a few things that need fixing in this old house. It's certainly well built, but everything experiences wear and tear, even classic Cape Cods."

Rose shuffled into the kitchen, moving her walker across the floor. Carmen resisted the urge to jump up and help. When she saw the twinkle as her mother's eyes landed on Mac, she suppressed a grin. Today was going to be a good day. Carmen could tell her mother still had a touch of her mischief left.

"You must be Mac. I can certainly see why my daughter is so taken with you. Aren't you a tall drink of water? They must grow them big and strong on the farm. What is this I hear about you rattling around in this old house to fix things? We'll talk later. I've been meaning to spruce up the place, especially this outdated kitchen. While the bones are good, the old wallpaper and linoleum floor really have to go."

It seemed as though Mac couldn't stand quick enough. "It's a pleasure to meet you, Mrs. Torre." Mac hesitated, and Carmen imagined she didn't know how to offer her hand without causing Rose to lose her balance. "Thank you for allowing me to invade your space and visit."

Rose lifted one hand from her walker and appeared to wobble. Mac was right there, placing a steadying hand on her back. "Pith-posh. It's not an invasion. Or at least if it is, we're both opening our arms to the invaders. I'm just going to sit at the kitchen table, if you two don't mind. Sometimes, I lose my balance, and those stools are too high. Not enough padding either."

Mac pulled out the chair for Rose and gently guided her into the chair. "I'll join you after I help Carmen with the food. Those cushions on the chairs look awfully inviting."

Once Mac had helped Rose settle into the chair, she held her arms open. "I'll take that hug now. We aren't hand-shakers in the Torre family. We're huggers."

Mac smiled and gently hugged Rose. "Same with the Sullivans. Probably why your daughter loves my pops."

"Is he as charming as you?" Rose asked.

"More. And single too." Mac winked.

"Oh, my romance days are long gone. Besides, I had the love of my life. Carmen's father might have had his faults, but I loved him, and no one could ever replace him in what's left of my life. In my current state, I doubt I would attract a homeless man."

"That's not true. You're still beautiful, Mom. You'll always be gorgeous because you have that classic Mediterranean look. We need to help you add a few pounds, not only for your vanity but also for your health. Speaking of which, the food is ready to go. I just need to unpack it and set it on the table. I prepared a variety of cold foods that I could simply set out. Mac, sit with Mom. I don't need any help."

"If you show me where the plates and eating utensils are, I can at least set the table. I'll be doing the dishes as well. No arguments," Mac insisted.

"All right." Carmen pointed to the cabinets on the right side of the range. "The dishes and glasses are there. And the silverware is in the drawers below."

†

Mac had noticed the kitchen floor had definitely seen better days. She thought to herself that it must drive Carmen crazy to not be able to get the floor to shine anymore. She knew for a fact that one stain was never coming out, no matter what Carmen tried. Mac had gone room to room in the old farmhouse in Moses Lake and updated most everything, leaving the insulation, roof, and the large jobs for last. Here, she could easily put in a new tile floor and remove the old wallpaper, adding texture to the walls and repainting them. A new faucet would also be a piece of cake. It looked like Rose had already upgraded the counters to something more contemporary. The cabinets were solid, and she could make them look new again with a little bit of sanding and refinishing. Mac smiled to herself as she thought about how she'd easily be able to keep busy over the next couple weeks.

Mac had been so pleased that Rose seemed to enjoy her cheese. She wished she'd brought more. Perhaps she could see if Evan would ship some to the house. Rose had retired for the evening, and Mac sat with Carmen in the small family room.

"What are you smiling about?" Carmen asked. "You have that scheming look on your face."

"After my tour of the house, there are a few easy fixes, but I thought I could remodel the kitchen for your mom. You know, replace that old linoleum floor that is driving you nuts. I bet you'd both love one of those kitchen faucets that turns on and off with a simple touch. No need to replace the cabinets. They're solid. But a little elbow grease, and I'll have them looking like new."

"I'm not going to get you to relax and enjoy what's probably the first vacation you've had in years, am I?" Carmen asked. "Will you at least leave a little time for me to take you into the city one day?"

"Of course. I want to have some of this world-famous deep-dish pizza."

"I would love to give this gift to Mom, but I am a little concerned about the dust and everything while you take on this project. It's not like it will be a quick job. The kitchen is my happy place too. How long will you need to kick me out of there?"

Mac wrinkled her nose and looked to the ceiling. "Three days if I work long hours."

"How long?" Carmen asked, suspicion dripping from the corners of her gorgeous mouth.

Mac cringed. "Maybe eighteen-hour days."

"Mac!" Carmen exclaimed. "Any chance I can help and cut those down to only twelve-hour days?"

"Maybe. I could teach you to do some of the grouting. It isn't that hard. And I suppose you could help with the removal of the linoleum. I need to inspect the floor. It's possible to install the tile on top of the linoleum. That might actually be better, in case there's asbestos below." Mac nodded. "Yeah, now that I think about it, I'll make that work. I'm not going to lie; removing the wallpaper and painting will probably end up being a bigger job than I think, and messy."

Carmen frowned. "Maybe this isn't such a good idea after all. If only I had a place to hang and take Mom while the remodel is happening."

"Would your friend Allison be able to put the two of you up for a few days? You could cook your gourmet meals for her as payment," Mac suggested.

"I wouldn't want to impose on her. I know she'd do it, but I'd feel funny asking. Plus, I doubt Mom would go for it."

"How about going to a nice hotel with access to a kitchen?"

"Maybe. I suppose I could use the front door instead and just get take-out. There are a few places with food that my mother used to love. Okay, let's do it. Can you block off the kitchen completely, so the dust and other harmful particles don't leak out? Mom has a hard enough time with her pulmonary embolism. She doesn't need to be coughing any more than she already does."

"I'll make sure of it. And I'll work as quickly as I can to ensure it's done in as little time as humanly possible," Mac assured.

"I love you," Carmen said.

She was excited now. Mac had something to occupy her time. Plus, anything she could do to cement her relationship by offering this gift to Rose as someone important to Carmen was a bonus. Of course, this might make it even harder to convince Rose to move to Washington, but Rose's happiness was more important.

"Can we go to the store tomorrow and get paint and tile samples for your mother to look at?"

Carmen chuckled. "Yes."

Chapter Fourteen

The renovations were going along swimmingly until they weren't. Mac wiped the sweat from her brow and let out a string of curse words. The old wallpaper proved more stubborn than her pops or Carmen's mother. At that thought, she allowed herself to smile. She liked Rose. Despite how ill she was, she had spunk. Mac only wished she could convince her to move, but after a brief time with her, she knew that wouldn't be the best option, and Mac didn't want to force the issue.

Thankfully, replacing the old faucet was a straightforward job that took less than an hour. The cabinets would also be a simple task. Knowing that sometimes wallpaper was stubborn and messy, Mac decided to remove the wallpaper and paint before laying her tile. She'd prepared the floor already and decided it was best to tile over the linoleum in case, as she suspected, the vinyl flooring had asbestos backing. Any paint drops on the old floor would be no big deal, and she could work on the walls without worrying about damaging the floor.

"Fuck, I'm going to need to repair that," she muttered after applying a little too much pressure with the scoring tool she'd bought.

She heard a chuckle from behind and turned her head. Carmen had snuck into the kitchen and was watching. "Need some help?"

"I thought you were at work," Mac answered.

"Low census today. I volunteered to go home. The other nurses need a full paycheck. I don't. Besides, I couldn't resist watching you battle the wall. You look positively yummy in those old overalls."

Mac chuckled. "Only you would find me attractive as I curse out an inanimate object. But you know, I'm not too proud to accept help. You'll probably have more finesse with this scoring tool than me. Better change into something you can get dirty, and I'll show you how to use it."

"Deal. Do you think this will all be completed before Thanksgiving? I'm going to need my mother's kitchen to prepare the meal."

"With your help, yes. How are you at painting?" Mac asked.

"Remarkably efficient," Carmen responded with a broad smile.

"Good. Maybe we'll be able to finish removing the wallpaper, and I can prep the walls today or tonight. Are you working tomorrow?"

Carmen shook her head. "Not likely. Unless there is a rush of patients coming in today."

"I could start cutting the more difficult tiles along the edges while you paint. That will save a lot of time." Mac nodded to herself. "Yeah, I think we can have everything done in plenty of time for you to have the kitchen bright and shiny."

"Good. I felt a little guilty leaving the entire job to you. Not that I didn't think you could handle it, but I'd love to work side by side with you. I feel so useless sometimes on the farm. I want to help more."

"You feeding us is more than enough contribution. Besides, you already have a full-time job. The farm is my full-time job, not yours," Mac argued.

"I better get changed so I can help." Carmen approached Mac and kissed her before squeezing past to run upstairs to the bedroom.

Mac smiled, thinking how lucky she was to have a partner like Carmen. Despite their current situation, which was proving to be more of a challenge than she had anticipated, she wouldn't change a thing. Mac had been sure that, along with Carmen, she'd be able to convince Rose to move to Washington. Now, Mac would need to alter her entire way of thinking. But it was the hard times that made the good times sweeter. No couple had smooth sailing for their whole life. She knew that. It was the bumps along the way and how each couple worked through them that defined the strength of any relationship. Mac knew Carmen was strong. They'd beat the odds for sure.

†

On Thanksgiving, Carmen knew she shouldn't have complained about the smell lingering in the kitchen before starting to prepare the big meal. The hurt look on Mac's face was enough to stop her cold.

Continuing to chop the celery and onions for her stuffing, Carmen backpedaled and offered a quick apology. "Goddess, I'm sorry, Mac. I know how hard you worked and how late you stayed up in the evenings to finish the job. I've no doubt that as soon as the bird starts cooking and I reheat the sauce for the lasagna, no one will notice the smell."

Mac ran her hand over her face. "No, I'm sorry. I promised it would be done days ago. I'd also forgotten how the smell of a freshly painted wall can linger for days." Mac

151

sighed. "We can't even air out the room because it's so cold outside."

Carmen stopped chopping, walked around the breakfast nook to where Mac was cutting apples for the pies and offered a chaste kiss. "I'm an ungrateful ass. Forgive me."

"Nothing to forgive." Mac lifted her eyes and looked hopeful. "Whenever you cook, you get the kitchen smelling sinfully good. You're right that after a few hours, all anyone will detect is the aroma of bubbling cheese, garlic and tomatoes, or the turkey and all the fixings."

Carmen smiled, returned to the nook's other side, and finished chopping. "Count on it. Thanks for getting up so early with me. I needed to put those pies in the oven before the bird."

"I'll bet those pies will gobble that paint smell right up." Mac chuckled.

Carmen laughed and added her ingredients into a large bowl. "Gobble up the paint smell? You really do have Thanksgiving on your brain."

"Clearly. I didn't notice the smell because I had visions of turkey, stuffing, cranberry sauce, lasagna and pies dancing through my head. I have a very active imagination that includes smells and sights. Should I worry about that? Isn't that a sign of mental illness?" she joked.

Carmen glanced at the clock on the stove. "Shit, I'm falling behind." She shifted her focus to the apples. "You almost done there?"

152

Mac nodded. "Just a couple more apples to peel and cut up. I suppose it would have been easier if we'd had one of those fancy contraptions like at home to peel and core the apples. Doing it by hand sucks."

"Aw, poor baby." Carmen grinned. "Yeah, Mom was never one for kitchen gadgets. She doesn't even use a garlic press. Everything has to be chopped and prepared by hand. I bought a press, though, because there was no way I was going to chop the garlic by hand. I suppose I should have picked up the same apple corer I use at home when I discovered that awesome kitchen store. But then I wouldn't have needed your help so early in the morning, and it would have been lonely in this kitchen without you."

"No chance I would have continued to sleep while you toiled away in the kitchen."

Carmen smiled. "And that's why I love you."

†

Allison was the first to arrive, and when she handed Carmen two bottles of what Mac suspected were very expensive Washington wines, Mac tried not to let that bother her. She also brought a large bouquet. The two gifts seemed awfully intimate to Mac.

Carmen leaned in to hug her friend after accepting the gifts and setting them on top of the breakfast nook. Allison

153

appeared to know where to go as she made her way into the kitchen. Mac noted her familiarity with Rose's home. It was no secret that the kitchen was a focal point in most households who valued a good meal above all else when entertaining guests. Rose's kitchen was larger than most, especially for an older home. Mac felt a sense of pride that she'd been a part of making the space even more special for Rose and Carmen.

Allison glanced around the kitchen. "Wow! This is amazing. Any chance you can rent out your girlfriend? My kitchen could use a facelift. Clearly, she is a woman of many talents."

"Sorry, I have plans for Mac. While she doesn't do idle easily, I'm taking her into the city. We're going to play tourist for a few days as long as Mom's health remains stable." Carmen waggled her eyebrows. "As for the rest of the time she's here, I'm sure I can think up a few things to keep her busy that doesn't include home improvement."

"Is your mom resting before the big meal?" Allison asked.

"Yes. I thought I would leave her until shortly before I serve dinner," Carmen answered. "She was up for a brief time this morning, and I got her to eat a little something."

"That's good. Any luck on encouraging her to gain weight?"

Mac appreciated the concerned look on Allison's face. She had to remember that Allison was a good friend and a great support to Carmen. Mac couldn't let her insecurities get in the way.

Carmen frowned. "Unfortunately, no. But at least she hasn't lost more weight."

"What can I do to help?" Allison asked.

"Nothing. I told Mac the same thing. I've put everything together, and the bird went into the oven. Both of you would just be in the way. It's all about timing now. You'll just crowd the kitchen." Carmen opened the oven and basted the bird, checking the thermometer and nodding to herself. "Perfect, another thirty minutes should do it." She pushed a lock of hair aside and leaned against the counter. "I'll wait to prepare the gravy." Her focus shifted to the wine as she turned the bottle to look at the label. Squealing in delight, Carmen announced, "You got my favorite Washington wine. How on earth did you manage that?"

That's what Mac wanted to know, but she kept those thoughts to herself. How did Allison know Carmen's favorite wine, and how did she arrange to have the wine shipped to Elgin?

Allison grinned. "I'm resourceful. You know that. The other bottle is something they suggested would be perfect for Thanksgiving. I have two more bottles in the car but only had two hands."

"That was very thoughtful of you," Carmen gushed. "I did purchase some wine for dinner, but I'm sure yours will be much better. You know you didn't have to do that."

"Of course I did," Allison insisted. "It's the least I could do. I'm getting a free meal out of the deal. Just to be clear, I also meant, can I help with your mom? I know I'd just be in the way in the kitchen. Not my forte, but while you're putting the finishing touches on the meal, I can help your mom get dressed."

"Oh, that would be a big help. Thanks," Carmen answered.

Mac cleared her throat. "I can get the wine if you want."

Allison shifted her eyes to Mac and smiled. "Thanks, my car is unlocked. They're in the back seat."

Not bothering to put on a coat, Mac shuffled to the door leading to the garage, listening to Allison and Carmen talking about something related to the hospital and the people they worked with. Suddenly, she felt like she didn't belong in Carmen's world. It was an uncomfortable feeling.

CHAPTER FIFTEEN

Mac returned to Moses Lake, and two months later, nothing had changed. Mac was getting worried. It seemed like there was no end in sight. Mostly, the time crawled by without Carmen by her side, but in some respects, it also seemed like it couldn't possibly have been that long because surely, a decision one way or another would have surfaced. Mac and Carmen made a fragile agreement—neither would broach the topic of the future. She knew Carmen needed to inform the hospital of what was happening. They wouldn't hold her job forever. Mac dreaded receiving that call.

The tearful goodbye at the airport had been almost too much for Mac to bear. Each day without Carmen took another small piece of her heart. It didn't help that this was the slow season for Mac, and she had way too much time on her hands to think about everything. Unfortunately, having that much time did not work to her advantage as much as it should have because she couldn't keep visiting Carmen in Chicago. Her financial situation made that nearly impossible unless she was willing to sell some land. It would break Pop's heart, and she couldn't do that to him. The farm had been in their family for generations.

Sensing her foul mood over the last several months, even Evan gave her a wide berth. She seemed content to pursue the nurse she'd been seeing, although everything Mac observed indicated that Evan was simply biding her time with the woman—merely scratching an itch. Evan talked about having needs and sex, and love didn't always have to go hand in hand. Mac disagreed, but they were both consenting adults, so who was she to rain on their parade? Whatever floats your boat and all that nonsense.

Her day brightened when her cell phone rang in her pocket, and she noted who was calling. "Hey. This is a pleasant surprise."

"Hi, love." Carmen's defeated tone should have been Mac's first clue.

"You sound, oh, I don't know, sad?"

"I need to tell you something, and I don't know how to say it," Carmen sniffed.

"Are you crying?"

"Maybe a little. I won't be able to come home anytime soon. I didn't see any other option but to resign from my job at the hospital and take a part-time job here."

"Okay," Mac responded hesitantly. Her heart beat so fast in her chest that she thought she might have a heart attack. "It's not like we hadn't considered that possibility."

"I know, but the reality is so much worse. The physicians won't give me a definitive timeframe but have hinted at years. Not months, Mac, years. I guess I didn't quite believe that was actually what I may have to consider. I can't expect you to wait for me for years. I would totally understand if you wanted to, uh, take a break. You know, the old saying about letting someone go and if they make it back to you, they were yours, but if not, they were never meant to be."

Mac swallowed the lump in her throat and held her tears at bay. "Is that what you really want?"

"No." Carmen's response came back so quietly that Mac had to strain to hear the rest of her answer. "None of this is what I want, including my mom being so ill that she hints at wanting it all to be over."

"I wish I was there to wrap my arms around you. For the record, this is not what I want either. On the other hand, I can hear the stress and anguish in your voice. I don't want any part of adding to your worries. I'll abide by whatever you need."

"I need for you to be happy and healthy, not someone who pines for a lover who lives thousands of miles away. Live your life, Mac. Love freely."

"I do love freely. I love you. I'm not going to start dating just because you're far away for an indeterminate amount of time. You can't ask that of me," Mac insisted.

"I don't know how to do this, Mac. Talking with you, yet not being able to touch you or see your smiling face, kills me a little more every time you pop up on my phone screen."

"We can see one another. It's not the nineteenth century. We video chat with one another all the time," Mac argued.

"It's not the same. That tiny little screen sucks. It's just another reminder of the distance between us. I can't do it. It's breaking whatever spirit I have left, which doesn't leave me any energy for Mom. It's like I've turned into a completely different person. I've always been so optimistic."

Mac had noticed the subtle changes but tried very hard to ignore them. Carmen *was* a different person. Now she knew what was behind that almost imperceptible transformation. There was no way she would contribute any more to those changes, even if she had to suggest something so outrageous that certainly Hollywood would consider it a ridiculous plot for a romance.

"All right. I'm going to make a totally off-the-wall suggestion. Remember the movie *An Affair to Remember*?"

"Of course. You know it's a favorite of mine," Carmen responded.

"Our situation is a little different, but in some ways similar. No contact until you're ready. One year, two years, ten years. I don't care. We'll live our lives, and when you call, I know it's time for us to take back our relationship. Together. I'm going to wait for you, Carmen. I don't care how long it takes. In the meantime, I'm going to make this farm something for you to be proud to return to. My cheese will become internationally acclaimed," Mac boasted.

"I believe that. All right. Don't change your phone number. And don't get into a car wreck and go into a coma so that you can't answer my call," Carmen joked. "I can't believe I'm even considering this. Can we really do this?"

"We can and we will," Mac stated with authority. "We are going to have our happily ever after. It just might take a little longer and travel through some alternate reality of love to get there. You don't think it's the craziest notion you've ever heard of?"

"Oddly, no. I want you to remember something that will keep you going for however long this takes." Carmen paused. "I love you more than I can ever put into words. And the only way to prove that to you is to make that call. I don't know when, but I do know it will happen."

"That's enough for me," Mac said. "I love you too, so much it hurts. But in a good way. Well, not this shit that we're having to deal with," she quickly amended.

"I understand."

"What do you want me to do with your car?" Mac asked. "I could ship it, but that might be expensive."

"Keep it at the farm. It'll be insurance and a reminder that I'm coming back someday."

Mac smiled. That gave her hope. "I'll make sure to run it every couple of weeks and keep it in good working condition."

†

Carmen knew she wasn't very friendly to her co-workers, and they would have had to be blind not to notice she'd been crying. On her way out of the hospital, Allison grabbed her arm.

"We're going out for breakfast. No arguments. Then you can tell me what the hell is going on?"

"I can't. Martha is only there for another hour or so. What if Mom needs me?"

"She has a phone with your number on speed dial. We'll go somewhere close to the house."

Carmen sighed. "All right. Mom has been complaining about me hovering and making her feel like a bloody invalid. Her exact words."

"Follow me in your mom's car," Allison ordered.

Carmen followed Allison to their favorite breakfast place and parked before stepping inside with Allison by her side.

The hostess showed them to a booth, and Carmen sat across from Allison.

Sally approached immediately, holding a pot. "Coffee?"

"Yes, please," Carmen said as Allison nodded.

"I'll be back in a few minutes to take your order unless you already know what you want," Sally said.

"I need some comfort food," Carmen admitted. "I'll take the French toast. Nothing like carbs to start my day off right."

"You got it, hon. I've noticed you've been down a little lately. Anything to do with that tall drink of water back in Washington?"

Allison glared at Sally as Carmen nodded, then looked away and wiped a tear from her eyes.

"Make that two orders," Allison redirected.

"Okay, I'll bring you some extra strawberry compote." Sally patted Carmen's shoulder. "Sorry, hon."

After Sally left, Allison waited patiently until Carmen pulled herself together, then asked, "Lay it on me. Did something happen between you and Mac?"

"I think I made a huge mistake," Carmen blurted. "I told Mac that we should take a break. I don't even recognize the person I've become. I'm cranky and sad all rolled into one. That's a terrible combination. Every time I talked with Mac, I lost a little more of who I used to be. It would remind me how much I longed for her to be by my side. I actually started blaming her for not being willing to live here with us and hire someone to take care of the farm. Of course, I never said that to her but just thinking it made me feel like a complete bitch."

Allison looked sympathetically at Carmen. "Yeah, that doesn't sound like you at all. I guess the old saying you're damned if you do and damned if you don't is more prophetic than I thought. You don't want to be without her, yet you can't handle staying in touch."

Carmen blinked back tears. "Uh-huh. But do you think Mac understands?"

"What exactly did she say?" Allison asked before taking a package of sweetener and adding it to her coffee along with the creamer already on the table.

Carmen could feel her heart swell with pride. "She's the ultimate romantic. I could tell she was struggling. Mac doesn't cry, and I clearly heard her swallow back tears. She suggested we do something similar to what the lead characters in the movie *An Affair to Remember* did."

"How exactly will that work?" Allison asked skeptically.

"She basically offered to put her love life on hold for however long it takes. I'm supposed to call when I'm ready to join her." Carmen grabbed the cream, poured a generous amount into her coffee and added stevia.

"Aw, that's so sweet. Not to be a nay-sayer, but how in the world are you going to keep yourselves from breaking the agreement before you're prepared to move back? I'd be drunk dialing her the first time I had too many." Allison sipped on her coffee.

"What if it takes two years or three years? I mean, you met Mac. She's the total package rolled into the yummy body of a goddess. She'll have women lining up to take my place. Hell, Evan is undoubtedly drooling over the prospect of Mac being single again."

"Who's Evan?" Allison asked.

"She's Mac's right-hand person on the farm. How can I compete with someone who has far more in common with Mac than me? I'm completely useless," Carmen lamented.

"You are not. If Mac wanted to be with Evan, she would have chosen her long ago. Instead, she was with you, and from what I could tell, that woman French kisses the ground you walk on," Allison insisted.

"Ew." Carmen chuckled.

Allison smiled. "There it is."

"What?" Carmen furrowed her brow.

"Your smile. I thought the damn thing ran off with my eyeroll," Allison joked.

"Funny. I guess I have noticed you trying to be better with your nonverbal responses since our boss called you out."

"In my defense, it's second nature. I think I was born with that go-to response to stupidity. I don't even realize I'm doing it." Allison grinned.

"The only bright spot to this whole situation is reconnecting with you. You always could bring me out of my funk. You're a great friend. So, do you honestly think Mac will wait for me?"

"I do. Even though it isn't great for my prospects of wooing you away. If I was a lesser woman, I'd do a full-court press right now."

Carmen playfully flicked Allison's hand. "Stop flirting. You know we're better as friends."

"I know no such thing. Whoops, and there it is…I guess I am a lesser woman." Allison grabbed Carmen's hand and squeezed. "I'm mostly kidding. Mama did not raise a stupid child. I know I have no chance with you. But I can be a good friend. I'll be here for you. Whatever you need. You can be Ms. Cranky Pants with me all you want."

"Thanks, Allison. Will you also be my wing-woman and keep me from drunk dialing Mac? That would only confuse her."

"It would be my honor. I'll steal your phone any time alcohol touches those luscious lips of yours," she quipped.

†

As Mac headed to the chicken coop, she saw Evan approach. "Fuck," she muttered under her breath. After splashing water on her face, she had looked in the mirror at her bags and bloodshot eyes, which were a sure sign that not all was right in Mac's world. The last thing she wanted to do was admit to the harebrained plan she'd devised. *What the hell was I thinking?*

"You look like shit. What's up? Carmen break your heart?" Evan's tone was joking, but there was an edge of something that Mac couldn't put her finger on. She'd like to think that despite Evan's innocent crush, she was still in her corner.

"I don't want to talk about it," Mac squeaked out as she choked back tears.

"Shit. I'm sorry. Look, no matter what, I am your friend. It might help to talk it out. Let's go into the house and have another cup of coffee. It looks like you could use one. Did you get any sleep last night?"

Defeated, Mac followed Evan into the large kitchen and made a beeline to the coffee pot. She emptied the carafe into Evan's travel mug. "I'll make some more."

"Sit," Evan directed. "I think I can handle making a new pot of coffee." Scooping the grounds into the filter, Evan added an extra half scoop.

"Well, that should get me moving or tear out the lining of my stomach," Mac weakly joked.

As the coffee percolated, Evan sat beside Mac and directed, "Okay, spill. What's going on?"

"I think I blew it?" Mac hung her head.

"What are you talking about? There's nothing you could possibly do or say that will result in sending Carmen away."

"She was so distraught, and the stress had been too much for her. I only wanted to lighten her emotional load. She's feeling extra guilty. I came this close," Mac held up her thumb and forefinger close together, "to having a long conversation with Pops about putting the farm operations on hold. They might need attorneys with my specialty in Illinois."

"Don't you need a law license in Illinois, and won't that take time?" Evan reasoned in an even tone, but Mac could see the panic in her eyes.

"Don't worry. I went in another direction. An idiotic one."

"What exactly did you do?"

"I suggested that we not have contact with one another until Carmen is ready to return to Moses Lake."

"You what?" Evan exclaimed in surprise. "You gave Carmen an ultimatum. Harsh. That doesn't sound like you at all."

"No, I didn't give her an ultimatum. I gave her the freedom to do what she needed without guilt. I kind of likened it to the agreement made in that old movie, *An Affair to Remember*. I promised her I would wait for her no matter how long it took."

Evan nodded. "That sounds more like you. So, what's the problem?"

"Have you looked at Carmen? Shit, she'll have every eligible woman lining up to date her. Women that have a lot more to offer her than my undying love. You should have seen her around Allison. As much as I wanted to dislike the woman, I couldn't. She's nice and beautiful and clearly crazy about Carmen. Who wouldn't be? Plus, she's a nurse. They have so much more in common than Carmen and me. I'm an unsophisticated farmer."

"Psht. You have a law degree and own an up-and-coming business. I forgot to tell you about the fancy chef at that Michelin-star restaurant in Seattle who wants to talk to you about supplying him with cheese. Before too long, I can see people fighting over our product. We're already selling out of cheese faster than you can make it. Besides, I'm not blind. Carmen loves you. She's not going to stray. Resolving things with her mom can't take much longer than a year. Nuns who are devoted to God spend their entire lifetime without sex, and I don't think they have access to vibrators. I've never seen a more devoted couple than you guys. If you can't do it, no one can."

"Goddess, I hope so. How am I going to stop myself from calling her?"

"Simple. Lock up your phone and only carry it when Pops or I am with you," Evan answered.

"I can't do that. In fact, I want this phone with me at all times. I can't afford to miss the most important phone call of my life—Carmen calling to say she's coming home."

"Oh, right." Evan shrugged. "Will power, my friend. You'll just have to exercise tremendous will power, knowing the prize of your life is waiting for you in that distant future. You can also keep busy on the farm. I have a feeling our business will explode this coming year."

Mac noted that was the second time Evan had referred to the farm as their business, insinuating a partnership that she hadn't exactly offered. But she was aware that if she intended to make good on her promise to Carmen, that by the time she was ready to return, the farm would be an international success, Mac needed Evan by her side to make it happen. Evan had a knack for the work as well as a keen head for business. She also had better marketing skills, and Mac needed someone like that to grow the business, including a web presence that caught people's eyes.

"I did promise Carmen I would work to make the farm something she'd be proud to be a part of and return to."

Evan frowned but quickly replaced that with an encouraging nod. Mac didn't have the energy to clarify that the only partner she ever intended to take on was Carmen. She'd have to brainstorm a way to give Evan a role that would satisfy her ambitions without developing a legal partnership.

CHAPTER SIXTEEN

Mac was sure she'd never been this sick in her entire life. She groaned and opened her eyes. Pop sat several feet away in a chair, snoring away, wearing what Mac suspected was full isolation gear. He looked like a scientist prepared to enter a contamination unit to observe an alien life. Maybe not that dramatic, but he was wearing a gown, gloves and a full mask, complete with one of those plastic shields she knew the nurses wore in the COVID units back when the disease was spreading like wildfire.

Oh shit. Mac's awareness of her current predicament became clearer every minute she was awake.

Evan had complained of a sore throat the previous week and developed mild cold-like symptoms that cleared in a couple of days, so Mac hadn't given it a second thought until her hacking cough arrived. She remembered thinking she didn't have time to be sick.

It had been six months since Mac had made that hasty agreement with Carmen. Not a single day went by without her thinking about Carmen and doing everything in her power to keep from reaching for her phone to see how things were going. In the meantime, her business had exploded. She'd purchased more goats and had been forced to hire another cheese maker. At first, she had scoffed at Evan, who wanted to advertise for a cheese artisan, but fortunately, Amanda was a true artist. Not only had she been eager to learn Mac's recipes, but she also came up with a few new ones of her own. They were selling cheese faster than they could make it and had recently hired an apprentice to learn and prepare them for Phase II of their planned expansion. Technically, Mac had taken the business international because a famous restaurant in Vancouver had learned of their cheese and had added it to their menu. Canada was a different country, so Mac convinced herself that counted.

She'd been ready to welcome Carmen back and had already begun renovations to make the farmhouse more comfortable and inviting, including a gourmet-style kitchen. Mac hadn't the foggiest idea about stoves and other gadgets, so she'd hired an expert to help her ensure Carmen would have everything she'd ever want or need to satisfy her creative talents in the kitchen.

When Mac had felt like it wasn't merely a simple cold that she had, it had almost been too late. Evan had discovered her on the floor and helped her to bed. She'd reluctantly agreed to take a day of rest. But things had unraveled quickly.

Evan had called Deb, who rushed over, took her temperature, and determined her blood oxygen saturation was dangerously low. By then, Mac was far too sick to make much of a fuss besides nixing the idea of needing an ambulance. The entire scene came rushing back, jolting her into acknowledgment her current predicament.

"She needs to get to the hospital, pronto," Deb ordered.

"Should we call an ambulance?" Evan asked, her eyes wide with worry.

"No ambulance," Mac protested.

"I'll take the stubborn ass," Evan declared.

"Pretty sure it's COVID," Deb stated. "You might want to stay clear."

Even in her miserable state, Mac saw the sheepish look on Evan's face. "Yeah, I thought it might be. I probably gave it to her. When I had that cold, Marcia insisted I test myself. She wouldn't get near me until I had the results. Then, when I tested positive, she said she wouldn't come over until I was negative," Evan grumbled.

"And you didn't think it was important to tell Mac?" Deb asked with a fair amount of incredulity. "Do you have any idea how irresponsible that was of you?"

"I was fine after a few days. I've had far worse with a bad cold. Mac got the vaccine. She made a big production of ensuring everyone associated with the farm was vaccinated. Said it was our civic duty," Evan defended.

Mac wasn't about to share that she'd neglected to get the follow-up vaccines. It wasn't like she was an anti-vaxer. Clearly. Especially with the lecture she'd given to Pops and Evan. She'd simply not prioritized the follow-up vaccines in her busy life.

Deb shook her head and began muttering something too low for Mac to hear in her compromised state. Her voice increased in volume as Mac clearly heard her take control. "We don't have the time to argue about this. Evan, help Mac to your car, and let's get her to the hospital."

"I'm so sorry, Mac," Evan whispered as she helped Mac from her bed and walked her to her car.

†

Against her better judgment, Carmen returned home after getting her mother settled into the ICU. Allison promised to call if there was any change in her condition. Her cell rang loudly on the nightstand, and Carmen jumped before she grabbed her phone to answer.

"Hello."

"Carmen, it's Allison. I'm so sorry. Your mom has taken a turn for the worse, and we had to vent her this morning."

Carmen glanced at the clock, noting the time. It was barely four in the morning. "I'll be there in thirty."

"Don't drive like a maniac. You have time. We've stabilized her for now," Allison said in her calm and soothing voice.

"You're her nurse, right?"

"Yes, so relax. Your mom will get the best care possible. I'll make sure of it," Allison reassured.

Carmen rushed around her bedroom, pulling on jeans and a T-shirt before running down the stairs and into the kitchen where she'd left the car keys. At the last minute, she patted her pockets to discover she hadn't grabbed her cell phone. Returning to the bedroom, Carmen quickly stuffed the phone in her back pocket and walked to the garage. While she didn't drive like a maniac, she did exceed the speed limit and made it to the hospital in record time.

As soon as Carmen entered the room and looked at her mother, she knew. She hadn't noticed Allison come into the room until she touched her arm.

"Prognosis?" Carmen asked. "No bullshit, Allison. Be honest, please."

"Without assistance, your mother cannot survive on her own. Not only will she need to remain on the vent, but she'll need a feeding tube at some point if we can't clear the infection and bring up her oxygen saturation. There's evidence that some organs are failing and shutting down. Honestly, it's not great, but it's not entirely hopeless either. We have a few things we could try. The team will be in later this morning to discuss those options with you. You know she signed a DNR form?" Allison reminded.

Allison's sympathetic gaze was enough to release the cascade of tears. She promptly gathered Carmen into her arms, rubbed her back and stated, "I'm here for you. Do you want me to call Mac?"

Carmen broke free from Allison's embrace and shook her head. "No. I know it's stupid of me, but I don't want to rig the outcome. Maybe there is only a slim chance Mom will pull through, but it's all I've got to hang onto right now. I can't drag Mac to Illinois during her busiest time of the year for something that could linger for weeks."

Allison opened her mouth, then promptly shut it. Carmen could guess what she might say. She knew all too well that it would only stretch into weeks if Carmen allowed her mother to stay on the vent for that duration. And that was clearly not what her mother would want. She'd pray for a miracle and hope for the best, even if that meant she'd need to remain in Illinois for a lot longer as her mother recovered from this latest bout of pneumonia. The signs of sepsis were everywhere. As a nurse, Carmen knew that. She'd only needed to look at her mother to recognize the reality of the situation.

"I'll let you sit with your mother. I promise to come and get you when the doctor arrives. Of course, we'll invite you to morning rounds when we pull the team together to discuss her case." Allison touched her arm and then exited the room.

Carmen sat and took her mother's hand, gently caressing it. Releasing it for a moment, she gathered her phone from her pocket, briefly debating whether to call Mac, then shaking her head. She pulled up her mother's favorite playlist and turned down the volume, setting it on the nightstand close enough for her to hear but not disturb the rest of the patients on the wing. She'd have to borrow a charging cord from Allison before her phone completely lost its charge.

†

Mac wasn't exactly sure if she'd heard everything correctly because she'd teetered in and out of consciousness. She tried to focus as she listened to the heated whispering beside her bed.

"I called Carmen, but she didn't answer. Allison did."

"What?" Pops exclaimed.

"Yeah, I thought that was kind of odd too, but *her friend*, Allison, explained Carmen was meeting with the healthcare team to talk about her mother's care. She's in the hospital again. I got the feeling it was serious."

"No, Evan, I meant you went directly against Mac's wishes. She specifically told you not to call Carmen. When she is back to full health, don't come running to me if she chews you out."

"Don't you think she deserves to know?" Evan defended. "I'd be on the first plane back to Washington if it were me. Mac almost died."

"That's not fair. You have no idea what's happening with her mother. You already said it sounded serious. Carmen has enough to deal with. And that's one reason Mac didn't want you to call her. The more important thing you need to understand is that she is fiercely independent. She doesn't want Carmen to see her like this. Mac is strong. She'll bounce back. However, the last thing she'd want is Carmen hovering over her and treating her like someone who needs constant nursing care. That would just about kill her. She won't want Carmen to have any part in nursing her back to health."

"Well, if it's any consolation. I didn't even have a chance to talk to Carmen. Allison said she'd tell her when the time was right. Whatever that means. Goddess, both of you have blinders on regarding Carmen. It's always all about her needs and wants," Evan grumbled. "What about Mac's? For once, Carmen could make Mac a priority. I would. She's a nurse, for fuck's sake. I don't understand why Mac would be so stubborn not to accept her help. Isn't that what solid partnerships are based on? If they ever get married, it's supposed to be through sickness and health. No one remains healthy their whole life."

Mac tried hard to turn her head and focus. "What's going on?" she mumbled.

"Don't you go making any trouble," Pops hissed.

"Nothing," Evan answered.

If this wasn't some hallucination or weird dream since she'd been having a few of those lately, Mac vowed to confront Evan and Pops. But for now, exhaustion once again overtook her body. Fighting COVID was incredibly challenging.

Hours later, when Mac finally had enough strength to have a brief conversation, she confronted Evan.

"Was I dreaming, or did I overhear that you called Carmen?" Mac asked.

"I thought she deserved to know that you're in the hospital fighting for your life," Evan relayed. "But if you were lucid enough to overhear the conversation, you already know that Allison answered the phone."

"Promise me that if Carmen calls back, you'll respect my wishes. She cannot know I'm in the hospital. I didn't even want her to learn that I'd gotten sick." It took every ounce of energy to continue the discussion with Evan.

"So, you want me to lie for you?" Evan asked with a touch of aggravation in her voice.

"I expect you to find a way to unravel the mess you created. I don't care how you do that." With that final declaration, Mac lost her fight to stay awake.

Throughout the rest of the day and night, she awoke occasionally and caught snippets of conversation. She knew things were not good, and it was touch and go several times. They'd debated whether to put her on a vent, and she heard Deb arguing against that. *Thank fuck for that.* She'd heard the horror stories. Once a person was placed on a vent, it was just a matter of time before they went completely downhill.

In one of her semi-lucid moments, Mac mumbled, "I won't be Sophie's choice."

"Mac, you aren't making any sense. Sophie's choice?" Evan asked.

Evan had tried to get her to explain her fevered ramblings. Mac felt it was too hard to help anyone understand that if Carmen chose Mac over her mother and came home prematurely to take care of Mac at the expense of helping her mother, their relationship was certainly doomed. Like in the movie *Sophie's Choice*, when Sophie had to make a choice between which of her children got to live, Mac would never make Carmen choose between two people she loved. Mac needed to be strong and healthy when Carmen finally came home. She fretted that she'd experience the lingering effects of the illness that some unlucky people endured. Long COVID was no joke. Mac would not be someone's invalid to care for, especially not Carmen's. That would most certainly break her.

If only she had enough strength and breath to help people understand, but the illness was making it difficult to think and speak clearly. A nurse entered the room after Evan pushed the button, and soon after, it was lights out again.

Chapter Seventeen

After trying a new chemo drug—a last-ditch effort—Carmen resigned herself to making the tough decision. The team had been hinting that palliative care was all that was left, and Carmen did not want to go against her mother's wishes. What remained was finding the best hospice facility in the area. Carmen stepped from the room to allow them to remove the vent before accompanying her mother to the facility.

Allison took the day off and was by her side when Carmen's mother took her final breath. Carmen wondered if it was selfish of her to want to have Mac by her side instead of Allison. Thinking out loud, she blurted, "I need to call Mac."

Allison took her by the arm and led her to the hospice chapel. "I have to tell you something."

Something wasn't right. Carmen couldn't pinpoint her friend's expression, but she was sure whatever Allison was about to tell her, she wouldn't like.

Carmen didn't even have the emotional bandwidth to cry anymore. She'd been doing that nonstop, and now that her mother had passed, she felt numb. More tears would come later. She knew that.

As they sat in the small chapel, Carmen turned her bloodshot eyes to Allison. "Okay. It can't be anything worse than my mother dying."

Allison sucked in a large breath. "Right when your mother took a turn for the worse last week, and you were meeting with the team, I answered your phone when I saw it was a long-distance call. I thought it might be Mac."

"And…" Carmen prompted.

"It wasn't Mac. It was Evan," Allison explained.

"Evan? Why would Evan call me?" Realization hit, and Carmen could barely get the words out. "Something happened to Mac," she stated.

Allison nodded. "I've been monitoring the situation. She's finally turned a corner; they believe she's out of the woods for now. Although, reading between the lines, there is a possibility she'll be one of the unlucky ones who might struggle with long COVID. Your friend Deb and I have been talking. She wasn't able to give a lot of details without violating the law, but I could glean most things from what she shared. I made an executive decision that you had enough to deal with. Besides, from what I hear, Mac was pretty pissed at Evan for calling."

"You should have told me," Carmen stated without malice. "But I sort of understand. Is she still in the hospital?"

"She is. Although it sounds like they may discharge her in the next couple of days. If you want to fly back, I can help with arrangements. Whatever you need," Allison offered.

Carmen slumped and bowed her head. Her hands grabbed each side as if it were the only thing to keep her head intact. "I just don't know what to do. I need to be the one to plan the memorial, call my idiot brother and put the house up for sale. I'll have to go through Mom's papers and figure everything out. At least Mom was always very organized. But I also need to see Mac for myself to make sure she's okay."

"Why don't you call first? It sounds like Mac has a lot of pride. She may not want you to see her like this," Allison gently suggested.

"Oh, if I know Mac, and I do know her well, she'll hate it for sure. Mac never wants anyone to see her as weak and unable to take care of every little thing. It's a miracle she lets me show my love by cooking for her. She's as stubborn as her pops and my mother."

As soon as those words came out, Carmen remembered her mother was dead, and the tears flowed freely again. Numbness thawed.

Allison gathered Carmen in her arms, and Carmen let herself be held as she cried. After what felt like forever, Carmen gathered herself and pulled out her phone. She dialed the number branded into her memory.

"Carmen? It's about fucking time you called," Evan stated with unrestrained anger.

"Hello, Evan." It took every bit of Carmen's restraint not to bite back a response, but Carmen did not need to justify anything to Evan. "Can you please put Mac on the phone?"

Carmen heard Mac's muffled voice in the background but not her actual words.

"She's sleeping," Evan answered.

"If you don't put Mac on the phone right this second, you tell her I'll be on the next plane, and it will take the National Guard to keep me from playing her nursemaid for however long she requires care. I'll be sure to tell her when I get there that you're the reason I caught the next plane versus handling my mother's funeral arrangements."

"Oh shit. I'm sorry, Carmen. I...I...didn't know..." Carmen heard a little rustling, then Evan's muffled voice as she said, "I think you really need to talk to her, Mac. She's threatening to take the next plane, and, um, her mother died."

"Oh, love. I'm so sorry." Mac's raspy voice came through the speaker. "I wish I could be there with you. Look, I'm fine. Whatever you've heard, it's a complete exaggeration. Let me see what I can do to catch a flight out in the next few days."

"I didn't know, Mac. Allison only told me today after Mom passed. It was peaceful," Carmen explained. "I would have come earlier…"

"Don't, please don't. I didn't even want you to know," Mac answered.

"You listen to me, Mac. There is no way they will let you get on a plane and travel to Chicago. I won't let you. If you even try…" Carmen chuckled. "Well, I'm not sure what I'll do. I haven't thought through an adequate threat. But please, stay in Washington and continue to regain your health."

"How about I make you a deal?" Mac asked.

"I'm listening," Carmen said.

"You stay in Elgin and get everything settled with your mom's estate, and I'll work hard to get back to fighting shape. This time, I'll call you when I'm ready. Don't come back until I call, okay?"

"I don't know if I can agree to that," Carmen hedged.

"Then I'll be on the next plane to Chicago," Mac insisted.

"Good luck with that. Let me talk to Evan," Carmen ordered.

"No way. As soon as I gain my strength, I'm going to wring her neck. I'm still pissed at her for calling."

Carmen heard a scuffle, and Evan returned to the phone. "I'm guessing you two are arguing over who is going to jump on the next plane."

"Can you keep her in Washington, please? Tell her she's adding more stress, and I can't take much more," Carmen suggested.

"Oooh, good one. Guilt. I like it. But don't worry, Carmen, there is no way they'll release her to travel. I'll make sure of it. If, you know, you wanted to speak with Deb, nurse to nurse, you may be able to help with that. Wink, wink. I'll take care of the rest. Do what you need to do."

"Got it. I'll call Deb next and get them to keep her in the hospital for the next few days." The wheels were turning. At least Evan was on her side now. "You aren't giving away our plan, are you?"

"Nope, I'm out in the hall right now. Want to talk with Mac again?"

"Yes, please."

After a short time, Mac pleaded, "Carmen, if you ever loved me, would you please not worry while you handle your mom's memorial and estate? Take the necessary time you need. I'm begging you."

"That I can agree with. But as soon as I settle everything here, I'm coming home. And I plan on using my nursing skills when I arrive. I love you."

Mac sighed. "I love you too."

After Mac ended the call, Allison raised an eyebrow and asked, "Mac wanted to jump on a plane, huh?"

Carmen nodded.

"Are you sure she doesn't have a twin or a sister? You are one lucky woman. Although, I don't know how you're going to convince her that providing care is like oxygen to you. It will kill you to hold back and delay that for however long it takes." Allison looked away and wiped a tear from her face. "I am going to miss you so much. I can't believe you're going to leave, and I'll never see you again."

"Don't be ridiculous. You've been the best friend a person could ever hope for. If it wasn't for you, I don't think I would have survived. Any chance you're interested in moving to Washington?"

"Really? You'd want me to move. Won't I just get in the way of you re-establishing your relationship with Mac?" Allison asked. "I'd consider it if I thought you were serious. I don't have anything keeping me here. Besides, I absolutely hate the weather in the midwest and the boring landscape. I've always wanted to move out west. I've just been too lazy to do anything about it."

"I am serious. After my call to Deb, I'll touch base with her sister, Kathleen, and ask about jobs. They are always looking for nurses, especially ones with critical care experience."

Allison smiled. "Maybe I'll find my own delicious farmer. What's Evan like?"

Carmen frowned. "She has her moments. I know she cares deeply for Mac, so I suppose that's enough for me. Plus, she is a hard worker. I suspect she's helped a lot with marketing. That was never Mac's forte. Evan is no dummy. Intelligent, attractive, and I sense she has the capacity to love deeply when the right one comes along. I suppose you could do worse."

†

Three days after the first call from Carmen, the doctors finally discharged Mac from the hospital, but she still had a long way to go to return to optimal health. Shortness of breath and extreme fatigue were two of the challenges Mac had to endure. She wasn't able to return to a full day's work, but she insisted on spending a couple of hours a day making cheese or else she'd go nuts.

Carmen called daily, and while Mac loved hearing her voice, she staunchly refused a video call. There was no way Mac would allow Carmen to see how much weight she'd lost and how horrible she looked. The illness had ravaged her body and left Mac looking fragile and pale, the opposite of a robust woman in good health.

Today was the day of the memorial, and Mac wanted to be there for Carmen. She could agree to a video link without allowing access to her camera. A photo would have to do. Evan had helped Mac arrange a large donation to the Lupus Foundation per Carmen's desires versus flowers, which Carmen insisted were a waste of money.

Connecting to her laptop, Mac joined the memorial where Carmen had arranged for individuals unable to participate in person, even if that was merely to watch the service. Mac noted Carmen's brother was one of those who was not at the service. He also chose not to activate the video, which seemed odd to Mac. *What was he hiding?* When the priest extended the offer to those joining via video conference to speak, Mac noticed Carmen's brother remained mute. Carmen gave a brilliant eulogy, and Mac couldn't help but feel moved by her words. She'd be sure to tell her that later.

Allison stood by Carmen's side, and Mac was grateful that she could be there for Carmen, despite the nagging discomfort. Clearly, from what Mac observed, Allison cared deeply for Carmen. Once again, Mac wondered if Allison would be a better fit, especially now that Mac had received information about the possibility of developing long COVID. The next few months would reveal any future health challenges because of the devastating pandemic.

After the video feed ended, Mac received a call from Carmen.

"Hello, love."

"Thank you for being there. I wish I could have seen your beautiful face."

"You don't want to see my ugly mug," Mac joked.

"I hope it's not because you don't want me to assess your health," Carmen responded.

Mac sighed. "I'm not going to lie to you. COVID took a toll on me. Yes, I still look like shit, but I'm getting better every day, and I don't need you rushing back to take care of me."

Carmen chuckled. "Now, was that so hard to admit?"

Mac smiled. "Yes, it was, and you know it. Let's talk about something else. Are you doing okay? Your eulogy was beautiful."

"Thanks. Yeah. I'm doing okay. Coming to terms with everything. Mom was miserable before she passed. I'm trying to look at her passing as a blessing. Her suffering ended, even if she was taken from me far too soon. Mom was only sixty-six," Carmen added.

"I don't even know what to say other than I agree that she was far too young. I wish I was there with you."

Carmen sighed. "You were, just not in person. Your presence on the video call was enough. I swear I could feel your love and energy like a warm blanket."

Mac chuckled. "Liar. If only that were possible. Listen, I'm going to let you go now because I'm sure you have a lot to do. Please pass along my thanks to Allison for being physically present to support you. Don't rush to get back to Washington. I know you have a lot to do. We have our whole life ahead of us. I love you."

"I love you too."

Mac only hoped she wouldn't develop long COVID because that would change everything. There was no way she would burden Carmen with caring for someone with a lifelong illness. She'd rather be single for the rest of her life.

CHAPTER EIGHTEEN

"That money-grubbing bastard." Carmen rarely lost her temper, but her brother was getting on her last nerve. He didn't want to lift a finger to pack up the house and ready it for sale, but he sure had a lot of opinions about what price they should list it for. None of them realistic.

She'd met with the realtor, who had suggested 50,000 less than the lowest number Daryl insisted they should accept. Since Carmen had been named executor of the will, she didn't believe Daryl had any say in how she handled her mother's estate, so she'd signed on with the realtor and listed the house for slightly above what the realtor thought they might get for a quick sale. When he saw the listing, Daryl had called and pitched a fit, threatening to challenge everything. Carmen didn't give two shits about the money, so she offered a more significant cut of the proceeds just to get him off her back. Carmen suspected she hadn't heard the end of his complaints. Not wanting to burden Mac with her woes, she sat in her kitchen and unloaded on Allison.

"Mac's an attorney. Why don't you ask her for some help? Call his bluff. No way does he have the money to hire an attorney and fight you on this," Allison advised.

Carmen lifted her cup of coffee to her lips and sipped. "Mac is not that kind of lawyer. Besides, she has enough to deal with. I had to call Deb to weasel out of her the real scoop. Mac has been downplaying her bout with COVID, and Deb thinks there is a better than fifty percent chance she'll develop long-term COVID. She says Mac has lost a lot of weight and is struggling to regain her strength. I just want everything tied up so I can return and give her all the support and care she deserves."

Allison furrowed her brow. "Tread lightly, Carmen. I didn't spend much time with Mac, but she didn't seem like the type who would appreciate any form of coddling. She'll hate the fact that she needs any assistance."

Carmen sighed. "Of course, you're right. What am I going to do? It's like second nature to me. I'm a nurse, for shit's sake."

"Yes, and Mac is a proud, independent woman. You'd be the worst person to provide care to her. She won't want to seem weak around you."

194

"So, what do you suggest? How do I handle the situation?" Carmen asked.

"Good question. I see some challenging conversations on the horizon for you, my friend."

"Thanks, you are not helpful at all," Carmen grumbled.

"One thing you might consider. Call Mac and ask for her advice on these legal issues. It doesn't matter that she isn't that kind of lawyer. My guess is she's feeling very useless right now. You'll be giving her something to show she can still be a good partner despite the setbacks to her health that she's sure to experience."

"Hmm. You have a point. I suppose you're not useless after all," Carmen teased. "How did you get so smart about relationships?"

"Trial and error. Mostly error. But at least I can learn from my mistakes."

"And I don't?" Carmen asked.

"Have you made many mistakes?" Allison asked.

"Only one. Agreeing with Mac's crazy plan for no contact. If we'd been regularly speaking to one another, I would have known about her landing in the hospital and almost dying. I'm not sure I can ever forgive myself for that."

Allison shook her head and smiled. "Self-flagellation does not look good on you, Carmen. It clashes with your gorgeous face. Get over yourself. You did not make that decision in a vacuum. Wasn't it Mac who suggested that stupid plan? If you ask me, which you didn't before agreeing to it, that was about the dumbest thing I ever heard. I know you thought it was romantic, so I kept my mouth shut."

"You did not exactly keep your mouth shut," Carmen argued. "You warned me about the temptation to drunk dial, which hadn't crossed my mind until you put the idea in my head. It's going to be so much fun to have you in Washington with me. Who else would throw harsh reality into my face? And with such tact and finesse."

"Ah, but remember that I did say she would wait for you and French-kisses the ground you walk on," Allison reminded.

"Ew, did you have to repeat that gross descriptor?"

"I'd like to think it was more memorable. I think I'll tell Mac I said that. She might appreciate that assessment."

Carmen shrugged and laughed. "She might."

"I sure hope Mac and I become good friends. She isn't stupid. I'm guessing she picked up on my little crush, but honestly, I'm over that. You and Mac are meant to be together. Anyone with eyes can see that. Plus, I think we make better friends."

"I do too. Thanks, Allison. You've been my lifeline."

"I'll remind you of that when it's my turn to fall apart."

†

By the time Mac reached the kitchen, she was so out of breath she slumped into a chair to gather her strength. The door swung open, and Evan glared at Mac.

"What the hell are you doing out of bed?" she yelled.

"I thought I might spend a few hours in the cheese shed. We'll lose momentum if we turn new businesses down."

"Are you out of your fucking mind? Don't think I don't notice how winded you get. You let me worry about cheese production. The apprentice we hired is doing exceptionally well. We can hold off on Phase II. At this point, we haven't lost any of our regular customers and have even added a few more. Granted, we may need to hire another apprentice and formally promote Tiffany to keep up. I don't mind working long hours to keep up with the rest of the chores. Deb suggested this ointment for Pops, which has worked well enough for him to pitch in more. At least with the less physically demanding tasks. We have it handled."

"The farm can't afford to hire another apprentice and promote Tiffany," Mac argued.

"Oh, yes, it can. Pops and I reworked the price structure of the cheese. No one even batted an eye. You might not know it, but your cheese is famous now. NPR wants to do an interview when you're up to it. And that television show where the guy goes around the world to taste different cuisines, he called too. We have a tentative date for next month, provided you feel well enough to do the show."

Mac blinked. "I knew you were good with the marketing stuff, but…" Tears pooled in Mac's eyes. "Thank you."

"This farm is just as important to me as it is to you. Look, I know I may overstep the boundaries sometimes, and it's obvious I'd like nothing better than to become a full-fledged partner. I also understand that might never happen. I'll admit to being jealous of your connection with Carmen, but I've been thinking about things lately, and most of all, I want you to be happy. Carmen makes you happy. I hope to find that with someone someday. Before I learned that Carmen's mom died and she had no idea you were in the hospital, I thought she wasn't good enough for you. I was angry with her. I thought she was being selfish."

"She wasn't. We were in a no-win situation. I couldn't leave the farm and Pops, any more than she could abandon her mother. Family is everything to us. I'm so sorry your family is a bunch of asswipes. I hope you know that not all families are connected by blood. You are a part of our family. I suppose I'm just realizing that, which makes me want to reconsider the partnership idea. Can you give me time to think on this?"

Evan rushed to Mac's side and hugged her. "I can't tell you how much that means to me. That you'd even consider it is beyond my wildest dreams. I have money saved to put into the business to help Phase II happen more quickly. Not that your illness was a good thing, but one positive that happened is that it's helped me grow as a person and businesswoman."

Mac smiled. "Yes, it has."

Mac wondered what Carmen would think of a three-way partnership. Four, if you counted Pops, but he'd made it clear when Mac first took over that he was handing over the reins to her. Other than helping out, Pops wanted no part of the business. Mac ensured he had everything he needed for a comfortable life and had been depositing money into a personal account for him for months. They were on the cusp of making more money than she ever dreamed possible—if Mac could kick the lingering effects of the illness. No way would she allow Carmen to settle back at the farm until she was at one hundred percent.

CHAPTER NINETEEN

Carmen and Allison sat at the kitchen table in Allison's condo, drinking hard lemonade. Although Allison put her condo up for sale, it wasn't getting many bites. After Carmen had an estate auction company take over the sale of every item inside the house, except for her father's antique gun collection that Daryl insisted her deceased father promised him, Allison had offered for her to stay at her condo until they moved. Carmen still couldn't believe both of her parents were dead now. Neither got to enjoy their old age and retirement. She wondered if she would suffer the same fate. Of course, her father's heart attack had been entirely preventable if he'd changed to a healthier lifestyle. Thirty years of smoking had not helped.

"Is that jackass brother of yours still giving you fits?" Allison asked before tipping the bottle and taking a sip.

"You have no idea. Pick a topic, and he's been contrary to it. First, he balked at me hiring the probate attorney. He didn't want me to use the money from Mom's estate. Finally, I called his bluff. I was tired of fighting with him."

"Good for you. What did you say?" Allison asked.

"I told him I would spend every penny I currently have access to on lawyers to fight any ridiculous challenge to the will. Which, for the record, is a significant amount since Mom put my name on all of her cash accounts. I intimated it could take years. I get the impression he's in a bind and wants money as quickly as possible. That shut him right up, until he found a new topic to argue about."

"What bee is in his bonnet now?"

"I told him if he wanted Dad's antique gun collection, he'd have to come and get it himself. Otherwise, I would let the company I hired sell the collection and give him the money. I think Mom was trying to be fair since she specifically noted all her jewelry would go to me to pass down to my children. At least she was smart enough to know that Daryl would have sold every piece, taken the money and run. My guess is that the gun collection is worth a pretty penny."

Allison grinned and gave Carmen a mischievous look. "Did you get the collection appraised?"

Carmen shook her head. "Nope. Don't really care. He'll just piss away the money no matter how much it's worth. But there was no way I would violate the law and ship the collection. If he doesn't arrive soon, I'll have to drag the lot to Washington. I despise the thought of having to drive a box full of guns across the country."

"So don't. Sell the guns and give your brother the money. Or, we could add your stuff to my U-Haul, and you can drive with me."

Carmen considered the offer and answered, "Maybe. When do you plan on leaving?"

"Two weeks. After I decided to rent my condo, that got me thinking about renting something in Moses Lake. So, instead of buying something immediately, I signed a lease for a condo on the lake next to a golf course. Perhaps I'll take up golf. Who knows, maybe I'll meet a hot lesbian golfer who can show me how to swing a club," Allison joked. "I want to get there a few weeks before I start at the hospital. Thanks for the introduction to Kathleen. Honestly, I was surprised she made an offer on the spot over the phone, especially with all the hoops I had to go through to get licensed in Washington."

"I'm not. The hospital is lucky to recruit you. Kathleen is a good boss. You'll love working with her," Carmen answered.

"If you come with me, we can start at the same time. You don't need to hang around until everything goes through with the house. DocuSign makes the process a lot easier."

"True. I suppose you're right. But what if the offer falls through at the last minute?"

Allison narrowed her eyes. "I call bullshit. What's really going on? I thought you'd jump at the chance to get there sooner rather than later?"

Carmen sighed. "Mac doesn't seem all that thrilled for me to move back. I know her well enough to detect that hesitation in her voice."

"I don't believe it. What do you think that's about?" Allison asked.

"Her stubborn pride. I called Evan, and I think I know exactly what's going on in that beautiful head of hers."

"And that is what? Because I can't think of a reason that she wouldn't be doing cartwheels right about now." Allison finished her drink and pointed to Carmen's empty bottle. "Want another?"

Carmen shook her head. "Better not, or I'll want to numb myself. I guess Mac still gets winded and hasn't been able to work a full eight hours. Evan says there are times when it sounds like she's coughing up a lung. She's worried about her."

Allison opened her refrigerator and took out another lemonade. "Okay, that makes sense. Mac doesn't want you to be her nurse. If she needs care, maybe I could offer my services."

Carmen frowned. "I doubt that would make it better. First, no way would I let someone else care for Mac when I'm right there. And two, you offering to be her private nurse would be almost as bad as me caring for her."

"Well, that's just stupid," Allison argued.

"Tell me about it."

"You'll just have to convince her she's acting like a baby."

Carmen laughed. "No wonder you're single."

Allison playfully slapped Carmen. "Hey now. I just call it like I see it. Maybe you could give her a little time and space. The condo I'm renting has two bedrooms. Stay with me until Ms. Stubborn feels like she's back to full health."

Carmen pursed her lips. "That's just it. She may never return to her previous state of health. The doctors suggested it was a good chance she would develop long COVID."

"Damn," Allison blurted.

"Yeah, damn is right, and a few other choice swear words. But maybe your idea has merit. I'd rather be close enough to touch her, even if it means we won't be living together again until she's ready for it. Perhaps that is the compromise we'll need to make."

"I better call the rental place and ask what I need to do to make Onyx legal." Allison glanced at the sleeping feline.

"It's been nice having you and her around. Maybe I'll get my own fur baby. Kittens attract women. Right?"

"Allison! You shouldn't adopt a kitten to snag a woman."

"Well, it wouldn't be the only reason. I'll need something to snuggle with until I can get my own hot farmer," she teased.

†

Mac was having a dreadful week. After working six hours a day last week and believing she was on the road to full recovery, she had started coughing again and ran a fever. Despite wearing protective clothing and a mask, she had to admit defeat because she didn't know if it was possible to contaminate the cheese.

When her phone rang in the middle of a coughing fit, she glanced at the screen and muttered, "Fuck."

Trying to control her coughing proved difficult, but she finally answered on the fourth ring. "Hi, love."

"Good news," Carmen said. "I know you weren't expecting me for another month or so, but Allison offered me a place to stay until you're ready to have me back at the farm."

Shit, now she thinks I don't want her here. "Oh, hon, not that I don't want you back at the farm…" Mac allowed her words to dangle.

205

"I understand more than you think. I'm still going to hover a bit, but not as much as if I were living in the farmhouse. It's in my DNA, you know."

"I know," Mac responded wearily. "I was just hoping to gain a little more strength." The urge to cough overcame Mac, and she cringed, knowing that Carmen would fully understand how fragile Mac's health remained when she couldn't contain the long coughing fit.

"Have you taken your temperature today?" Carmen asked after Mac finally settled.

Mac groaned. "It's a little elevated, but I'm fine."

"Please promise me you'll stay on it, and if either your temperature gets too high or your oxygen level too low, you'll let Evan know. If not, I'll be on the next flight, and I will move in, whether you like it or not. This is the best deal you'll get from me. Take it or leave it."

Mac chuckled. "I'll take it. But I reserve the right to alter our agreement once we see how it's working out. So, are you two driving here then?"

"We are. I don't have much, but Allison thought it wasn't cost effective to hire a moving company, even though the hospital offered to pay for moving expenses. She opted for a sign-on bonus instead. The condo she's renting wanted first and last month's rent. It's actually a good thing that I'll be along to help with the long drive."

"It is." Mac chuckled before launching into another coughing fit.

"What's so funny about us driving a truck across the country?"

"Oh, it's not that," Mac answered after her coughing had stopped. "I know you both are competent women. I was just picturing Onyx howling the whole way."

"If it was Midnight, I might be worried, but Onyx only cares about food. She'll be fine. I'll just keep feeding her treats along the way."

"True," Mac agreed.

"Hey, when is that show *Culinary Arts* coming to the farm? I wish I could be there for that." Carmen sounded genuinely disappointed.

"Next week. Yeah, me too. Evan made all the arrangements. She's been the one holding this place together. I don't know what I'd do without her. I'd like to talk to you about an idea I had regarding partnership, but I'd rather discuss that in person."

"Okay, but if it's that you want to make Evan a partner. I think you should. Honestly, a year ago, I might have had concerns. Not that I have any say in the decisions you and Pops make for the farm, but Evan is like a different person. I talk to her sometimes because I know she'll be straight with me and give me the unvarnished truth."

"I'm not sure I like knowing that the two of you are conspiring behind my back," Mac teased. "And, just for the record, you do have a say in what happens on the farm. A big say."

Mac could hear the smile in Carmen's voice.

"I like the sound of that. It speaks to our future. As for Evan and I finding common ground, you know it's because we both love you. I promise, neither of us is hiding anything from you. I should let you get some rest."

"Okay. You probably have things to do, like helping Allison pack up her condo. Have fun with that. I hate moving."

"It isn't fun. That's why I hired that company to handle Mom's house. It didn't keep me from having to go through all her files and drawers. Unraveling everything I needed to stop payment on and attend to existing bills was not a barrel of laughs. Of course, Daryl was absent through the entire process, only bitching about it after it was complete. But that's a story for another day. Bye, Mac, I love you."

"Later, love. I love you too."

Mac ended her call and ambled around the farm. The new cheese shed would be at least twice the size of her original. Mac needed to decide how much she could handle before finishing Phase II. Evan had caught Mac during a time when she'd almost felt like herself again, and she had convinced Mac to go ahead with the plans. Then Mac relapsed, and she had worried the expansion was a terrible idea. Evan was unfazed by Mac's setback, arguing they could easily hire more apprentices, especially after that television show aired, which wouldn't be for several months. It wasn't like they filmed the show, and it aired the next day. The delay didn't matter because, apparently, Evan was good at promoting the farm and recruiting promising young women who wanted to learn the art of cheese-making.

Mac wanted to be the one to occupy the new shed and spend her days inventing innovative cheeses to sell. With the Brie and Camembert market in serious disarray resulting from the overuse of the essential fungus that was a key to make those famous cheeses, Mac's creamery had a golden opportunity to offer an alternative gourmet cheese that would astound the tastebuds of cheese connoisseurs without looking like a block of unappealing mold.

†

Midnight's routine kept getting interrupted, and nothing had been the same since Carmen had taken her sister away. No amount of protest on her part had made any difference. Onyx never returned. And neither had her other mother. Mac was always sad, and then she left her alone with Pops and Evan for two whole weeks. It was excruciating. She'd taken to eating more than she should and imagined her rotund little tummy was probably as big as Onyx's. And that brought her back to thinking about her sister and how much she missed her.

Then Mac wasn't just sad anymore; she'd gotten sick and left again. Pops and Evan barely even acknowledged

Midnight's presence. She'd taken to roaming the farm on her own and had made friends with the new workers. At least they cooed over her shiny black coat and bent to pet her occasionally, but it wasn't the same. She wasn't allowed inside the cheese shed, which had always been okay because that was nap time when Mac entered her shed. However, the workers spent most of their time in the shed, and Midnight had no one to play with.

Mac was home now but spent a lot of time in bed. Not that Midnight objected to frequent naps, but that wasn't who Mac was. She didn't even look or feel the same. She certainly was not as comfortable to snuggle against with her sharp bones sticking out. Mac was never fat, but at least her muscle was more comfortable than bone.

Midnight's ears perked up this morning when she heard her sister's name. Midnight was smart enough to know that Mac was talking with her other mama, and finally, they were coming home. But it sounded like Carmen wasn't returning to the farm immediately. That made no sense to Midnight. She'd have to take matters into her own paw. Surely, Onyx would help. Midnight would simply need to figure out how to get to Onyx. It couldn't be that hard if they were in the same city.

Midnight trotted along next to Mac, but it wasn't the same as before Mac got sick. Mac rested on the wooden bench, and Midnight jumped into her lap, purring. She wanted to let Mac know she'd be there for her, even if they didn't have grand adventures anymore.

"Meow."

Mac ran her hand through Midnight's fur. "Your other mama and sister are coming home soon. Well, almost. They'll be living with Carmen's friend Allison for a bit, until I'm strong enough to…"

Midnight tilted her head, waiting for Mac to finish, prompting her with a quiet *meow*.

"Ugh. I don't know, Midnight. Maybe I'm being ridiculous. I know you miss Onyx and Carmen as much as I do. And it isn't fair to keep Onyx from you, but I wouldn't dream of suggesting that Onyx come live at the farm before I'm ready for Carmen to be here. You understand, don't you?"

"Meow, meow, meow, meow."

Mac was smart, but Midnight wondered if she knew that her irritated meows roughly translated to, *No, I do not.* At least Midnight didn't add, *you stubborn idiot,* to the end.

"Well, I thought at least you'd understand and be supportive. Seems like no one else on the farm does."

Midnight was impressed. Midnight supposed she hadn't given Mac enough credit for understanding her response.

"Come on, let's head back to the house. You like afternoon naps."

"Meow." Midnight did enjoy her afternoon naps, but she liked following Mac around the farm even more. However, there was no way she'd say a word. She wasn't about to add to Mac's misery.

CHAPTER TWENTY

Two weeks later, Carmen placed the litter box into the back of the U-Haul and grabbed Onyx's carrier. Most of the time, Onyx was a mellow cat, but the minute she saw her carrier, she ran in the other direction. Carmen understood. Poor Onyx had experienced so much upheaval over the last year. First, Carmen had dragged her across the country to Illinois. She'd finally settled into her mother's home, mainly because whenever her mother was awake, she'd sneak treats to Onyx. Then they'd gone to live with Allison so the company Carmen had hired could empty the house and ready it for sale. The previous evening, Carmen had locked her in the bathroom because she was afraid that Onyx would puncture the inflatable mattresses they'd used for sleeping so they could get an early start in the morning after packing the truck.

The minute Carmen opened the door, Onyx shot out of the bathroom, protesting loudly. Then she saw the carrier and looked around the empty room. Fortunately, there was no hiding place, and Carmen grabbed Onyx by the scruff to shove her into the carrier.

"Onyx, aren't you excited about seeing your sister?" Carmen soothed. "I promise I'll let you out when we get on the road, and you can curl up on my lap when I'm not driving."

"Meow brmmp."

Carmen stuck her fingers inside the cage and stroked Onyx's nose. "That's my good girl."

"Ready?" Allison asked.

Carmen nodded. "I am."

"We'll stop at that coffee place and get a breakfast bagel for the road," Allison suggested as she opened the heavy door and hoisted herself inside.

"They're open this early?" Carmen asked.

"Yup. They open at six."

"Perfect. It's okay if I let Onyx out of her carrier, isn't it?" Carmen set the carrier in the middle between the seats and climbed inside.

"Sure, as long as she doesn't roam in the cab of the truck. Um, I meant to ask how we'll know when she needs to use her litter box?" Allison asked.

"Good question. Maybe the next time we stop, I'll put Onyx in her box in case she needs to use it. Good thing it was the last thing I put in the back, so we'd have easy access to it. I suppose we could do that every time we stop."

Allison nodded and shrugged. "Sounds like a plan. When we get to Moses Lake and unhook my car from the back, why don't you take my car and go see Mac while I unload? Were you planning on taking Onyx?" Allison started the truck, checked her mirrors, and pulled away from the curb.

"Was it not okay to have a cat in the condo?" Carmen asked. "I thought you called and got the ok."

"I did. I just remember you telling me how much Onyx cried when you took her away." Allison held up her hands. "No judgment. I understand. She's such a sweet thing. I would have wanted her with me too."

Carmen frowned. "I'm being very selfish, aren't I? I didn't ask Mac about that. I suppose I should have. Unless you want me to try to get Evan to help, I'd rather not take your car. Mac will want to help us unload, and she probably shouldn't exert herself. Asking Evan will only put salt on Mac's wounds. I think it would be best to get settled before going to the farm. I'll call Mac when we arrive and talk with her about Onyx. See what she thinks. Maybe with Onyx at the farm, that will give me more reason to visit and won't look like I'm checking up on Mac."

"Devious. I like it," Allison teased as she glanced over at Carmen.

Carmen playfully pushed against her shoulder. "It is not devious." Letting Onyx out of her carrier, she patted her lap. "Come here, Onyx. If you need to pee, go over to your aunt Allison's lap and let her rip."

Onyx jumped on the floor and sniffed around, then hopped into Carmen's lap but wouldn't settle. She lifted her head and looked out the window, and when she jumped back to the floor and started to make her way to the driver's side, Carmen scooped her up and placed her on her lap, petting her head and trying to calm her.

"Mean, you're just mean." Allison grinned. "Find us a good radio station."

Carmen saluted. "Aye, aye, captain."

It didn't take long for Onyx to wail, and Carmen cringed. "She'll settle down soon once we reach the highway and the road is less bumpy. Be a good girl, Onyx, or I'll have to put you back in your carrier."

Allison quirked her eyebrow. "I doubt Onyx views it as a carrier, more like a cage. Maybe it brings back terrible memories from when she was at the shelter. Don't do that. It's fine. She's serenading to the music," Allison joked.

"You're a good friend."

"Damn tooting, I am," Allison answered.

Carmen's phone rang, and she shifted her body so she could retrieve her phone without letting Onyx roam again.

"Hello."

"Someone's unhappy." Evan chuckled.

"Is Mac okay?" Carmen asked in a panic.

"Yeah, she's fine. Actually, she's had a good week. No fever, only minimal coughing."

"Good. So why are you calling?" Carmen asked.

"Mac mentioned that you two were heading out this morning, and I wanted to offer our assistance when you hit town. You have a U-Haul to unload. Right?"

"That's awful kind of you." Carmen snickered. "Mac told you that Allison is attractive, didn't she? I'm guessing you and Marcia didn't work out."

Allison glanced over and raised her eyebrow.

"She was fun, but no, it didn't work out, probably for the best. I think she thought I was wealthy because my family owns one of the more prominent farms in the area. Ironically, Mac's organic farm is going to bypass my family's potato farm in a couple of years. Anyway, I thought our team could make quick work of unloading the truck, minus Mac, of course."

"And Mac was okay with this idea?" Carmen asked.

"Not exactly. That's why I was calling you. Mac is doing so well, and I didn't want to see her have another setback. I kind of hoped you'd call, and we could come over without telling Mac, then you could visit the farm after we unload the truck. You need to get your car anyway. I've been running it every few weeks to keep the battery working. I only started doing that after Mac got sick," Evan amended.

Carmen smiled. "Thank you, Evan. You're going to make some lucky woman very happy someday. Don't settle. You have plenty of time to find the one."

Allison poked Carmen and mouthed, *Is she cute?*

Carmen grinned and nodded before returning to her call. "I suppose that sounds like a good plan. I'll call when we arrive. We'll feed you after. But maybe not a home-cooked meal. Is pizza and beer okay?"

"You got yourself a deal," Evan answered. "I'm glad you're coming home, Carmen."

"Me too, Evan, me too."

†

Mac was both excited and anxious for Carmen to return to Moses Lake. Based on her knowledge of when they were planning on leaving and the call she'd received yesterday, she suspected Carmen and Allison would arrive sometime today. Mac assumed they would call when they hit town. She headed to the cheese shed to settle her nerves and thought she'd immerse herself in work as she waited for them to arrive. Midnight followed her and settled into her bed right outside of the shed.

When she opened the shed, she found it empty and scratched her head, wondering where the hell Amanda and Tiffany were. Come to think of it, she hadn't seen Evan either. And then the pieces came together. She stifled the urge to slam the door.

"Bloody hell. I'm not an invalid." As soon as the words left her mouth, she noticed Midnight lifting her head and meowing as if to say, "What, no nap today?"

She walked back into the house with Midnight on her tail and found her pops sitting at the kitchen table, eating a sandwich.

"Did you know?" Mac asked through gritted teeth.

"Know what?" Pops seemed genuinely confused.

Mac grabbed the keys to her truck. "Never mind."

"Where are you going?" Pops asked.

"To find that condo Allison rented. I'm not a betting woman, but I'd bet the entire farm that Evan, Amanda and Tiffany went to help Allison and Carmen unload the U-Haul."

"Oh, and your little pride is all bent out of shape now, right?" Pops shook his head. "Knowing your limitations isn't such a bad thing. Sure, it takes getting used to, but at least your limitations might not be permanent. And they aren't guaranteed to get progressively worse. Do you think it was easy for me to ask you to help with the farm?"

Mac crossed the room and slumped in a chair across from her pops. "No. I'm sorry, Pops." Midnight jumped into the empty chair next to Mac.

"Now you listen to me, Mac. That woman loves you. Let her."

"Let her what? Be my personal nurse? I can't do that," Mac argued. "I've been reading up on new drugs they're trying for long COVID. I need to get into one of those trials."

"No, Mac, let her love you. She's a caregiver at her core. Surely you can bend a little and allow her to show you that love. I agreed to that when my arthritis got so bad."

"I'll think about it. But right now, I need to prove to her and everyone else that I'm not an invalid. No fever today, and my fatigue is manageable."

"Just don't overdo it, or you'll be right back to square one. And that will not get you to the finish line."

Mac stood, walked over, and kissed her father on the cheek. "Thanks, Pops. Keep Midnight company while I'm gone."

Even though COVID had caused a small amount of brain fog, Mac remembered that Allison's condo was on the lake and by a golf course. She thought she knew exactly where that was. It would be easy to pinpoint which condo. Besides, they might still be unloading the truck, and she could help.

As soon as she pulled into Moses Point, she saw the truck with the ramp extended from the back. Noticing Evan's sheepish expression as she carried a large box was all Mac needed to know. Evan set the box on the ground and rushed over as Mac emerged from her truck and glared.

"Mac, don't blame Carmen. I called her and made the suggestion."

"We'll discuss this later." Mac marched to the truck and noticed that only a few boxes, along with other small items, including a floor lamp, remained. Everything was tucked into a back corner. Mac picked up a box marked, bathroom. She shifted her focus to Evan. "Which unit?"

"Um, 1103." Evan pointed to the stairs. "Up there and to the left."

Mac carried the box up the stairs and concentrated on her breathing. The last thing she wanted was to have Carmen see her short of breath after climbing the long set of stairs. Once Mac reached the top of the stairs, she took a few seconds before entering the condo with her box. Unfortunately, she didn't get the time she needed before the door opened, and she was face-to-face with a scowling Carmen.

"Hi, love," Mac said through somewhat labored breathing before quickly ducking inside and seeing Allison, who looked slightly surprised.

"Mac?"

Mac lifted the box a little higher. "Bathroom. Which way?"

Music blared through a Bluetooth speaker, and Mac thought she could hear the faint cries from Onyx.

Allison grabbed her phone and turned down the music before responding. "Um, there's two, so maybe just set it on the floor, and I can figure out which one to take it to later."

Mac nodded. "Sorry I'm late to the party, but my invitation must have been lost in the mail," she sniped before placing the box on the floor next to several other unopened boxes.

Allison had the good sense to cringe. Tiffany and Amanda stood awkwardly in the middle of the living room.

Evan barged into the condo and stated, "There isn't much left. Amanda, Tiffany and I can get the rest."

"Oh, good. That didn't take long. I'll pick up the pizzas," Allison offered.

"I'll come with. Just give me a few minutes. Can you guys handle the rest?" Evan asked.

Tiffany and Amanda both nodded and scurried out of the condo.

After everyone left, Carmen grabbed Mac's hand and pulled her to the back bedroom. "Come with me."

Mac noted the small number of boxes in the room as Carmen led her to the bed that was already set up but free of linens. She could hear faint meows from somewhere but couldn't pinpoint the location.

"I guess this is your room, huh?" Mac asked.

"Before you get your nose bent out of shape, Evan offered, and we accepted. I was planning to come by after we unloaded the truck. And had pizza," she amended. "Although

I probably would have encouraged Evan to eat quickly so she could bring me to the farm."

"I'm not an invalid." Mac couldn't keep the hurt from creeping into her voice.

"I never said you were," Carmen defended.

"But you thought it," Mac countered.

"No, I thought it didn't make a lot of sense to have you join the moving crew because we had plenty of help." Carmen waved her arms around the room. "You've seen the condo, or at least most of it. It's barely one thousand square feet. We'd be like those little silver balls in a pinball machine, bouncing into each other. Too many cooks in the kitchen."

Mac laughed. "You really should pick only one metaphor."

"All right. I choose the cooks in the kitchen. We had it handled," Carmen insisted.

Mac sighed. "It just hurt my pride. Pops yelled at me too."

Carmen arched her eyebrow. "I knew I loved that man. Don't be mad at Evan, okay? She's turned into quite the woman, hasn't she? Maybe she'll ask Allison out. That would be so perfect. Just between you and me, I didn't really like Marcia, but I encouraged that relationship because I was a little jealous."

"You were?" Mac asked.

"Yeah. Not my proudest moment. Remember when I told you Evan had a crush on you? It kinda started then."

"Well, I guess I should admit to being a little jealous about your close relationship with Allison, so, hell yes, let's hope that Evan asks her out and they fall madly in love. But you know you had nothing to worry about, and Evan is so over her little crush."

"So is Allison."

"I knew it," Mac exclaimed.

"Old news," Carmen insisted.

Mac stroked the side of Carmen's face and leaned in to kiss her. "Goddess, I've missed you. I should have done this the minute I set down that box."

"Yes, you should have," Carmen teased.

"Are we okay?" Mac asked.

"As long as you don't yell at anyone."

"I won't. Where's Onyx?" Mac asked.

"Locked in the bathroom. You were right. Onyx cried nearly the whole time, taking intermittent naps when she tired, only to start up again when she woke."

"Yikes. That must have been tough," Mac consoled.

"You have no idea. It's a bloody miracle that Allison is even still speaking to me," she joked. "I was planning on bringing Onyx to the farm, if that's okay."

"Of course, but don't you want her here with you?" Mac suddenly felt a rush of sadness. She was reminded of their arrangement to live apart until she returned to full health.

"Um, I meant for a visit," Carmen awkwardly replied.

"Right. I hope that won't be too hard on them," Mac responded.

"It couldn't be any harder than it will be for us."

If Mac didn't know Carmen as well as she did, she might have missed the slight bite to her voice.

"No, I don't suppose it will be more difficult. I've been thinking of getting into one of those clinical trials. I'd love your opinion on that."

Mac hoped that tossing this out would smooth over the tension. She remembered what her pops had said, and perhaps getting Carmen involved in her care without actually having her hover might work. Visions of Carmen wiping her ass kept invading her brain and making her more than a little queasy. Although that wasn't something she'd needed, even at her lowest point.

"I'll need more details, but I'd love to assist you with that. I might have some connections that will help get you into the appropriate study."

Carmen's face brightened, and Mac knew she had hit the right note.

"That would be really helpful. I'm so glad you're back to lend your expertise to the situation."

Carmen grinned. "Stop buttering me up. I know exactly what you're doing, but I'll take it. Feeling like I'm helping in some small way is better than nothing."

Mac smiled. "Damn. Why did I have to fall in love with someone so smart and strong? I can't get anything by you, can I?"

CHAPTER TWENTY-ONE

"Should we go into the living room and prove that we haven't killed one another?" Carmen joked.

"I didn't look that upset, did I? You, on the other hand, could have cut me in half with your laser vision," Mac teased.

"It's my superpower. I inherited that from my mother. Whenever we acted up, she'd give us what my brother called her bug eyes. I'll use it on our children." Carmen's eyes filled with tears.

Mac pulled her into her arms and rubbed her back. "I'm so sorry I wasn't there for you."

227

"It's just that neither my mother nor father will ever meet their grandchildren. I just realized that."

"You sound awfully sure that we'll have kids and a future with one another," Mac hedged.

"Aren't you?" Carmen asked. The sadness from the loss of her mother took a back seat to panic at whatever Mac was trying to convey.

Before Mac could respond, the sound of loud wailing from the master bathroom resumed after Carmen heard voices in the living room.

"We should let Onyx out. I'm eager to see her." Mac wouldn't look Carmen in the eyes.

Carmen took Mac's face in her hand and turned her, forcing Mac to make eye contact. "In a minute. I'd like an answer to my question."

Mac sighed. "I'm working on it."

"What does that mean?"

"It means that I won't saddle you or anyone with someone who will need lifelong nursing care. Getting into that study is my way of working on it. I can't be anyone's damaged goods."

Carmen abruptly stood. "This conversation isn't over, but I don't want to finish it right now lest I say something I can't take back."

Mac reached out to Carmen, who shook her head. "You're going to have to give me a minute. I'm sure I'll calm down, but right now, I'm ready for pizza and beer. Lots of beer."

"Okay. But you don't even like beer," Mac grumbled.

"Maybe Allison got hard cider for me. That goes well with pizza. At least she knows what I want and need, rather than presuming what that might be and deciding for me." Carmen glared at Mac before stalking out of the bedroom.

Before Carmen entered the other room, she heard Mac mutter, "Shit."

Two large pizza boxes sat on the coffee table, along with a twelve-pack of beer and a six-pack of hard cider. Allison looked up and smiled, then quirked one eyebrow. "Help yourself."

"Thanks for getting cider. You're a peach," Carmen said through a forced smile.

Allison furrowed her brow. "You don't drink beer. I knew you'd want the cider instead."

Mac sighed again and announced, "Although I don't believe I deserve pizza or beer after only carrying one box, I think I'll take a beer anyway."

"Do we need to send you two back to Carmen's room and lock y'all in there until you work everything out?" Allison teased.

"No," Carmen and Mac simultaneously grumbled.

"Good. Now act like you love each other and behave," Allison chastised before grabbing a piece of pizza and taking a big bite. "Oh, and would one of you please let poor Onyx out of the bathroom? It's breaking my heart to hear her cry like that."

Carmen rushed to the master bath next to Allison's bedroom and opened the door. Onyx darted out and promptly scurried under the bed. After five minutes of coaxing, she still wouldn't budge. Carmen finally admitted defeat and returned to the living room.

"She's hiding, isn't she?" Mac asked.

Carmen nodded. "This has been a traumatic experience for my poor baby. She's under the bed in Allison's room."

"Want me to try to coax her out?" Mac offered.

"Have at it," Carmen answered.

"It's the first door on your left," Allison instructed.

Carmen settled on the floor and grabbed a can of cider. After a few minutes, Mac returned with Onyx in her arms. She was talking in a low voice and scratching her head.

"It's okay, Onyx. I know how confusing all of this has been for you. Soon, we'll take you to see Midnight, and everything will be okay," Mac soothed.

Carmen hoped that was true. She wanted nothing more than to have everything go back to how it was before she left to take care of her mother.

†

Mac had limited herself to one beer since she offered to drive Carmen and Onyx to the farm. Carmen needed to get her car and have her own transportation, and Mac had promised Onyx that she would take her to see Midnight. It didn't matter that Onyx might not completely understand what she'd been assured, but a promise was a promise. Mac never broke her vows. That got her thinking about what she'd vowed to Carmen. She'd told Carmen she would wait for her as long as it took—one year, two years, ten years. It didn't matter how long. Now, without actually communicating directly to Carmen what she hoped for, she desperately yearned for Carmen to tell her she would wait for Mac as long as it took. That wasn't fair at all. Mac had no idea how long it would take her to resolve her situation, if that ever happened.

The ride back to the farm was eerily quiet. Onyx wasn't even crying anymore. *Shit, I've made a mess of things.* Mac opened her mouth to try to help Carmen understand but promptly closed it. What could she say?

Eventually, the frost thawed, and Carmen broke the silence. "You may not be sure about our future, but I am, and I have enough confidence in our love to get through this. I'm not giving up. If you think you're stubborn, the Torre genes have got you beat by a country mile."

Mac smiled and glanced at Carmen. "I haven't given up on us. I just need to work through some things. Will you give me the time to do that?"

"I'll give you all the time you need, but this isn't just your journey. It's *our* expedition. One that I'm sure will have a plethora of obstacles to overcome. Life is like that, you know. You have to let me walk beside you. Don't leave me behind. That's all I ask."

"We're going to have to talk about what that looks like." Mac took a chance and grabbed Carmen's hand. "Because I've no doubt your vision might differ a bit from mine." She was thrilled when Carmen didn't pull away. They still had a lot to work out, but it was a start.

"Fair enough. As long as it's a discussion and not you deciding for both of us," Carmen insisted. "Compromise and communication are two important building blocks to a healthy relationship."

"Agreed." A kernel of hope sprouted in Mac's heart. Now, if only her health would step in line, then she could make plans for the future.

†

Midnight was in the cat tree next to the window when she heard Mac's truck. She lifted her head to see Mac pull into the long gravel driveway. Pops had slipped her a treat before heading to the gardens, but Midnight didn't want to follow him. Instead, she climbed her cat tree to nap and pass the time. Jumping gracefully to the ground, she hurried to the

232

door to greet Mac. It always brought a smile to Mac's face when Midnight did that, and since smiles were so rare these days, Midnight wanted to do everything she could to cheer Mac up.

The last thing Midnight expected to see was Onyx and Carmen. Midnight ran over to her sister, and they touched noses.

"Onyx! Where have you been?"

"Long story. They locked me in the bathroom, and I was in a big truck for days," Onyx said indignantly.

"That doesn't sound like Carmen. Why would she lock you inside a truck?" Midnight asked.

"She didn't lock me in the truck. It was the longest car ride of my life. I cried and cried, but that didn't make it stop."

"Look how cute they are together. Maybe I shouldn't take Onyx with me after their visit," Carmen nearly whispered.

"Okay, full story later. Sshh, pay attention. I want to hear what their plans are," Midnight hissed.

"Midnight! That's your sister," Mac chastised.

"No, no, no, no," Midnight said. "They think I'm mad at you just because I shushed you and told you to be quiet." Midnight pushed Onyx onto her side and began grooming her. "Act like you're happy to see me."

Onyx put her paw over Midnight and began licking her back.

Midnight opened one eye and noticed Carmen smiling.

"I think they just worked out their differences," Carmen noted. "Midnight, I hope you don't blame Onyx for leaving you. Would you like her to stay here at the farm?"

"Meow. Yes, please," Midnight tried to answer in a way that her human would understand.

Mac touched Carmen's arm and said, "I'm sure they'll both be fine living apart. At least now, they'll be in the same city. We can arrange play dates for them," Mac offered. "I know Onyx has been as much of a comfort to you as Midnight has been to me."

Midnight stopped licking Onyx's fur and puffed out her fur proudly until she realized where this conversation was going. She started meowing and protesting loudly, but apparently, neither of her mommies understood.

"I *would* miss her. Can we have play dates too?" Carmen asked seductively.

Mac chuckled. "I sure hope so."

"Should we let them get reacquainted? Maybe we can have our first play date right now?" Carmen suggested. "Unless you need to rest."

Mac grabbed Carmen's hand and pulled on it. "I'm not made of glass. Come on, it's time we got reacquainted."

Midnight was torn between following Carmen and Mac and learning more from Onyx. She knew the situation and figured they would shut the door to keep the cats out of the bedroom. She decided to remain in the kitchen with Onyx, who blinked back at Midnight curiously.

Turning to her sister, she demanded, "Tell me everything you know."

"I guess you figured out that I'm only here for a visit. Carmen has her own room in this tiny place on the lake. I like the view of the lake because there are birds and a back deck. But it isn't the same as living on the farm. It isn't even as nice as the house I stayed in after Carmen took me away."

"Why aren't you and Carmen coming back to the farm?" Midnight asked.

Onyx began licking her fur. "I don't know. I think it has something to do with Mac being stubborn and prideful."

"It doesn't make sense. Clearly, they still love each other."

"I suppose. I'm learning that we don't have a lot of say in any of this," Onyx stated with resignation.

"Well, you're going to need to start paying attention so we can devise a plan to get our family back together again."

"Okay. What did you have in mind?" Onyx asked.

"When human kids are caught in the middle of a divorce, sometimes they run away and force the parents to work together to get them back."

"Mac and Carmen aren't married," Onyx answered reasonably. "I don't want to run away. Being a feral isn't a lot of fun. Don't you remember the stories we heard in the shelter? Even being in the shelter was better than living on the streets."

"Don't worry. You might not be a good mouser, but I am. We'll survive for a few days," Midnight soothed. "Do you think you can find your way to the farm?"

"Maybe. If I pay attention the next time that they bring me here. But it's a long way. Could we meet in the middle?" Onyx asked.

"If you give me detailed directions, sure," Midnight assured with a fair amount of bravado she wasn't sure she possessed.

"All right," Onyx agreed, but she didn't sound very convincing to Midnight.

"We'll finalize our plans next time Carmen brings you for a play date."

"You sure this will work, and they'll find us quickly?" Onyx asked with a quiver in her meow.

Midnight lifted her paw. "Paw promise."

Onyx touched Midnight's paw and answered, "Paw promise."

†

Mac wasn't lying to Pops when she'd told him that she was having a good day. Granted, her energy wasn't what it used to be, but that would not stop her from making love with Carmen. It had been far too long since she'd touched the love of her life. Carmen seemed uncharacteristically nervous, and Mac suspected she knew exactly what that was about.

"The house looks fabulous. You've done some renovations. You remodeled the kitchen. Were you expecting a chef to move in?" Carmen asked.

Mac chuckled. "I did those before I got sick. I just kept asking myself, what would make Carmen's life easier? I didn't know the first thing about gourmet cooking tools, so I asked the experts. If that specialty place next to Michael's Bistro didn't know, they would recommend a store in Seattle."

"Was that a new fireplace I saw?"

Mac approached Carmen and brought her finger over Carmen's clavicle. "I've missed this. It's one of my favorite spots on your body. Very sexy."

Carmen squeezed Mac's hand, then turned away and looked at the ceiling as if she was checking out the ductwork, like a building inspector. "You added central air too."

"Why are you so nervous?" Mac asked.

"I'm not nervous," Carmen answered.

"Liar." Mac pulled Carmen into her arms. "Look at me, Carmen. I promise I wouldn't have offered to drive you back to the farm if I wasn't up to it. Hell, I would have locked myself away and not rushed over. I feel good today. Not like the energizer bunny or anything, but certainly, there is enough gas in the tank to make love to you. I swear it will not cause a setback."

Mac leaned in and captured Carmen's lips, letting her mouth communicate all the desire and love she felt for this woman who had long ago captured her heart. The kiss started slow. Tentative. But with all that pent-up desire, it quickly turned into something almost desperate. Carmen melted into her embrace, eagerly accepting Mac's tongue as they reconnected.

But there was no way Mac would rush this. She'd waited too long to have Carmen in her arms again. After the kiss broke, Carmen admitted, "Goddess, I missed you. Us. This. But you got it wrong. It's me I don't trust. All I want to do is rip off my clothes and ask you to fuck me until I can't move."

"Will you settle for one of our less enthusiastic couplings?"

Carmen broke into a fit of laughter. "Couplings? Please do not tell me you've talked about this with your pops. Because that sounds like something he would say."

Mac made an exaggerated face of mock horror. "Oh, hell no. I do talk with him about other things, but never my sex life."

"Well, in that case, vanilla, it is. Actually, that sounds perfect to me. I've been dreaming of that tongue of yours almost as much as I've fantasized about seeing you on your back, moaning in pleasure while I take you to the edge so many times you're begging for release."

"That doesn't sound all that vanilla to me, but I think I can make that work." Mac pulled Carmen's T-shirt over her head and then deftly unsnapped her bra. Running her hands over Carmen's breasts, she declared, "So beautiful."

"No seductive strip tease. Just take off your clothes right now," Carmen ordered.

"After you," Mac retorted. "Ladies first."

"I'm no lady, but the last one to undress has to make breakfast."

"You're staying the night?" Mac asked. She was both confused and thrilled.

"Yes, I am. You got a problem with that?"

"No, ma'am," Mac answered and couldn't control her smile as she made quick work of removing her clothes.

The two women stood before one another, and Carmen stroked Mac's rib cage. "Oh, my love. You've lost so much weight. The first course of business is to put meat on your bones. No arguments. Even if I don't stay for dinner, I'm bringing you food."

"You'll get no push back from me. Pops would kill me if I turned you down. At least he'll stop complaining about my cooking," Mac joked as she pulled down the covers, and they climbed into bed.

Mac knew every one of Carmen's sensitive spots, and as she made her way down Carmen's body, she could feel

Carmen respond to her touch. Subtle changes in her breathing pattern and the movement of Carmen's hips let Mac know she was getting close. Carmen had always responded to the extremes. Either she loved it soft and teasing or hard and fast. Today, Mac would dance along the edges with the most delicate touch, forcing Carmen's body to lift for that elusive connection to the spot that would send her over the edge. Two could play the edging game. Mac was incredibly proficient at it.

"Stop teasing me, Mac."

Mac's tongue made small circles, only intermittently connecting to Carmen's clit. When she thought Carmen couldn't take it anymore, she entered using a slow rhythm while continuing to use her tongue and connecting with Carmen's clit more frequently.

"Yes, right there, don't stop," Carmen begged.

Mac continued her gentle ministrations until Carmen's body tightened and finally let loose. Every pulse that Mac felt on her fingers was like a declaration of love from Carmen. Feeling her pleasure was the most satisfying thing Mac had experienced in quite a long time. Mac stayed between Carmen's legs for a few seconds more, basking in the afterglow before making her way up Carmen's body to offer an unhurried kiss. She gathered Carmen into her arms, directing her to lie on top as she stroked her back. Skin on skin was the best feeling in the world.

"Thank you for loving me and letting me love you," Mac murmured.

"For as long as you'll let me." Carmen grinned. "My turn." She lifted her head and peppered kisses along Mac's neck before making her own descent down Mac's body, often stopping along the way to touch and caress nearly every inch.

CHAPTER TWENTY-TWO

After a couple of hours, Mac and Carmen let Midnight and Onyx into the bedroom, and it almost felt normal again. They both patted the spots next to them for Midnight and Onyx to jump onto the bed. Midnight closed her eyes, listening to the soft rumblings of her two mamas while Mac ran her hand over her fur.

After too short of a time, Midnight felt movement on the bed as Carmen pushed aside the covers and climbed from the bed.

"Do you still have our robes hanging inside the bathroom door?" Carmen asked.

"Yeah, why?"

"Well, I don't want to give your pops a heart attack while I grab my phone and call Allison. She'll probably figure out I'm not coming home tonight, but I know I would want a courtesy call."

Mac shifted her body and turned to look at Carmen, who stood naked in the bedroom. "Forget the heart attack; Pops would never let me hear the end of it if you walked into the kitchen in your birthday suit. Tomorrow morning, I'll pack some goodies for you to take back to the condo. A small token of my appreciation for Allison being such a good friend."

"That's sweet of you. If you let me harvest some veggies and snag some of your wonderful cheese, I bet I could come up with a nice dinner for your crew and Pops. Maybe we should invite Deb and Olivia. We could make it a homecoming party and introduce Allison to our dear friends here in Moses Lake. I will need to go to the condo because I hadn't planned on staying and didn't bring my travel bag. I know I still have some clothes here but not my make-up bag and other essentials."

"Only you would suggest planning your homecoming party and doing all the work." Mac laughed. "But I certainly won't turn down your cooking."

"I'll sweeten the deal and bake a few pies," Carmen added.

"You had me at dinner party."

"Should I bring my overnight bag?" Carmen asked.

"Two nights in a row. I must have won the lottery." Mac smiled. "I'd like that. You can leave Onyx with me."

Carmen reached over and scratched Onyx under the chin, then kissed the top of her head before moving to Midnight and doing the same. "That okay with you, Onyx? Want to stay here with your sister tomorrow?"

"Meow brmmp."

Carmen left the room and returned wearing the large, fluffy white robe.

†

"Maybe we won't need to run away to get them back together," Midnight communicated to her sister via a string of meows.

Mac lost her smile and furrowed her brow. "Carmen, as much as I loved being with you tonight and having you spend the night tonight and tomorrow night, this doesn't change a thing. I still need time to increase my strength."

Carmen sat on the edge of the bed. "I know, but let me enjoy these two days."

"Guess that was too easy," Midnight hissed.

"Midnight! Don't you want Onyx to stay with us?" Mac asked.

Midnight quickly started licking her sister. The last thing she wanted was for Mac and Carmen to misunderstand. If

Midnight could have meowed the word "fuck" she would have.

"I wonder what that was all about?" Carmen asked.

"Who knows? Cats are notoriously temperamental," Mac answered.

Both Onyx and Midnight glared at Mac with their ears pinned back. "We are not," they said simultaneously, but Midnight supposed to the humans it sounded more like a wailing meow.

"I don't think they like being called temperamental," Carmen teased, then stroked their fur.

"At least Carmen understands us," Onyx said to her sister.

"Hmpf, if Mac wasn't such a great mama, I'd bite her hand, just to teach her a lesson," Midnight complained.

"Don't do that. She might send you back to the shelter. Then we'd never see each other again," Onyx wailed.

"Relax. I wasn't going to. Just remember to pay attention to all the landmarks so that when we decide to run away, neither of us gets lost," Midnight said.

"I don't know about this. We haven't been on our own for a long time. I'm scared. There are coyotes out there. I've heard them yipping."

"Fraidy cat," Midnight taunted.

"Better that than a dead cat," Onyx answered.

"Cats are much smarter than dogs, and coyotes are just skinny dogs," Midnight shared with authority. "Besides, we're faster and can climb trees. I'll bet they'll find us before we even have to spend the night in the bushes."

"Okay, if it means having everything go back to how it was, I'll do it."

"If I didn't know any better, I would think the two of them are planning something," Mac joked. "I don't think I've ever heard either of them talk so much."

"Me neither," Carmen answered.

†

Carmen was in her element in the remodeled kitchen, preparing a feast for her closest friends and those she considered family—her only remaining family since she'd lost all respect for her brother years ago. Although she didn't know Amanda and Tiffany very well, they seemed to fit in with Carmen's chosen family. It was clear how much they revered Mac and her talents as a cheesemaker. Carmen was going to make it her mission to put weight on Mac, and hopefully, in time, she'd regain her healthy glow.

As the group sat around the fire pit, enjoying Carmen's Dutch apple pie, Carmen had never felt so much at home. Earlier, Deb had pulled her aside for a quick conversation.

"Look, I'm sorry I didn't call right away when they brought Mac into the hospital. You have no idea how much it took for me not to violate her privacy," Deb pleaded.

Carmen smiled. "Don't worry. I understand. Good thing Evan didn't have to comply with HIPAA."

"Mac still looks like she could use a month-long vacation, but honestly, she appears to be on the mend. I'm glad you're back but sorry to hear about your mother. Olivia and I were running out of excuses to drop by unannounced," Deb admitted.

"I really appreciate you monitoring Mac while I wrapped things up in Elgin."

"Are you actually going to be living with Allison?" Deb asked.

"Not by choice, but I agreed to this compromise. Mac is stubborn. She won't let me move back to the farm until she's one hundred percent free of any lingering effects from COVID," Carmen explained.

"Yeah, I heard. I just thought you'd be able to get through to her. Long COVID is unpredictable. If I didn't know any better, I'd think you two were back together and ready to plan your wedding."

"I'm working on it. Hey, does Kathleen still have contacts at the University of Washington Medical Center?" Carmen asked.

"She does. Why?"

"I hoped she could hook Mac up with one of their clinical trials. I've been doing my homework, and UW is at the forefront of this clinical research. What do you know about the study? Are they in Phase II or higher in the trials?" Carmen asked.

Deb crinkled her nose. "I'm so sorry. I should have looked into this, but I don't have any details. Kathleen will help you for sure. She adores you and Mac. She's even happier that you brought your very qualified friend along. Recruiting a critical care nurse with a lot of experience is like gold. She got a twofer, and you two aren't even a couple. Allison seems great. If I'm honest, I'm a little jealous. I thought I was your best friend," Deb teased.

Carmen grabbed Deb and hugged her. "You are, but in this instance, I've decided to embrace polyamory. I love you both. Can't I have two best friends?"

Deb laughed. "Polyamory, huh?"

Olivia sidled next to Deb and asked, "Did I hear polyamory? What the hell? Didn't know you and Mac were into that?" Olivia held up her hands. "No judgment."

Deb smacked Olivia playfully. "Stop it. We were talking about us."

"What?!"

"Polyamorous friends. Nurses have to stick together. Allison, Carmen and I are about to embark on a polyamorous friendship," Deb explained.

"That's the most ridiculous thing I've ever heard of," Olivia stated.

"Oh yeah, if guys can do it, why can't women? Ever heard of the Three Musketeers? What do you think that was?

Just because you always have sex on the brain..." Deb teased.

"I do not." Olivia smiled. "If anyone always has sex on the brain, it's—"

Deb wagged her finger. "Unh Unh Uh, don't you finish that sentence." Deb leaned in and kissed Olivia. "I think it's time we went home. You ready?" Deb waggled her brows. "All this talk about sex..."

Olivia chuckled. "Carmen, thanks for a wonderful dinner. Thrilled you're back. Someone needs to keep Mac in line," she teased.

Carmen hugged Olivia. "Thanks for looking after her while I was gone." She turned to hug Deb. "You too, bestie. Now go home and ravage your wife."

As Deb and Olivia started walking to their car, Allison approached. "I see the party is breaking up. Evan offered to show me the farm. Do you mind?"

Carmen arched her brow. "Why would I mind? Something I should know about?" she teased.

"Um, well, she did ask me to dinner," Allison confessed.

"Wonderful. You could do far worse than Evan." Carmen pushed Allison. "Go, have her give you the full tour, including her place. From what I understand, it's quite cozy now after the remodel."

"See you tomorrow?" Allison asked.

"Yeah, I'll be home tomorrow. Our first shift at the hospital starts the day after."

Annette Mori

CHAPTER TWENTY-THREE

Mac knew that she'd hurt Carmen when she suggested that making dinner for her every night was probably not the best thing for them, especially if it ended up with Carmen spending every night on the farm. But she was serious about wanting to be free of lingering health issues before jumping back into cohabitation. She'd also put her foot down about Carmen accompanying her to Seattle to start the clinical trial. She insisted she didn't need anyone to drive with her. They still saw each other, and Carmen would dutifully bring Onyx so she could spend time with Midnight. If Mac didn't know any better, she'd think the cats were plotting something with how much they chattered with one another. She had joked with Carmen about that just the other night.

When her phone rang at six in the morning, Mac noticed it was Carmen. She snatched the phone, knowing it was not like Carmen to call this early, even if she had the early shift at the hospital.

"Love, what's up?"

"It's Onyx," Carmen exclaimed in a panicked voice.

"What do you mean, it's Onyx? I'm going to need a little more, love."

"Well, there's this friendly feral cat that the community at the condo feeds, and Onyx took an interest in him. At first, I wouldn't let her out to play with him because I thought he might have some disease, but our neighbors assured us they've been caring for him and take him to the vet all the time for shots or whatever if they notice anything is going on with him. He's an outdoor cat because he likes it that way, but he might as well be their indoor/outdoor cat," Carmen explained in a rush of words.

"Okay, what does that have to do with Onyx? Did they fight or something?" Mac calmly tried to decipher Carmen's nervous rambling.

"No, no, nothing like that. Tom, that's what they call him, is the sweetest boy. Onyx was crying incessantly to go out to play with him. So, I let Onyx out last night and called and called for her, but she never returned."

"Okay, I'm on my way over. I'll bring Midnight. Maybe she can entice Onyx from wherever she's hiding. Sometimes cats get scared and hide when they are in unfamiliar territory. Onyx is chipped, so if someone finds her, hopefully, they'll take her to the shelter."

"Thank you. I'm really worried. Onyx doesn't get out as much as Midnight. I don't think she's prepared to be on her own. I should have known because she's been roaming with Midnight on the farm. It's like she's more confident now playing outside. Do you think she was trying to get back to Midnight? I know this sounds crazy, but maybe Midnight and Onyx were planning this or something..." Carmen's voice trailed off before she continued, "Never mind, that sounds completely—"

"Actually, it doesn't. I can't believe I've wondered the same thing. I know they're smart cats, but they're still cats. Although it may not be completely out of the realm of possibility that Onyx went looking for the farm. There are micro farms around the condo. They just aren't mine. That would be a hell of a distance to travel. I'll be there in thirty as soon as I get dressed."

After Mac ended the call with Carmen, she called for Midnight while pulling on her shorts and T-shirt. Typically, Midnight came running as soon as Mac called for her, but today, she failed to respond. After Mac checked all her favorite places, she tried not to panic, but now there were two missing cats. Could this be a coincidence? Mac shook her head. Surely, Midnight and Onyx hadn't run away so they could be together again. That would be impossible. Wouldn't it? Granted, they were heartbroken and had both cried for days when they'd been separated, but cats didn't plan escapes. Did they? She hesitated to tell Carmen about Midnight, but maybe her assessment wasn't so crazy after all. Reaching for her phone, she called Carmen to relay the disturbing update.

Although Mac had assured Carmen she was on her way, that didn't mean she wouldn't drive slowly, looking for Midnight along the way. Evan wasn't home yet, so she couldn't ask her to look for Midnight. Although they'd warmed a bit to each other, Midnight might not come for Evan. Mac forgot to ask Carmen if Evan had spent the night at their place. Maybe by the time she reached the condo, Evan, Allison, and Carmen would have found Onyx. Mac hurried to her truck and inched along the gravel road, rolling slowly down the path as she scanned for Midnight. Before she hit the main highway, she passed Evan's truck and waved her over.

Evan rolled down her window and asked, "What's up?"

"Carmen can't find Onyx, and Midnight is also missing. Could you see if Midnight will come if you call her? Check her favorite hangouts. I'm on my way to the condo to help Carmen look for Onyx."

"Okay. I'll get on the Moses Lake lost pet page and see if anyone found either of them," Evan offered.

"Thanks, Evan." Mac rolled her window back up and peeled away.

†

After Carmen had ended the second call with Mac, she saw Allison run down the stairs. Evan had already left for the farm a short time ago before Carmen even started calling for Onyx.

"You can't find Onyx?" Allison asked.

Carmen shook her head and started to cry. "Mac is on her way." Carmen continued to wipe her eyes while Allison rubbed her back.

"Should I call Evan and have her come back?" Allison asked.

"No, maybe she can look for Midnight while Mac helps me look for Onyx."

"Midnight's missing too? That's beyond odd. I'll help you look for Onyx until I have to leave for work. I remember our neighbor telling us that when her cat escaped, she found him huddled under the stairwell. He was terrified because he was an inside cat and pushed out the screen like a teen going for a joyride or something. We can check every building."

"Thanks, Allison."

Carmen and Allison had each taken half of the buildings and checked every hidey-hole that Allison described while

Tom, the feral cat, trotted behind Carmen. Next, they'd pushed aside all the bushes, hoping to find her curled up under a bush. By the time they'd thoroughly searched the property, Mac had pulled into the parking lot. Jumping from her truck, she rushed to Carmen and pulled her into an embrace.

"We'll find her. I talked to Evan, and she is going to look for Midnight. The good news is that I did not see her on the side of the road. So, I don't think she was hit by a car." Mac nodded to Allison. "Hey, Allison."

"Hi, Mac. Do you want me to make up some flyers? I think there may be a social media page for lost and found pets. I can check that. Although, it may be too soon since they both just went missing."

"Evan's on it. I should send her some pictures for her to post," Mac offered before she began scrolling through her phone.

"Goddess, if I get this upset over our cats, I cannot imagine what I would do if one of my kids went missing," Carmen lamented.

"That just means you're going to be an amazing mom," Mac assured.

"Or a helicopter parent that never lets her kids do anything fun," Carmen quipped.

"All right." Mac took control of the situation. She felt as helpless as she had when she'd gotten COVID, and the only thing to keep her distracted was to organize the search. "How about if we split up? I'll take the golf course. One of you should check out those side roads close to this complex. The other should continue to search the complex, maybe walk through the backfield that leads to the lake. Lots of interesting critters there that might pique Onyx's interest."

"I'm so sorry, Carmen. I have to leave for my shift. But I'll help you look tonight if you haven't already found her."

"That's okay, Allison. Thanks for your help. Go, you're going to be late," Carmen ordered.

Two hours later, Onyx and Midnight were both still missing, and Carmen's voice was hoarse from calling Onyx.

Mac's phone rang, and Carmen listened in when Mac stated, "Well, that's interesting. Okay, I'll ask Carmen if she wants to come to the farm to check things out."

"What? Did Evan find Midnight?" Carmen asked.

"Not exactly. But she found paw prints in the bed of her truck."

"Do you think it's possible that Onyx jumped into Evan's truck?" Carmen asked.

"I don't know what to think. But it's worth checking out. Too bad we don't know any trackers."

"Do you think Olivia could help?"

Mac shrugged. "Maybe. At least she understands animals."

"Okay. Let's go to the farm. Just let me put on a bra."

†

"Psst, over here," Midnight called. Onyx pranced over and greeted her sister by touching her nose.

"I'm hungry," Onyx whined. "I had to stay up all night and hide in Evan's truck. It wasn't comfortable at all. Plus, I heard the coyotes yipping all night long, and they were close."

"Quit complaining. Our plan is working. And at least you didn't have to walk halfway here to meet me."

Onyx lifted one paw and began licking. "Yeah, pretty smart of me to suggest catching a ride with Evan. Admit it, I'm the brains of this operation. Every time I came over with Carmen, it seemed like it took forever to get here, and there were miles of highway to run along. The cars move really fast on the highway. No way was I going to risk that. So, what did you hear?"

"Well, I only heard Mac's side of the conversation, but she sounded panicked. Then, by the time she went looking for me, her worry increased threefold. I kind of felt bad hiding from her. It was a close call, though, because I had to wait for Pops to get up and then sneak by him when he went to collect the eggs."

Onyx stopped cleaning her fur and asked, "So, how long do we have to hide? I'll waste away if I don't get my wet food pretty soon."

"I caught you a mouse to tide you over," Midnight offered.

"Ew, I don't want a mouse. They're mostly bones, and you have to gnaw around the gizzard. It's gross. I don't know how you can eat them."

"I'm getting in touch with our roots. I'm sure we come from a long line of badass hunters. And they certainly didn't survive on canned food," Midnight retorted. "Let's give it a day or two. Carmen hasn't spent the night since the day you came home, much less two nights in a row. Mac seems healthier, so maybe after a couple of nights together worrying about us, she'll soften her stance."

"Where are we going to hide?" Onyx asked.

"We're going to have to go into that field with the tall grass that isn't used much."

"Out in the elements?" Onyx exclaimed with a fair amount of horror in her voice.

"Yeah, toughen up, buttercup," Midnight taunted. "I can teach you to catch mice."

"I don't want to learn how to catch mice," Onyx whined. "I kind of feel sorry for them. They never did anything to us. Why should we kill them?"

"Because it's in our nature, and we have to eat. Come on, let's go before Evan finds us. Didn't you see her snooping around in the back of her truck? You didn't leave any paw prints, did you?" Midnight asked.

"Um, I didn't check, but there was a mud puddle I stepped into before jumping into the truck."

Midnight shook her head. "Well, now we really need to go." She started trotting through the field, with Onyx following close behind.

"Wait up, Midnight. I think I got a goat's head sticker on my paw, and it really hurts."

Midnight huffed and muttered, "How is it possible you were born in the same litter?"

"That's just mean, Midnight."

"I'm sorry, okay? Let me see your paw?"

Onyx flopped onto the ground and lifted her back paw. "I hate those things. I don't understand why you love following Mac around the farm. Don't you get those stuck into your paw?"

"I see it. Let me try to bite it off." Midnight began licking and biting at Onyx's paw in an attempt to remove the sticker.

"Ow, ow," Onyx cried out.

"Hold still, I'm trying to get it. Quit being a baby, I've almost got it." Midnight bit one more time, and the sticker embedded into her tongue. Whimpering, she said, "It's on my tongue now." She tried to hack it up like a furball, but the sticker wouldn't budge.

"Run your tongue along the grass; maybe it'll dislodge," Onyx suggested.

"Midnight," Evan called. "Come on, Midnight, your mama is really worried."

Midnight crouched into the tall grass. She heard Evan shaking a bag of treats. She'd just have to endure the discomfort and try to loosen the goat head sticker after they found a more secure hiding place. Slinking through the grass, she hissed, "Come on, let's go. I found a good place to hide by those trees."

"Midnight. Come on out. It'll be okay," Evan tried again.

Midnight heard a distinctive sound that stopped her short in her tracks as they neared the cluster of trees and bushes. "Oh, no," Midnight exclaimed, her words slightly slurred with the irritation to her tongue.

"What now?" Onyx asked.

Four tiny noses peeked out from the den their mother had created. "Those are coyote pups. We need to make a run for it. If their mother returns, we're as good as pup food."

"I don't want to do this anymore," Onyx whined. "Can't we go back to the house? It's safe there."

"Soon. I know another place. Follow me," Midnight directed.

CHAPTER TWENTY-FOUR

Mac didn't know what to think when she pulled up beside Evan's truck and inspected the bed. Sure enough, there were paw prints in the back and leading away in the patches of dirt beside the gravel. It was hard to follow the tracks because there were paw prints everywhere. Midnight played outside all the time.

Evan approached and offered a small wave. "I didn't find Midnight, but I swear I heard her hiss. I'm not sure why because I thought she had warmed toward me over the last couple of months. She even started following me around a little bit when you were in the shed. Although you aren't going to like where I heard that sound because it's close to that coyote den you found last month."

"Shit," Mac exclaimed. "I'm not going to shoot the mother with the pups still so helpless, even after her failed attempts to get inside the chicken coop."

"You want me to put up some cat posts in that field?" Evan offered. "Just because Midnight hasn't ever wandered that far out doesn't mean she won't in the future. We probably should have done that long ago."

"Fuck," Mac swore. "Yeah. Midnight and Onyx are smart enough to climb the posts to escape if they run into the mother. I'll help you."

"No, I got this," Evan answered. "You two keep looking." Evan pointed to the large open field with the tree line on the right. "Check out that area but be careful. The last thing you need is a protective mother coming at you. Don't worry about making cheese today. Tiffany and Amanda said they'd put in a few more hours to catch us up." Evan walked to the toolshed, where they kept their fencing supplies.

"Do you think Onyx did this because we separated them? This is all my fault," Carmen lamented. "I should have left her here with Midnight."

"You had no way of knowing she'd sneak into Evan's truck," Mac soothed. "At least she didn't try to make it to the farm on her own. I'm kind of impressed by her ingenuity."

"If we don't find them today, can I stay with you tonight? Maybe they'll come back if they hear us both calling them."

"Of course," Mac answered, then chuckled. "I just got this insane idea that they're doing this just to get us living together again. You know, like the movie *The Parent Trap*. We're smack dab in the center of *The Kitten Trap*."

"I don't think we have the luxury of laughing about this just yet. Maybe after we find the naughty little furballs."

"Let me get my gun before we head out."

Carmen frowned. "I thought you said you didn't want to shoot the mother coyote."

"I don't. It's a tranquilizer gun."

Carmen smiled. "When did you buy that?"

Mac scratched the back of her head. "Um, when I found the den. I got worried about Midnight because coyotes become brazen when they have a litter of pups to care for."

"Have you ever even used Pops' old shotgun?" Carmen asked.

"To scare them away, yeah, but I never actually aimed at them. Coyotes might be a nuisance, and they sure aren't helpful to have around with cats or small dogs, but I'd have a hard time killing one. They're just trying to survive like every other wild animal whose territory we've encroached on."

Carmen leaned in and kissed Mac's cheek. "Softie."

"After this, I'm installing wildlife cameras. Midnight and Onyx will never be able to go on another adventure without me capturing it on film and knowing where they've gone off to."

Carmen chuckled. "Right. It's just a way for you to spy on those adorable pups."

"They *are* pretty cute," Mac answered.

†

After another several hours of calling for their cats, Carmen reluctantly agreed to take a break. She was glad that they'd stopped walking the perimeter. The last thing Carmen wanted was for Mac to have another setback. She didn't exactly look sick, but Carmen could tell she was tired. Hell, Carmen was tired too. They probably had walked miles looking for Midnight and Onyx.

"How about I make us some lunch?" Carmen suggested.

"I could eat." Mac grinned. "Is it okay to invite Amanda, Tiffany and Evan?"

"Of course. The more the merrier." Carmen began preparing the meal, which took her mind off the missing cats.

As if the three workers sensed the meal was almost done, the door to the kitchen pushed open, and all three filed inside.

"I brought my lunch today, but no way would I pass up on a meal prepared by Carmen," Amanda said.

"Ditto," Tiffany added. "Thanks for the invite, Mac."

"I could smell whatever you're cooking a mile away," Evan noted.

265

"Well, perfect timing. It's almost done. One of you can set the table," Carmen directed.

"I'll do that," Mac offered as she retrieved dishes from the cabinets. "Did you get the cat posts up?"

"Three. I'd still like to put a few more up if that's okay with you?" Evan answered.

"After lunch, I'm going to run into town and pick up supplies to install wildlife cameras," Mac announced. "Maybe we'll discover the location of where the cats are hiding."

"Good idea," Evan answered.

"I'd like to come with, and then you can take me to the condo so I can pack a bag. I'll take my car to drive myself back to the farm," Carmen said.

Evan arched an eyebrow and winked at Carmen. "I think I can speak for all of us and say we'd love it if you came to stay for however long it takes to find those little rascals because we'll benefit from your culinary expertise."

Tiffany and Amanda both nodded with vigor.

"Who says I'll be inviting you to lunch every day?" Mac joked.

"I thought that was one of the perks of working here," Evan retorted. "Just because we haven't taken advantage over the last several months because, no offense, your cooking sucks, doesn't mean we'll pass up this golden opportunity now that Carmen is back. You are back, aren't you?"

Carmen looked at Mac and smiled sweetly while Mac shot Evan a warning look. "Instead of running your mouth, why don't you help me set the table?"

"Sure thing, boss." Evan shot Mac an unrepentant look.

Carmen decided to broach the topic with Mac as soon as they were alone. She'd wanted to ask how the clinical trial was going anyway. Mac had picked up a few pounds and looked significantly healthier than when Carmen had first returned to Moses Lake. Whether that was from whatever treatments came from the trial or simply that Mac's body was finally able to fight the residual infection didn't matter because a kernel of hope had sprouted. Carmen would tend the fragile green tendril of hope like her life depended on it because that's exactly how she felt. If Mac and Carmen were unable to come together again, she'd die a little bit at a time until nothing survived.

†

Mac was lost in thought as she drove Carmen to the condo after picking up the supplies to install the cameras. She wasn't sure if keeping Carmen at arm's length was necessary anymore. Although she still became fatigued more easily than before she'd gotten sick, Mac hadn't experienced another relapse in weeks. All evidence pointed to remarkable improvements in her health. The researchers seemed particularly pleased with her progress.

"Can we talk about what Evan said earlier?" Carmen interrupted Mac's thoughts.

"Evan has a big mouth and needs to mind her own business," Mac answered.

"This whole situation has been horrible for all of us. I've tried very hard to respect your decision because you were one hundred percent supportive when I ran off to care for my mother. I didn't think it was fair to impose my wishes on you, even though this has had a negative impact well beyond myself. However, I realize it isn't all that different from when I left. I see that now. Obviously, the months I was away did have an impact on Evan, Pops, the farm, and last but not least, Midnight and Onyx."

Mac sighed. "It isn't the same. Your situation with your mother and my stupid pride are not even in the same stratosphere."

"Does that mean I can come home now?" Carmen asked, her voice laced with hope.

"I guess what Evan said struck a nerve. You were taking care of all of us before you left. And yes, you were an integral part of the farm. We all missed you."

"Missed? As in past tense?" Carmen asked.

"No, it's damn near killing me to have you so close but still out of reach. Obviously, it's not past tense for any of us.

Do you think you can come home but not jump into nurse mode every time I sneeze?" Mac asked.

"I don't think I can completely shut off that part of me, no," Carmen answered sadly. "But that doesn't mean I'd treat you like an invalid. You don't need round-the-clock care. Let me ask you something," Carmen began, "if I was the one who had gotten COVID, the flu, or any other illness, would you have ignored me and gone about your day without the need to care for me?"

"Of course not. I might not be a great cook like you, but I can make tea, heat up a can of soup, hold your hair back while you puke, or whatever you need," Mac answered.

Carmen raised her eyebrow. "And that's different, how?"

"Okay, I see your point. But long COVID could be a permanent condition that requires ongoing care for the rest of my life. How is it fair to saddle you with that?"

"So, you're saying that if I contract an illness that requires care for more than a couple of weeks, you wouldn't stay with me? Good to know," Carmen teased.

"Don't twist my words. You know that isn't true. I think you missed your calling. You should have been an attorney or politician." Mac chuckled. "Okay, point taken."

"Mac, we were heading towards marriage before life became complicated. I know those old marriage vows of in sickness and health are dated, but I still believe them with every beat of my heart. Would you have kicked me to the curb if we had already been married?"

"No, of course not," Mac answered with a long sigh. "I'm so close to being back to full health. I'm not saying we have to wait, but can I sit with this a little while longer? Honestly, I'm almost there. I was just thinking about our situation and wondering if it was still necessary to keep living apart. And that was before this conversation where you masterfully painted me into a corner."

Carmen smiled. "How about if I pack a big suitcase?"

"I suppose that would be all right."

†

Midnight had managed to get most of the sticker loose, but like a splinter, a tiny part remained embedded in her tongue. She'd just have to deal with it because they had to eat, so she started stalking a mouse. Onyx crept alongside of her, watching. She wasn't crazy about learning how to catch a mouse, but Midnight insisted this was a useful skill.

Midnight was so intent on capturing her prey that she didn't notice the coyote creeping up on her until Onyx screamed.

As soon as Midnight turned her head, she saw the animal bearing down on her and barely managed to climb the cat post. Unfortunately, the next cat post was too far away for Onyx to reach, but if she slowed down the coyote, she might be able to reach the tree. Midnight had to do something quick

270

before Onyx was caught. Jumping down from the post, she ran as fast as her legs would take her and leaped on the mother coyote, earning a satisfying yip as her claws and teeth landed a significant blow, enough to stop her from chasing Onyx. Onyx scrambled up the giant tree while Midnight debated how to get to the tree without being caught in the powerful jaws of the coyote. Using her sharp claws, she swiped her paw across the coyote's eye before vaulting off her back and running for the tree. She almost made it too, until that jaw clamped down on her leg. But the coyote made the mistake of letting go so that she could lunge for Midnight's throat, giving Midnight enough time to use her front paws and her remaining uninjured back leg to climb higher.

Onyx jumped from one of the higher branches to make her way to where Midnight clung to the tree. "Are you okay? Can you clean your wound? I can do it for you," Onyx offered.

"I'll be okay. But you might have to run back to the house to get help. I don't think I can outrun a pack of coyotes with a bad leg. We're just lucky it was only one."

The coyote paced around the base of the tree, seemingly frustrated that she hadn't gotten her prize.

"I'm scared, Midnight. What if she stays there and waits for us to climb down?"

"She won't. She has to feed her pups, and when she leaves to hunt for something else, you can make a mad dash to the farmhouse."

"Maybe Mac and Carmen will come looking for us again. I know you said we needed to be quiet earlier when they called, but I'm going to meow as loud as I can if they return. I want to wait for them."

Midnight considered Onyx's suggestion. "Okay, Mac put something on that tree over there so she could return to this area to check on it."

"What is it?" Onyx asked.

"It's a wildlife camera, I think. I guess our mamas are smarter than I thought. I bet she wanted to see if she could catch us on camera, and then she would know where to look for us."

"I miss snuggling with Carmen," Onyx admitted sadly.

"Yeah, I miss hanging with Mac. If they don't find us in the next day or two, you're going to have to get them. We can't stay in the tree forever."

"Okay, Midnight. I'll be brave."

CHAPTER TWENTY-FIVE

Even though Carmen slept beside Mac, and it felt so right, Mac couldn't sleep. She kept thinking about the cameras she had installed. She wanted to check the footage captured over the last few hours. Slipping from the bed, she threw on some clothes and made her way to her laptop to access the smart app she had installed, intending to review the footage already captured.

Rubbing her eyes, she leaned back in her office chair as she scrolled through the videos from the various cameras she had installed. Moving close to the screen, she focused on the coyote trotting through the grass. Mac wasn't sure, but it sure looked like she'd been in a fight with some other animal.

Mac felt a light touch on her shoulder. She turned her head and smiled at Carmen, who sported a messy head of hair, as she blinked adorably at Mac.

"What are you doing? It's the middle of the night."

"I couldn't sleep. I wanted to see if I might catch a glimpse of our escape artists. I have a bad feeling."

"What do you mean?" Carmen asked.

Mac pointed to the screen. "See that coyote there?"

"Yeah. We know there are coyotes, which is why Evan installed more cat posts."

"It looks like she got into a fight with some other animal. I'm worried it might have been Midnight or Onyx."

"Oh." Carmen looked panicked. "Let me help you look through the video footage. I'll get my iPad and install the app."

"Thanks."

Mac continued to methodically scroll through the footage from the camera that had caught movement from the coyote. Carmen returned and sat in a chair next to Mac as she quietly focused on her tablet. "Which camera are you looking at?"

"Camera one," Mac answered. "Can you start on camera two?"

"Should we wake up Evan and have her help?"

Mac shook her head. "No, if we call her, it will wake Allison up too. Evan gets to the farm early. If we haven't found anything, we can ask for her help when she arrives in a few hours."

Thirty minutes later, Carmen exclaimed, "I got something! It looks like Midnight is stalking a mouse in the far field next to that copse of trees."

"I put a camera on one of the trees. Let me switch to camera four. What's the time stamp on that?"

"Seven fifteen," Carmen answered. "Shit, I think that's Onyx, and she's crying. I've never heard her meow like that before. Midnight took off and isn't in view anymore."

"Give me a few minutes. Let me see if there's anything on this camera within that same time frame."

Mac quickly accessed camera four and typed in the time parameter that Carmen had shared. "Oh, no." Mac jumped up. "We gotta go right now. Call Olivia."

"I'm coming with," Carmen stated, leaving no room for argument.

"You can meet me at the copse of trees next to that far field where we were looking earlier. It isn't far from the coyote den we found. I really need you to get Olivia here first," Mac directed as she moved quickly down the hall.

"Please tell me they're going to be okay. I don't need details…"

"I hope so." Mac grabbed her tranquilizer gun and the headlamp she kept in the drawer, then ran out of the house.

†

Carmen grabbed her phone and dialed Olivia's number. Putting her phone on speaker, she hurried to the bedroom and tossed her robe on the bed.

"Hello," a groggy voice answered. "Carmen? Is Mac okay?"

"Yeah, yeah, Mac's fine, but something is wrong with one of the cats. We didn't have time for me to get the details, but Mac told me to call you. Can you come out to the farm?" Carmen pulled clothes from the bag she had packed and tossed them on the bed next to her robe.

"Sure, sure. I'm on my way. I'll bring supplies and be prepared for whatever. Mac isn't prone to hysterics, so it must be an emergency. See you soon."

Dressing quickly, Carmen ran into the kitchen and searched the drawers for a flashlight. Finally, she found what she'd been looking for and pressed the button to test that it worked. Sighing in relief when the powerful beam created a circle of light on the wall, she dashed outside the house, using the flashlight to illuminate a path to the far field.

She didn't want to run and risk twisting her ankle, so she walked quickly through the tall grass. She saw a bobbing light in the distance and figured it was Mac. The light seemed to stop, then point upward. As Carmen got close, she heard Mac's soothing voice.

"It's okay, Midnight, Mama's here. Can you climb down for Mama?"

Carmen closed the distance and noticed Onyx sitting on the ground, patiently waiting.

"Onyx," Carmen cried out. She scooped the cat in her arms and hugged her. Feeling along her fur, Carmen couldn't find anything wrong with Onyx. "Onyx seems to be fine."

"It's Midnight," Mac answered. "The coyote caught her back leg. I saw the whole thing. I'm trying to get her to come down on her own, but her back paw must be really bad. I don't know how she managed to climb the rest of the way up. I might have to scale the tree to get her."

Onyx let out a pitiful *meow,* followed by Midnight, who sounded even more desperate.

Carmen held out Onyx for Mac to take. "I climbed a lot of trees in my youth. Remember that big oak tree in my mother's backyard? I used to climb that all the time. Let me try to get Midnight. I'll grab her and hand her to you."

"Okay. But be careful. Midnight is terrified right now," Mac answered.

"I'm coming to get you, Midnight. Don't be afraid. Your mamas are here. Everything is going to be okay. Olivia will fix you right up," Carmen soothed as she climbed the enormous tree. Midnight crouched on the branch but didn't try to get away. As soon as she was close enough to touch Midnight, she gently stroked her fur, carefully avoiding Midnight's back legs.

A weak *meow* from Midnight nearly broke Carmen's heart. Carefully, she grabbed Midnight by the scruff and hung on with her dominant hand as she lowered her into Mac's now empty arms.

"I got her," Mac said.

Carmen quickly scrambled down the tree. "How's her leg?"

"Hard to tell, but it looks bad. Is Olivia on the way?"

"Yeah, she said she'd be here as soon as possible," Carmen answered.

"Okay, grab Onyx, and we'll head back to the house. I'm just glad they're both alive." Mac sounded as relieved as Carmen felt.

Carmen lifted Onyx into her arms and felt the rumble of her motor. At least Onyx wasn't scared anymore as she purred in her arms. Carmen only hoped Mac could soothe Midnight enough to make the trek back to the farmhouse comfortable for the injured cat.

†

Although Mac's headlamp provided enough light to look at Midnight's paw in the almost pitch black of the night, it wasn't enough to inspect the injury as thoroughly as she wanted to. Since it would take Olivia some time to reach the farm, Mac didn't want to rush to the house, potentially irritating Midnight's wound. She could hear the young cat pant in her arms.

Finally, they made it to the house, and Carmen switched on all the lights in the kitchen after setting Onyx on the ground. "I'll get a fluffy towel," Carmen offered.

Mac set Midnight on the counter and tried to inspect her mangled paw, but it was hard to determine the extent of the damage. She feared the paw might have to be amputated. Surely that was the worst-case scenario. Midnight continued to pant and was doing something strange with her tongue. She kept pushing it out and pulling it back in, almost as if something awful tasting was in her mouth. Onyx paced the kitchen floor, not exactly weaving in and out of Mac's feet, but close by. She looked up at Mac who was attempting to calm Midnight, and meowed.

"Don't worry, Onyx, Olivia will be here soon, and she'll fix Midnight right up."

Midnight's ears twitched, and Mac heard tires on the gravel. *Thank the goddess, Olivia is here.* Carmen returned to the kitchen with a large bath towel. She set it on the counter, unfolding it before Mac gently lifted Midnight to place her on the soft towel.

Two quick knocks came in rapid succession before Olivia entered the kitchen. She set a large bag on the counter before cautiously approaching Midnight. "Hello, pretty girl. Remember me?" Olivia stroked Midnight's fur before separating the fur around the dried blood.

Midnight let out a pitiful cry.

A frown formed on Olivia's face as she inspected the wound. She looked up at Mac. "For now, I'd like to clean things up a bit, but I recommend we go to my clinic for some X-rays. Can you help hold her down while I clean the wound?"

Midnight continued to pant as Olivia cleaned the wound. Mac observed Midnight resuming the strange behavior with her tongue.

"I think there might be something on her tongue too," Mac said.

Carmen had gathered Onyx in her arms and sat in a chair, placing the cat on her lap while she continued to pet and pacify Onyx, who seemed almost as distressed as Midnight.

"Yeah, I noticed that. After I finish with the wound, I'll take a look. It's pretty deep. From what I can tell, her flesh is torn down to the bone. I'm just unsure if the bite caused a break."

Mac nodded. "Whatever she needs. Do you think you'll have to amputate her back leg?"

Midnight wailed again as if she understood what Mac had just asked. Onyx quickly joined in and began crying on Carmen's lap.

"Ssh, ssh, it's okay, Onyx, Olivia is going to fix your sister right up," Carmen soothed.

"Too early to tell. Even if there is a break, it might be clean enough to cast. Plus, we're attending to the bite soon enough that I hope we'll be able to head off any infection.

Normally, we only have to resort to amputation when the wound has developed an acute infection, or the fracture is so severe it's the only option. That typically occurs with injuries not attended to right away," Olivia explained. She gently probed Midnight's mouth and announced, "I think I know what's wrong with her tongue. It looks like she has a goat's head sticker embedded deep inside. I don't want to put her under, so I'll try to get it out, but I might need your help keeping her mouth open."

"Okay," Mac answered. "I can do that."

"It might be easier for me to do that at the clinic, where the lighting is better. Let's get her wrapped up and ready for travel," Olivia directed.

"Carmen, I know you probably want to go with, but maybe it'd be better for you to stay with Onyx and keep her calm," Mac suggested.

Carmen nodded. "You'll call as soon as you know more?"

"Of course," Mac answered, then walked over and kissed Carmen before returning to Midnight and gently wrapping her in the towel.

"It might be better if you ride with me while holding Midnight versus putting her in a carrier and driving over yourself," Olivia suggested.

"Good idea. I'll call Evan to give me a ride back to the farm. It's kind of on the way. I'm sure she won't mind."

"If that doesn't work out, I'll take you back," Olivia offered.

"I owe you," Mac answered. "Tell Deb that I plan on arranging to have fresh vegetables and my cheese delivered to y'all for at least the next year, maybe a lifetime."

Olivia chuckled. "It isn't necessary, but I sure won't turn down the occasional delivery."

"I'll throw in a few pies," Carmen added.

"I'm pretty sure I'm getting the better end of this deal."

†

Olivia helped Mac wrap Midnight in the towel before Mac followed her to her truck. Once they'd settled into the vehicle and were on their way, Olivia glanced at Mac and arched an eyebrow.

"What?"

"Is Carmen back at the farm now?"

"Not exactly," Mac answered.

"But she stayed over, right?" Olivia asked.

"Onyx and Midnight were missing. Evan found paw prints in the back of her truck that suggested that Onyx caught a ride to the farm in her truck. We were searching for our bad kitties, so it just made sense for her to stay."

Olivia smiled. "How big of a bag did she pack?"

Mac shrugged. "Enough clothes for more than a day or two."

"I sure hope you were happy about that. Not that it's any of my business, and I usually stay out of people's personal affairs, but why are you being such a bonehead?"

Mac sighed. "Deb's been bending your ear, hasn't she?"

"Every single night. She's Carmen's best friend, and Carmen is miserable without you."

"I'm lost without her too," Mac admitted. "I'm not exactly sure, but I think I might have signaled that it would be good for her to come home to the farm."

"Might have?" Olivia quirked her eyebrow again. "Either you did, or you didn't. Step up to the plate, woman, and make it clear. You don't want to let that one slip through your fingers. Trust me, I know what it's like to drag your feet and almost make the biggest mistake of your life."

Mac nodded. "You're right. As soon as Midnight is fixed up, I'll make it clear that I want Carmen to move back to the farm. I hope Allison isn't depending on Carmen for half the rent. She's been a great friend, and I would hate to put her in a bind."

"Oh, I wouldn't worry about that. It sounds like she might enjoy having more privacy. She's quite smitten with Evan."

"How do you know that?" Mac asked.

"Oh, please, Deb, Carmen, and Allison are thick as thieves. No topic is off-limits to them. You're just out of the loop because you're being such an ignoramus with Carmen," Olivia teased.

"I knew they were seeing each other. I just didn't realize it had gotten serious," Mac defended.

"The point is that you don't need to worry about Allison. Besides, nurses make decent money. I doubt she'll have any problem paying the entire amount of rent. You know, it wouldn't be the worst idea to make it crystal clear that you want her back at the farm with a proposal. Big gestures go over extremely well," Olivia suggested.

"Hmm, maybe I will," Mac answered with a bit of swagger.

Midnight meowed, but it didn't sound like she was in pain. It was different.

"See, Midnight agrees," Olivia said.

Mac chuckled. "Carmen and I talked about this ridiculous notion that Midnight and Onyx ran away just so they could get us back living together."

Olivia laughed. "Goddess, I'm envisioning that old movie, *The Parent Trap*."

"I know, right? That's what I thought of too. Crazy, right?"

"Meow."

"I don't know. Sometimes, I think our pets know exactly what we're saying or at least have a pretty keen sense of the emotion behind our words. And they're a lot smarter than we think," Olivia explained. From my interactions with your fur babies, I can tell you that Midnight is one of the smarter cats I've cared for."

"Meow."

"She definitely knows her name," Mac answered. "And I suspect she just acknowledged your assessment of her intelligence."

CHAPTER TWENTY-SIX

Carmen had a whole lot of time to kill before she could make a call to the hospital. Hopefully, they would understand that she couldn't come in today for her shift. Pets might not count in some people's eyes as sick or injured children, but to Carmen, they absolutely did. That was why she felt so guilty separating their fur babies. They'd been no better than those couples who divorced and made it nearly impossible for the other parent to see their children on a consistent basis. If this incident did not convince Mac they belonged living under the same roof, she didn't know what would. Fortunately, it seemed like Mac was softening to the idea.

"Meow brmmp!"

Onyx reminded Carmen she was still there and needed attention.

"Oh, my poor baby. That must have been so scary. Let Mama find you a treat." Carmen walked to the refrigerator and looked inside. "How about some chicken?"

She pulled out the Tupperware container with the grilled chicken breasts Mac must have stored for quick lunches or dinners. She had preferred tossing cut-up chicken on a salad and calling it good whenever Carmen worked the rare twelve-hour shift to cover for Deb in the critical care unit before she'd left to care for her mom. It hadn't seemed important to get her job back on the medical surgical unit, and now, Carmen almost exclusively worked twelves.

Carmen smiled, knowing that old habits died hard. Except now, she probably had to do this more often because Carmen hadn't been living at the farm and wouldn't be preparing gourmet meals after her shorter shifts on the medical surgical unit like she used to. She wondered if Kathleen would be upset with her if she asked to transfer out of the critical care unit to work eights again. Proceeding to cut the chicken into small pieces, she placed the tiny chunks on a dish and set it on the floor for Onyx, who had been weaving in and out of her legs while meowing loudly.

When her phone rang, she snatched it from the counter and answered, "How is she?"

"There's a minor fracture, and Midnight might want to incessantly lick the wound after biting off the bandage and splint, so Olivia is sending her home with the cone of shame. She gave her a shot of antibiotics, but we'll need to give her more. Olivia gave me some pain medication in case Midnight is still in pain. She also had a sticker embedded in her tongue that Olivia removed. As long as we keep on the wound and make sure it stays clean, Olivia doesn't think it will be necessary to amputate. The biggest challenge will be keeping her subdued. I might go to the pet store and buy a large kennel or something. She'll hate it, but I want the paw to heal, and if she's jumping around or following me all over the farm, it won't."

Carmen pushed out a large breath of relief. "Thanks for the update. Will you be home soon?"

"Yeah, I called Evan, who will swing by to pick us up."

"I'm waiting until six to call Kathleen so I can stay with Midnight today," Carmen stated.

"Oh, um, that won't be necessary. Deb called Olivia to get an update. She's taking your shift. I hope it was okay. I just thought you'd be too tired to work a twelve, not that I needed you to stay with Midnight because I can do that."

"We'll both do that," Carmen answered. "Maybe she'll want to nap with us on the bed."

"Oh, I'm sure she will. She's a little loopy right now. I don't think she'll be zooming around the house in the next couple of days."

"I want to stay with you until Midnight has completely healed," Carmen hesitantly proposed.

"Okay," Mac answered.

"Okay? That's all?"

Mac chuckled. "We can talk more when we're face-to-face."

"I'm going to hold you to that."

†

Mac held Midnight in her lap while the truck bounced along the rural route on their way to the farm. Evan glanced over with an expectant look on her face.

"So, is Carmen staying at the farm?" Evan asked.

"Mmhm," Mac answered.

"For how long?"

Mac smiled. "She brought a large suitcase. So, I suspect for more than a couple of days."

"Good." Evan grinned. "When are you going to ask her to move back?"

"Soon. I've got to buy a ring first."

Evan chuckled. "Go big or go home. Or, in this case, go big and bring the girl home. Who are you asking to be your best woman? Olivia or me? Granted, Olivia just came to the rescue and saved Midnight's paw, but I've been managing all the marketing on the farm with outstanding results that will give you the money to buy that enormous diamond." Evan brushed her knuckles against her chest.

"I see they bypassed you when handing out the humility gene," Mac teased. "How about if we don't label it, and you can both stand next to me? It works out perfectly since I imagine Carmen will want Allison and Deb by her side. That is, if she says yes."

"For someone so smart, you sure are a dumbass. Of course she'll say yes. You could present her with a cigar ring, and she'd scream yes after you asked the question. How are you going to do it?"

Mac frowned. "I don't know, but I'm going to do it soon. I told her I needed to pick up a large kennel to keep Midnight in until she's fully healed. Maybe I'll go ring shopping while I'm out."

"Take Allison. She's off today."

"Why? You don't think I have good enough taste to pick out a ring?"

Evan shook her head. "Actually, no. Girlie stuff isn't your thing. Hey, it's not mine either, so don't get your knickers in a twist. When I get to the point where I need to pick out a ring, I'm asking Carmen to help me."

"I guess that wouldn't hurt," Mac grumbled. "Maybe she has some ideas about making the proposal special."

"Speaking of marketing, are you ready to take the farm to the next level yet? I have some thoughts about weaving Carmen into our plans."

"What makes you think Carmen will want to be included in the farm's operations?" Mac asked. "She loves nursing."

"She loves to cook and bake too. I just think it's worth asking," Evan argued.

"I've got to get the woman to say yes first. And I don't want her to feel pressured about anything."

Evan removed her hands from the wheel temporarily and held them up. "No pressure, promise."

"Put your hands back on the wheel. The last thing I need is to be involved in an accident."

Evan laughed. "There is literally no one on this road."

"Wildlife sometimes dashes in the middle of the road."

"All right, all right, Grandma."

"You know, I'm rethinking who to have as my best woman," Mac teased.

†

Carmen hadn't wanted to return to the bedroom until Mac and Midnight came home, so she paced the kitchen until she sensed it was making Onyx nervous. Moving to the living room, she pulled out her tablet and patted her lap for Onyx to cuddle with her. She made a half-hearted attempt to read a book on her tablet, but as soon as she heard Evan's truck, she quickly put Onyx on the ground and jumped up.

Mac looked even more exhausted than Carmen, and she thought that could not be good for her health. Mac carried a sleepy Midnight in her arms, holding the cone of shame in one hand. Carmen brushed her hand over Midnight's head.

"You both look like you could use a nap," Carmen said. "I wouldn't mind getting a few hours of sleep either. Do you think if we brought her up to the bed she'd sleep?"

"I think so. Let's try. Although, I want to pick up that kennel later today. So, I'll only allow myself to sleep for a couple of hours. Maybe you can stay in bed with Midnight while I'm out?"

"I can go into town and pick one up," Carmen offered. "That way, you can get the rest you need."

"No, no, I have to go to the feed store, and before this happened, I planned a long list of errands for today. It's just easier for me to make the run versus explaining everything to you. You'll be a big help by staying with Midnight and Onyx," Mac countered.

"Okay, but will you let yourself take the rest of the day off after you get all the necessary supplies?"

"I will. I promise," Mac assured.

"Right, then. Let's take the kids to the bedroom and settle in. Come on, Onyx, come nap with Mama and your sister."

Mac followed Carmen, and Onyx trotted behind. She gently placed Midnight on the bed, taking the soiled towel with her and tossing it into the laundry hamper. Next, she stripped and added her dirty clothes to the hamper.

Midnight didn't move after being placed on the bed, but Carmen heard a weak *meow* escape. Onyx jumped on the bed and sniffed her sister. She tried to lick her bandages, but Carmen gently pushed her away. "No, Onyx. No licking. Maybe we should put the cone of shame on Onyx since she seems more alert than Midnight."

"Perhaps she'll settle after you climb under the covers. We can put Midnight between us, and hopefully, Onyx will just cuddle beside her. I'd rather not put the cone on either of them. It isn't very comfortable."

"All right." Carmen pushed aside the covers, readying the bed for her to climb inside. Mac moved Midnight to the middle and carefully lifted the other side of the covers, settling next to Midnight and automatically stroking her head.

Onyx carefully approached and meowed before settling beside her sister. It almost sounded like Midnight answered, but her meow was so faint that Carmen barely heard it. While Mac soothed Midnight, Carmen rubbed Onyx's head and eventually heard the soft purring from both cats. It didn't take long for Carmen to fall asleep beside their two cats. The next time she woke, Onyx and Midnight were still sleeping peacefully, but Mac had slipped from the bed. Carmen touched the empty spot and felt how cold it was.

†

Although Mac was tired, she'd only been able to sleep for less than two hours. She smiled to herself as she remembered the vivid dream, which had been the primary reason she'd decided to get up and drive into town. Hopefully, the call to Allison wouldn't be too early on her day off. The dream offered a glimpse into her wedding. She saw herself walking down a path lined with flower petals. She recognized her farm as a backdrop to this idyllic vision of a wedding. Carmen was on one side, with Mac on the other. Pops grinned proudly as he led his two daughters down the path. Midnight and Onyx trotted happily behind, and Mac caught the glint of gold attached to each of their collars, right next to the silver bell. Seeing the cats carrying the rings like tiny ring bearers must have subconsciously given Mac an idea. Her eyes flew open, and she carefully slipped from the bed, trying hard not to disturb Carmen or either cat. She pulled on a pair of pants and a T-shirt. Before she lost all the details of the dream, she found a scrap piece of paper and jotted down a few notes, then glanced at the clock.

Shoving the notes into her pants, Mac grabbed her keys and hurried to her truck. She was on a mission. On the way to town, she called Allison, who seemed surprised to hear from Mac.

"Hello," Allison answered.

"Hey, Allison, it's Mac—"

"What's wrong? Please tell me Midnight's okay. Evan said she was giving you a ride to the farm this morning because you were at Olivia's clinic."

"Everyone's fine, well, not exactly fine, but Midnight's going to be okay. That isn't why I'm calling."

"Okay…" Allison answered hesitantly.

"I need your help," Mac said.

"My help?"

"Yeah, can I swing by and pick you up? I'm going to buy a ring today, and according to Evan, I'm shit at picking out girlie things."

"Are you telling me you need me to go ring shopping with you because you plan on asking Carmen to marry you?" Allison chuckled.

"Yes, I am. Will you help?"

"Hell yes! Count me in. But you know Carmen won't care what you pick out. You could buy her a lollypop ring," Allison teased.

"That's what Evan said, only she told me I could use a cigar wrapper. I may suck at picking out girlie stuff, but I am not going to offer the woman I love anything that won't absolutely delight her. I live for seeing that beautiful sparkle in her eyes, and unfortunately, I haven't seen that too much lately."

"Well…" Allison began.

"I know, I know," Mac interrupted. "I'm the reason she's lost that sparkle. I'll admit to having too much pride, but I will fix that with your help."

"I need to jump in the shower, so I'll see you soon. This is going to be so much fun," Allison excitedly replied. "Can't wait to help you guys plan the wedding."

"She has to say yes first," Mac answered.

"She will," Allison noted with confidence. "So, I take it that Evan knows your plans?"

"Yeah, she was the one who not so delicately suggested I ask you to help me pick out a ring."

"Smart woman. Okay, I've got to get ready."

"Thanks, Allison."

Mac ended the call and smiled. Hopefully, she'd find something today. If not, she'd have to wait until her next treatment and suffer through the crowds in Seattle. She couldn't ask Allison to travel that distance. That would be above and beyond the call of duty.

†

Carmen slipped from the bed and was thankful that both Onyx and Midnight apparently weren't ready to get up yet. Onyx raised her head and slowly blinked, but she settled down beside her sister when Midnight didn't wake. Carmen threw on some clothes and headed to the kitchen to see if

Pops was up and about. She would offer to make breakfast if he hadn't already had his. She was happy he hadn't woken up with all the commotion early this morning after Mac returned with Midnight.

A fresh basket of eggs was on the counter, and Pops sat at the table drinking a cup of coffee. His smile widened when he saw Carmen enter the kitchen.

"Morning, Carmen."

"Morning, Pops. How about if I make us some breakfast?"

"I sure won't turn that down. Where's Mac?"

"She said she had errands to run."

A wrinkle formed in his brow. "You didn't want to go with? I assume you have the day off. Why aren't you both still looking for our bad kitties?"

"We found them last night. Well, technically, early this morning. Mac and Olivia took Midnight to her clinic, and she's in the bedroom resting. A coyote did some major damage to her leg, but she'll be okay. Of course, Onyx isn't about to leave her sister's side. I stayed back to keep an eye on her."

"So, will you be staying for a few days?"

Carmen smiled. "I will."

"Good. You know I don't agree with Mac. I think she's being a stubborn ass, and I told her that."

"Thanks, Pops. I see a big thawing, so who knows, maybe she's almost ready."

"You just let me know what I can do to help push her along, and I'll do it."

"An omelet okay with you, or would you like a quiche or maybe a frittata?" Carmen asked.

"Oh, you don't have to go to any trouble. I'd be happy with fried eggs, bacon and toast. Save your fancy meals for Mac or Evan," Pops answered.

"Speaking of Evan, I should probably see if she wants something this morning. Have you seen her yet?"

"Yeah, she was tending to the goats. She sure appreciates it when I gather the eggs. After all this time, she still doesn't know how to avoid their sharp beaks. Not sure if Tiffany and Amanda are here yet. They usually head straight for the cheese shed."

"I'll go see. I might as well make breakfast for everyone. I don't do idle very well, and with the day off, cooking and baking will keep me out of trouble." Carmen stepped into the morning sunshine and went to the goat pen to find Evan.

Evan was milking the goats and looked up when Carmen entered the pen. "Hey. How's Midnight doing?"

"She's good, resting. I'm going to make breakfast if you're interested."

"Absolutely. Count me in."

"Do you want me to call Allison and ask her over for lunch? Mac's running errands, so I don't know when she'll be back, but I know Allison has the day off. It sounds like she enjoys coming to the farm," Carmen teased.

Evan blushed. "Um, she might be busy today. She mentioned taking care of something on her day off," Evan hedged.

Carmen furrowed her brow. "Okay… I'll call and check, just in case. Besides, I should probably give her an update on our errant kitties."

Carmen wondered why Evan was suddenly acting strange, but she left to knock on the cheese shed and offer breakfast to Amanda and Tiffany if they had started their shift. She knew that most of the staff on the farm began their day early. It was all a part of farm work. Tiffany poked her head out after Carmen knocked and answered they were going to pass since they both had already grabbed a bite to eat and were in the middle of a batch of cheese.

Before Carmen began cooking, she grabbed her phone to call Allison.

"Uh, hi," Allison sounded strange, and she heard faint music in the background. It almost sounded like Allison was in her car.

"Sorry, are you driving right now?" Carmen asked. "You shouldn't answer your phone while driving unless you're on speaker."

"Um, no, I'm not driving. I'm with a friend."

Carmen sensed Allison was being purposely evasive and had no idea why. Unless Allison had met someone else and was dating them at the same time she was seeing Evan. But that didn't sound at all like the Allison she knew.

"A friend? Do we need to have a girl's night so I can find out why you're being so cagey right now? Please tell me you aren't cheating on Evan."

"Absolutely not. How's Midnight?"

"She's good, resting. Evan mentioned you had something going on today. Come to think of it, she was acting strange too. What the hell is going on? You aren't sick, are you? Why wouldn't you tell me that?" Carmen couldn't keep the hurt from creeping into her voice. "I know I've been a little preoccupied with my own drama, but you could have told me," Carmen insisted.

"Whoa, nothing like that. I promise I would tell you if I was sick. You're my best friend." Allison sighed. "Why don't we get together after things settle with Midnight? You're staying at the farm for now, right? I'll call you, but right now, I have to go."

"Okay, but you owe me a night of gossip and catching up on whatever you're hiding from me."

"You got it. Talk to you later." Allison abruptly disconnected the call.

Carmen looked at her phone like she'd just been conversing with an alien. "How odd."

†

"Carmen?" Mac asked as she cringed.

300

"Yeah, and I don't think I did a very good job evading her questions," Carmen answered. "You better plan on asking her soon because Carmen is like a dog with a bone. She won't let up, and I can't lie to my best friend. You need to keep her at the farm too. It's a darn good thing I'm working the next three days. Twelve-hour shifts might be a killer, but at least they'll keep me too busy to go to the farm and visit Evan or find time to get together with Carmen."

"I have an idea, but it involves Onyx, and she won't likely wander too far from Midnight until she knows her sister will be okay."

"Now this, I gotta hear." Allison chuckled.

"I hope you won't think I'm out of my mind, but I had this vivid dream. We were walking down this path lined with flower petals. It was clearly our wedding, and my pops was giving us both away. Midnight and Onyx were trotting behind us, and I saw the glint from the gold rings attached to their collars. They were like little, tiny ring bearers." Mac chuckled. "Anyway, I thought that since we need to know when Midnight is moving around anyway, I'm going to buy a collar with a bell attached. I don't want Onyx to get jealous that Midnight has this special collar, so I'm buying her one too."

"Okay, that's cute. But what the heck does that have to do with how you plan on asking Carmen to marry you?"

"Don't ask me how this thought got into my brain, but I'm convinced that Onyx and Midnight sped up the process of Carmen and I getting to the place we were before she left to take care of her mom. So, in my convoluted brain, I thought at least one of them, probably Onyx since she doesn't have a bad paw and tends to stick closer to Carmen, should be involved in the proposal. I'm going to attach the ring to her collar and let Carmen find it. Then, once she sees the ring, I'll ask her to marry me." Mac chanced a glance at Allison to gauge her reaction.

Allison smiled. "I think it's perfect."

"You do?"

"Yeah. Now let's find the perfect ring." Allison glanced at her watch. "What time did you say the jewelry store opens?"

Mac frowned. "Um, I didn't really say, and I don't know. I just assumed everything would be open by nine. All the stores I usually go to are open early."

Allison shook her head. "You're a farmer. Regular people don't get up at the ass crack of dawn."

"You and Carmen do, and you aren't farmers," Mac argued.

"No, but we're in healthcare, and day shifts start early at the hospital. We know not to shop for anything besides food early in the morning."

"Oh. If it isn't open, you can help me pick out a kennel and collars for the cats. I know the feed store is open now, and they have dog and cat supplies."

Allison chuckled. "Maybe, but I doubt they have cute collars. You probably have to go to Petco for that, and I'll bet that store isn't open until ten either. Will the feed store at least have baby chicks?"

Mac smiled. "Yeah, I'm sure they will."

"Great, I love watching the baby chicks. I'm in. We can also kill some time at the Bistro. They have yummy baked goods for breakfast. You're buying. I'll do a quick search to find out when everything opens. My guess is ten, but I'll confirm my suspicion."

"Thanks, and I will happily buy breakfast." Mac sighed. "Carmen is probably making a big breakfast for everyone back at the farm, and I'm missing out."

"You've been missing out for a long time. I would have thought you'd break long before now. She's right. You are stubborn and prideful to the point of stupidity."

"She said that?"

"I'm paraphrasing. Evan was harsher and might have used similar words. On the other hand, Carmen shared her frustration in kinder terms."

"I'm never going to live this down, am I?"

"Nope. But we all still love you," Allison stated.

†

303

Carmen had done her best to wiggle more information out of Evan regarding Allison's strange behavior, but Evan wasn't budging. She just kept saying that Carmen should talk with Allison if she thought something was off. Giving up, Carmen cleaned the kitchen, then settled into the overstuffed recliner and began reading. When she heard the cats meowing, she rushed into the bedroom to find Midnight attempting to get off the bed by scaling down the sides as she clung to the comforter.

Onyx sat patiently on the floor, waiting for her sister to somehow perform this acrobatic feat. Carmen rushed over, gently pulled Midnight's claws from the comforter, and set her on the ground. She limped around and appeared slightly woozy as she approached the litter box.

"Good girl," Carmen praised. She felt terrible that she hadn't considered how Midnight might want to move around and have a need to use the box. Midnight was probably hungry too. Carmen would cut up some chicken for her as a special treat like she did with Onyx. After she finished, Carmen scooped Midnight into her arms and carried her to the kitchen.

"Are you hungry, my sweet baby?"

Both Onyx and Midnight meowed.

Carmen set Midnight on her fluffy bed, but once she opened the refrigerator and pulled out the container with chicken, Midnight left the cozy bed and hobbled over to join her sister as both patiently waited for their treat.

Carmen chuckled. "Onyx, I gave you chicken earlier."

Stereo meows increased in volume until she'd finally cut up enough and set the pieces on two separate plates. Carmen waited for the cats to devour their treat, then settled Midnight into her bed. Onyx promptly joined her sister. Midnight tried to bite her bandage.

"Midnight, no. I don't want to have to put on the cone of shame," she warned. Carmen sat on the floor, stopping Midnight from trying to work the bandage off. Finally, Midnight gave up, and her eyes blinked a few times before she settled into the bed.

Carmen looked up when she heard Mac's truck. She sighed because she had settled Midnight and Onyx not too long ago, and now Midnight lifted her head. Obviously, she heard Mac's truck in the gravel as well.

Carmen heard Mac come inside and saw her carrying the large kennel. "Do you need help?"

"Nah, I got this," Mac answered. "I thought maybe we could put it in the living room during the day, and then at night, I'll carry it to the bedroom."

Carmen laughed when she saw the two fancy collars with bows. "You bought collars with bows?"

Mac blushed. "I thought it would be a good idea to put collars on both of them with little bells, so when they move, we can hear it. I thought the bows were cute, like they're wearing little bow ties to attend some fancy event." She set down the kennel.

Onyx was the first to sniff the large container, then Midnight hobbled over, curious about the kennel.

"Fancy event? What happened to my girlfriend? Because you clearly know nothing about fashion."

"I can clean up nicely when the occasion calls for it," Mac defended. "Just you wait and see. I'm going to plan a special date night and get all gussied up, and then you'll have to eat your words," Mac teased.

"I so look forward to that."

The cats continued to poke their noses around the kennel but seemed to decide it wasn't something they were interested in going into, even after Mac moved their fluffy bed inside.

"We should put the litter box in there and maybe some food to entice them to crawl inside, otherwise we'll need to shove them inside against their will. I think I have some leftover chicken in the refrigerator. That should work. They both love chicken."

"Um, I already fed them the leftover chicken," Carmen confessed.

"This probably reminds them of the shelter, but I don't want Midnight to use her paw too much. She'll want to follow me around, especially after the medication wears off and she starts feeling more alert."

"I'm sure they'll forgive you," Carmen said.

"Me?" Mac chuckled. "You're going to make me be the bad guy, aren't you?"

"Damn right I am." Carmen laughed.

"Fine, but next time they need disciplining, that's all on you," Mac retorted.

"You know we never discipline them. They've got us both wrapped around their little paws. Goddess help us when we have tiny humans. I love you," Carmen exclaimed.

"I love you too."

CHAPTER TWENTY-SEVEN

It had been a week now, and Allison had called, insisting she couldn't hold Carmen off any longer. She pointedly stated that if Mac didn't get her ass in gear and ask Carmen to marry her, she was going to do it for her.

Mac rolled onto her driveway with Midnight snuggled in her carrier. She'd taken Midnight to Olivia to check the wounds, ensuring everything was healing properly and Midnight wouldn't have any long-lasting challenges. She'd been moving around more and meowing loudly to be let out of the kennel every time Mac left to take care of things on the farm.

After settling Midnight inside and greeting Carmen, who was baking several pies, Mac walked back outside and waved Evan over. "I need a favor."

"Sure, anything you need," Evan answered.

"I'm going to do it tonight. You know, pop the question. I already talked with Pops, and he's going to play poker with his buddies. Not to be indelicate, but can you get lost tonight and head over to Allison's early?"

Evan clapped Mac on the back. "Absolutely. But you know Allison and I will need a play-by-play as soon as she says yes."

"I was going to wait a little longer, but Allison threatened me. That woman's got spunk. Good luck with that," Mac teased.

"Don't I know it. But honestly, that's what I love about her. She's the first woman not to let me get away with any of my shit. I respect that," Evan admitted. "I'm not ready to pop the question like you, but I can see a future with her. That's a first for me."

"Excellent. She's been good for you."

"Yeah, she has. Okay Romeo, I'll even cut out early in case you need time to set things up."

"Thanks, I appreciate that," Mac answered.

Now for step two. Mac needed to set the stage and devise a reason to stop Carmen from planning dinner. Carmen had given her the perfect opening when she teased her about her lack of fashion sense. She'd have to brush off the tailored suit she'd worn in her days as an attorney when she'd attended one of those fancy fundraisers that enabled her to network with prospective clients.

Resting her hip against the counter, she waited until Carmen looked up. "Hey."

"Hey yourself. Do you need something?" Carmen asked.

"Pops told me he's going to play poker tonight, and Evan is leaving early for a date with Allison. I thought maybe I could show you how well I clean up. I can't take you to a fancy restaurant because I'd feel bad about stuffing them in the cage while we're having a night out. But I can whip up something for dinner, and we can have a candlelight dinner right here?"

"Why not have me prepare the meal?"

"Because I want to do this for you. It won't be anything fancy, but I think I can handle grilled fish and marinated asparagus. I'm pretty sure I can make the marinade since I've watched you prepare it numerous times. I'll add a few roasted red potatoes in a foil pouch that I can also throw on the grill. I will, however, not turn down a piece of that pie for dessert." Mac pointed at the pie crust that Carmen was filling.

Carmen smiled. "Sold. You had me at the whole insistence on how well you can clean up. I have the perfect dress to slip into."

"Wonderful. As long as you let me help you slip out of it tonight after dinner."

"That's a guarantee. I have to admit that sometimes it's nice to not be the one planning a nice dinner. Thank you for making me feel special."

Mac frowned. "I've been a horrible partner. You deserve to feel special all the time. I'm sorry for taking you for granted."

"Oh, Mac, that isn't at all what you should believe. You don't take me for granted. This little blip that I feel confident we'll work through, is the only thing that's been frustrating. I've been trying very hard to exercise patience until you're ready to talk it through. Maybe we could do that tonight?" she asked hopefully.

"Yes, let's do that." Mac pushed off the counter and gathered Carmen in her arms, kissing her as if her life and future depended on it. A swell of excitement nearly overwhelmed her. It all had to work out tonight, or she didn't know what she would do because letting this woman walk out of her life was not an option.

†

Carmen watched with amusement as Mac busied herself in the kitchen. She wanted so badly to step in and help, but it meant so much to Mac to do everything herself. Finally, Mac offered a crooked smile and made a gentle suggestion.

"Why don't you get ready? You're making me nervous, hovering like I'm going to mess it all up. Besides, you take a lot longer to get ready."

Carmen chuckled. "All right. Sorry. I didn't realize how hard it would be to simply sit and let you do all the work. I'm going now."

After showering, Carmen put on a robe and blew dry her hair before applying her make-up. When Mac showed up, ready to shower, she moved to the bedroom and used the mirror above the dresser to finish. She didn't want to put on her dress until Mac returned to the kitchen. She knew it was silly, but she envisioned making a grand entrance.

Mac didn't take long to dress, but Carmen was surprised that she was drying her hair and had clearly taken the time and care to style it. Her mouth dropped open when she saw her emerge from the bathroom. Mac had finally regained nearly all the weight she had lost after COVID hit her so hard, and the suit fit her perfectly. Mac left the top three buttons open on the crisp white tuxedo shirt. It was the sexiest thing Carmen had ever seen.

"Holy shit, you weren't kidding. Why have I never seen you in this?" Carmen waved her hand up and down Mac's body.

"Good to know I still have a few tricks up my sleeves to woo the woman of my dreams."

"Sweet talker."

"I'm going to borrow that apron of yours. I'd rather not get anything on this suit while grilling. Can you give me thirty minutes to set everything up?" Mac asked.

"Sure. I'll make my grand entrance in thirty."

"Perfect. Mac grinned as she leaned in to kiss Carmen on the cheek before exiting the bedroom.

Carmen checked her phone, and after thirty minutes, she walked into the formal dining room. Mac had pulled out her mother's china and good silverware. Two candles flickered in the middle of the table on either side of the vase filled with flowers. Mac had probably picked them from the garden.

Mac whistled. "You are beyond gorgeous. That dress is…I don't have the words to describe how good you look." She pulled out Carmen's chair.

Tears glistened in Carmen's eyes. "Everything is so beautiful. Thank you." She glanced at the kennel when she heard the pitiful meows from Onyx and Midnight. "Someone is irritated right now. Can we let them out, please?"

Mac chuckled. "Sure. I suppose you'll sneak them pieces of salmon, won't you?"

Carmen smiled. "They've been so good. Even going into the kennel without us having to fight much with them. I think they deserve a few treats."

Mac went to the cage and opened the door as the two cats scrambled out, their tiny bells tinkling before they sat beside Carmen, patiently waiting for their mama to slip them a tasty morsel of fish.

"At least wait until you've had a few bites before you sneak some to the cats," Mac requested before filling Carmen's wineglass, then her own. She lifted the glass and said, "To enduring love through life's many challenges."

Carmen smiled as she touched her glass to Mac's.

Apparently, the cats had waited long enough. Both began meowing, so after Carmen had taken a few bites and complimented Mac on her grilling acumen, she broke off several tiny pieces and put them on the small plate already on the table. Carmen chuckled to herself. Mac knew Carmen so well that she'd planned for Carmen to give the cats small pieces of fish. The empty plate was all the evidence Carmen needed. As she bent to place the plate on the floor, she caught a sparkle on Onyx's collar. At first, she thought it was the tiny bell attached, but upon closer inspection, she saw the ring and gasped.

Grabbing the cat to take a closer look, she heard Mac's chair squeak across the floor. Suddenly, Mac was on one knee as Carmen got a good look at the princess-cut diamond ring.

"Is this what I think it is?"

Mac nodded. "I might have been an attorney in a former life, but now I'm just a humble farmer without any pretty words. All I know is that if you don't agree to be my wife, I will surely shrivel up and die," Mac stated nervously.

"Does that mean I can come home now?" Carmen asked.

"Yes. Sorry, I've been such a stubborn ass. So, will you marry me?"

"Yes, a thousand times, yes. Now help me get this ring off Onyx before she bites it off, swallows it, and we have to take her to Olivia to get it out."

Mac laughed. "I'm pretty sure Olivia would just tell us to wait for her to poop it out, and then I'd be the one digging through cat shit."

"Ew, okay, can we strike that from the record? I want to preserve remembering this romantic proposal without visions of you poking through Onyx's poop."

Mac quickly undid the collar and pulled the ring off, slipping it on Carmen's finger before kissing her. "I love you."

"I love you too. Always and forever, through good times and bad, and sickness and health. I am going to recite those words in our vows. I don't care how old-fashioned they are."

"You can say whatever you want as long as you don't leave me hanging at the altar," Mac insisted.

"Never."

"I had this dream about our wedding. Can I tell you about it? I'm hoping you agree to what I saw in the dream."

"As long as it has Pops giving both of us away and the cats are involved, I'll agree to anything. Oh, and can we have the wedding on the farm?" Carmen asked.

"You just described my dream almost to the last detail. The only thing remaining was to have Onyx and Midnight be our little ring bearers."

Carmen laughed. "I can totally see that. But cats aren't the same as dogs. We'll be forced to entice them with treats. They are our tiny overlords after all."

"What do you think, Midnight, Onyx? Do you want to be our ring bearers?"

"Meow. Meow."

"I'm going to take that as a yes."

EPILOGUE

Midnight squinted at her sister, who kept licking her fur. "It's good already. Geez, you'd think you were the one getting married. Remember, we aren't walking on the path until someone coughs up the good treats."

"I know, I'm not stupid. I get more treats than you do from Carmen," Onyx answered.

"That's only because you're with her more than me," Midnight replied.

Onyx stopped licking and shot Midnight a pointed look. "Now look who's the smart one. I knew which human to sidle up to from the very start."

"You did not. I was the one who told you to offer your cute meow," Midnight argued.

"Whatever. Admit it. I'm the one who sealed the deal with our mamas with my meow. It isn't my fault your meow is more irritating than it is cute," Onyx taunted.

"Don't forget that I thought up the plan to get them back together. I can't believe you were more than content to stay with Carmen and forget all about me," Midnight huffed. "Besides, I risked my life and paw for you."

"I was worried," Onyx defended. "I cried my little heart out until they heard us. And don't forget I willingly climbed inside that big prison just so you would have someone to play with."

Midnight looked over as Mac and Carmen entered the bedroom. "Are you guys ready for your close-up?" Carmen asked.

"Aw, they look so good. Carmen's dress is so beautiful. I'm trying not to play with those pretty baubles. She didn't sound too happy when I pounced on the dress before. Do I look okay?" Onyx asked.

"Yes," Midnight harrumphed.

"All you have to do is follow us around like you always do," Mac instructed. "Come on, Midnight, we're going outside now."

Midnight jumped off the bed and followed Mac, while Carmen picked up Onyx and carried her outside.

"Do you have the treats?" Carmen asked.

"Yeah, they're in my pocket," Mac answered. "I'll hand them off to Evan and Olivia as soon as we reach the gazebo."

Midnight dutifully followed Mac until Pops held out each arm for Carmen and Mac to take hold of. "Are you two ready?"

Brandi Carlile's *You and Me on the Rock* blared from the speakers as Carmen and Mac walked alongside Pops, down the path generously littered with flowers. Midnight had listened when they talked about the wedding plans, and Carmen played the song way too many times for her liking. It looked like everything was going well.

The chairs set on each side were filled with guests as Kathleen, Deb's sister, stood at the Gazebo waiting for the couple to approach. Midnight remembered the night that Deb had suggested Kathleen as an officiant because she'd gotten her certificate a few years back when a fellow nurse needed someone to perform a ceremony and was having difficulty finding someone to do it. Moses Lake had taken a very hard right, making same-sex weddings a focal point for the radical Christian Nationalists. Whatever that all meant. Midnight didn't understand human politics.

"Okay, time to act disinterested," Midnight called out. "We can get halfway there, then just stop and start cleaning yourself again."

"I know, I know. You don't have to keep harping on me. You've only told me the plan like a million times," Onyx huffed.

Mac passed over treats to Evan and Olivia, then handed a handful to Carmen, who gave them to Allison and Deb.

Midnight almost rolled over with laughter while all four women bent, holding the treats in their hands, attempting to entice Onyx and Midnight to trot down the path to the gazebo.

"Come on, you know you want these," Allison cajoled.

Midnight and Onyx continued to look bored with what was occurring on the gazebo.

Evan wiggled her hand. "Come on, Midnight, Onyx, give us a break and be good kitties. I'll let you lick the yogurt container."

"We should wait until they give the treats to Bri and Sierra. I love those two," Onyx stated.

"You only say that because they made your fur look so good today. Face it, you're a total princess. I don't even know why you had to lick your fur after they bathed you," Midnight grumbled.

Onyx lifted her head with pride. "I was just making last-minute adjustments. This tiny patch sticks up like a cowlick on occasion."

Olivia waved over Bri and handed her the treats. "If anyone can entice them to walk the path, it's Bri. She's an animal whisperer," she explained to Evan. Sierra followed Bri and accepted a handful from Deb and Allison. The young women crouched, calling the cats and giggling.

"All right. I think we made them wait long enough. You know how important it is to show them who's boss," Midnight declared.

"Good, because those treats look awfully delicious. And we get to lick the yogurt container too. Bonus."

"It sure is good to have our mamas back together."

"Yeah, life is good," Onyx agreed before following her sister down the path.

"Aren't they adorable?" Carmen said.

"Yeah, they sure are," Mac agreed.

Onyx quickly gobbled her treats while Midnight took her time to savor the special morsels. Since they'd agreed earlier not to cause more delays, both sat patiently while Deb and Olivia removed the rings from their collars and handed them to the brides.

Thankfully, the ceremony was short because Midnight was bored with the whole affair, looking for something to do now that she and her sister had successfully engineered their mamas to get married. With Onyx's help, she grudgingly admitted.

"Let's go bat at those pretty ribbons on Carmen's bouquet," Midnight suggested. "It looks like she's finally ready to play. She's swinging it around for us."

"Okay," Onyx happily answered.

Carmen looked over her shoulder and grinned at Allison, who stood with a group of women in a cluster behind Carmen. As the bouquet went flying, Midnight and Onyx launched into the air, hoping to catch the ribbons fluttering. A surprised Allison caught the bouquet.

Carmen turned around and winked at Allison. "Guess you're next."

Midnight caught the tail end of one ribbon, pulling hard as her claw caught the end, causing Allison to release the bouquet and let it drop to the ground. Onyx finally reached another ribbon as she pounced on top.

"It doesn't count now because Allison couldn't hold on," Evan remarked with a smirk on her face.

Allison playfully smacked Evan and announced, "Don't be so sure of that."

An initial shocked look on Evan's face turned soft before she leaned in to kiss Allison and mumbled, "Goddess help me, but I do love you."

"I like Evan a lot more now. Allison is really nice. She's been good for Evan. Maybe they'll let us be their ring bearers when they get married," Onyx said excitedly.

"I suppose we could agree to that if they offer us more treats," Midnight haughtily answered.

"The cats are talking a lot again. I wonder if they're plotting to get you two engaged?" Mac joked.

"I wouldn't put it past them," Carmen answered. "Watch out, Evan, you're next in their little kitten trap."

AUTHOR'S NOTE

Thank you for your support of my books. You are the reason I continue to write and am inspired to spin these tales. If you enjoyed this book, I hope you will consider leaving a review or rating the book wherever you are comfortable. I can't tell you how much reviews make a difference to authors. I finally left the world of intrigue with this contemporary romance, and now I've ventured into a whole new sub-genre with a healthy side of romance. Enjoy this sneak peek of my superhero tale, titled: **The Invisible Woman**! If you want to read about Bri and Sierra, and Deb and Olivia's love stories, be sure to check out Unconventional Lovers. Additionally, as a thank you to all my subscribers on my mailing list, I occasionally offer links to free short stories. Here is the link to subscribe: http://eepurl.com/cS7nr9. I promise not to bombard you with messages but will only send an email when I have a new book release or a new offering of a free short story.

Peace,
Annette

SNEAK PEEK FOR THE INVISIBLE WOMAN-A LESBIAN SUPERHERO STORY

Prologue

Being the Invisible Woman isn't such a bad thing. I've been invisible all my life—metaphorically speaking. Now, I am the literal Invisible Woman.

It's easy to fade into the background if you're average. I was average in almost everything except my giant brain. I don't say that as a braggart; it was simply a fact. I liked being average. I had a few friends. It wasn't like the cool kids ostracized me. Mostly, they ignored me.

Unfortunately, people notice you if you're on the fringes, so I politely declined to be the valedictorian. My friend,

Annalise, wasn't average and got picked on all the time. If you weren't one of the beautiful people, but you also weren't what society deems ugly, life was bearable. Unfortunately, Annalise had scars from the fire that burned the entire left side of her body, including part of her face. She was on the fringe and scorned for something she had no control over. In fact, most ostracized people don't have control over the reasons for banishment.

Annalise could have easily hidden the scars on her face with her hair, but that wasn't Annalise. She preferred a close cropping of her hair, signaling to the world she wasn't afraid of being labeled a lesbian. With her shaved sides, even though the scars on her jawline were visible, in my opinion, they didn't detract from her good looks. Her arm and hand took most of the brunt of the fire and attracted the most attention, especially during gym class.

I became a scientist because I was determined to find some miracle cure for her scars. Practicality led me to forensic science, specializing in skin. Looking at the skin can tell a person a lot about the cause of death, the identity of the victim, and sometimes, when we're lucky, who is responsible for the homicide.

Annalise overcame all the obstacles and became an FBI agent. I think she enjoys unraveling puzzles. Even though she's never been able to unravel the mystery of who started the fire that caused her scars. Annalise has had to overcome all the rash judgments from others regarding her looks and almost didn't make it into the FBI. But Annalise is strong. Her perseverance is legendary. She says the same thing about me. I suppose she's right because eventually, I found something that completely removed all her scars. And that is where our story begins.

They say most scientific breakthroughs are part tenacity and a healthy dose of old-fashioned luck. I quite literally stumbled on my discovery. I never dreamed of making a mark on the world like Annalise, so maybe that's another reason we kept the discovery hidden.

I wouldn't exactly say I'm an unlikely superhero because don't a lot of them tend to originate from outcasts and geeks? Most would undoubtedly consider me a geek. But transforming from average to exceptional seems a stretch. Annalise insists I was never average. We disagree on that point, which isn't unusual because, despite our affection for one another, we are very different people. Annalise believes in soul mates and love. I believe in science. But you aren't interested in our differences; you want to hear our story. It all started with the strange purple pod that literally glowed at night.

Chapter One

"What are you still doing here, Doctor T?" my assistant Reggie asked.

"Psychotic killer still on the loose. Every minute counts, Reggie. I've been experimenting with a new chemical substance that might be able to lift prints on a badly decomposed body. I wanted to treat the tissues with my cocktail and see what happened. Why are you still here? I told you I didn't need you anymore tonight. I understand it is common for people to have dates on Friday night."

Reggie chuckled. "Can I ask you something?"

"Yes, of course, Reggie. I am always happy to explain the science behind what we do. I'd like to think that being my assistant provides you the opportunity to learn and grow. Forensic science is an exciting field."

"It's not about work. It's about Agent Taylor."

I could almost feel my face contort in confusion. "Agent Taylor?"

"Yeah. Is she seeing anyone?" Reggie asked. "I know I'm no prize, but Annalise is nice, and that's all that should matter anyway. She's also wicked good at her job, and that's incredibly sexy. Not everyone can be a beauty queen. I just think that maybe I'd have a shot because, you know..." Reggie's voice trailed off.

"You aren't suggesting that because Annalise still has visible scars, that makes her less desirable?" My voice held a warning edge.

"No, no, sorry, Doctor T. I barely even notice them anymore. They seem to be less prominent. I'd like to ask her out, but I don't know if she'd say yes or no." Reggie stumbled over her words as her face flushed.

I tended not to feel comfortable with conversations in the workplace that weren't directly related to work. Still, my discomfort seemed different from Reggie's line of inquiry, and I couldn't figure out why. Fortunately, I didn't need to analyze this too closely or answer Reggie because Annalise barged into the lab and interrupted our conversation.

"Tamara, come on, let's go. It's Friday night, and we have a Marvel comics marathon to get to," Annalise blurted. Her eyes turned to Reggie. "Oh, hey, Reggie. How come you're still here?" She jerked her head to me and stated, "This one spending her life in the lab is typical, but surely you have somewhere better to be on a Friday night."

Reggie blushed and stammered, "No, not really. My social calendar isn't exactly bustling with activity."

"Well, you could join Tamara and me if you want. We're just going to order pizza and watch a few movies," Annalise offered with a smile.

Something foreign bubbled up inside of me. At the time, I thought it had something to do with how insensitive Reggie's comments about Annalise's scars were, but it was something far more unexpected. Whatever it was must have shown on my face because Reggie's eyes widened before politely declining the invitation.

"No, that's okay. I wouldn't want to intrude. Maybe another time?" Reggie asked hopefully.

Annalise shifted her eyes between us, and a wrinkle formed on her forehead. "Okay. Did I interrupt something here?"

I opened my mouth to say something, but Reggie was already heading to the door, waving and denying our previous conversation. "No, I'm honestly a little tired."

As soon as she left, Annalise asked, "What the hell was that all about?"

"Reggie wants to ask you out," I answered.

Annalise's mouth curled up on one side. "Really? Hmm, I never would have guessed that. She's nice but not really my type."

"You don't have a type. But that's good because I don't think you and Reggie should start seeing one another."

"I do too, have a type. Just because I haven't been ready to date again doesn't mean I don't have a type. I'm waiting until you find the miracle cream to eliminate all my scars, then watch out because I'll sow my wild oats like a freshman in college away for the first time." Annalise slung her arm around my shoulder. "After I'm done getting that out of my system, I'll force you to go out with me, and we'll fall madly in love, proving that love is not simply a chemical reaction resulting in an increase of endorphins."

"The notion of love is as silly as any organized religion that assigns an idol-like status to something a person cannot see, hear or touch." The familiar argument settled me. I knew what her next dispute would be, and the customary response further mended whatever was causing so much distress.

"Atoms can't be seen, yet scientists acknowledge their existence," Annalise argued as her arm dropped from my shoulder, and I felt the absence of her touch.

I chuckled. "Stop teasing me with the same argument. You know I can see atoms through an electron microscope." I began organizing my space, readying the lab to lock up and leave.

Annalise leaned casually against the table. "And you know scientists didn't always know they existed. Perhaps science has to catch up to religion. Never say never. Also, what about dark matter? Most scientists believe it exists but have never seen it."

After Reggie's earlier comment insinuating that Annalise had an inferior appearance, I studied my best friend. Objectively, Annalise had above-average looks, exceptional in some ways. Her dark, thick, slightly wavy hair would look good in any style despite how she preferred it on the shorter side. A strong jawline and prominent cheekbones gave her a slightly masculine appearance that caught the attention of many young women on the rare occasions we would visit a gay bar, especially in a darkened room where her scars were less visible. But the features that generally charmed most women were her smoky gray eyes and cocky half smile. If she had more of a feminine appearance, I might describe her lips as almost pouty. They were certainly plump enough to satisfy our modern notion of attractiveness.

Yes, without her scars, Annalise might be considered an apex predator at the top of the heap, able to attract any mate she desired. Although I'd finally grown out of that awkward stage and did all right attracting other women, especially those who preferred a more delicate appearance, I was an objectively less striking individual. Whoever said blondes had more fun wasn't scientifically accurate. I mentally shook my head and returned to our debate.

"You're just trying to get a rise out of me. Well, it won't work." I laughed at our familiar discourse.

"I didn't have to try to get a rise out of you because you were already agitated. What's got your panties in a twist?" Annalise arched her brow.

"You know I don't wear panties. They're an unnecessary garment with the items of clothing I tend to wear." I grabbed my sling pack and headed for the door. "We're watching the ones with strong female leads, right?"

"Duh," Annalise answered as she pushed off the table and followed me out of the lab. "Stop changing the subject. You know you can't hurt my feelings, right? Let me guess, Reggie said something about my scars that you didn't like. It can't be that bad if she wants to date me. Nothing can compare to what everyone said in middle and high school. I've grown an exoskeleton that prevents harm no matter what anyone says or how they stare at me."

"Exoskeletons are wearable structures that support and assist movement or augment the human body's capabilities. They have nothing to do with how uninformed comments intended to hurt a person's feelings affect an emotionally vulnerable person. If you were more logical with your arguments, I wouldn't have to worry," I argued rationally.

Annalise burst into laughter. "If I didn't love you so much, I would take offense at what you just said. Forget it. I'm going to take it as a win that anyone wants to ask me out, regardless of whatever uninformed comment Reggie made."

We walked to the parking lot and got into our respective cars, mine a practical hybrid, hers a gas-guzzling monster SUV—a Toyota Sequoia SR5, what Annalise called a quality car with an engine powerful enough for a truck. I never understood why she didn't buy the truck with the same engine. It seemed more suited to her, but she insisted she didn't want to be a walking, talking lesbian stereotype. The RV I planned on buying after I retired got better gas mileage. A fact that didn't seem to register with Annalise.

✝

Annalise rested her long, lean form against her pride and joy, waiting in the extra paved space perpendicular to my driveway as I hit the remote to open my garage door. Her cocky smirk telegraphed her superiority at finding the fastest route and pushing the speed limit. I always groused about her knack of constantly wiggling out of those speeding tickets. Of course, having FBI credentials didn't hurt.

"Pizza should be here in about ten minutes," I called out.

Annalise pushed away from her car and greeted me inside my garage. Her brow furrowed as she shook her head in rebuke. "You really shouldn't order pizza while driving."

"Says the woman born with a lead foot," I parried, but with very little oomph. "I believe crashes related to distractions like texting make up thirteen percent of all motor vehicle accidents, while speeding is attributable to nearly one-third. You can lecture me all you want after you decide to drive the speed limit, Speed Racer." The familiarity of our recycled arguments helped to settle me.

I didn't want to admit it, but the latest case had gotten to me. The body count was not only increasing, but the age of the victim seemed to reduce by one year with each new find. The last victim was two years younger than the previous one. Either the killer had slightly altered their pattern, or there was a missing body the FBI had yet to find. The press had dubbed him The Hunter because he strung up his victims, gutted and skinned them. The killer had removed the victim's head, hands and feet with precision, leaving what looked like slabs of meat attached to the tree with meat hooks. I'd yet to pull prints from the bodies, or rather skin, carefully hanging next to the body, meaning he'd probably used gloves. The forensic bone expert hadn't found any useful clues either. The only significant clue I'd discovered was an anomaly in the skin. After comparing it to the place of the body where it was apparent he'd removed something from the deltoid muscle, I suggested it might be a tracking device. The killer was hunting his prey using technology to give him the upper hand.

Annalise must have noticed the lackadaisical way I engaged her in the debate. "The facts are all present, but where is the passion? What's wrong?"

I led Annalise into the house and pushed the button to close the garage door. Tossing my keys into my junk drawer, I turned to face my best friend, who looked at me with concern. "You're working The Hunter case. How do you do it? Remain unaffected," I clarified.

Annalise gently grabbed my arm and led me to my couch. She took my hand and answered, "Don't be so sure about that. Many things bother me, but I refuse to let the world see. I've been practicing all my life. Practically made it my own personal Olympic sport."

I saw the tenseness around her eyes and wanted to jump into a time machine and rewind the entire conversation. "Oh, Goddess, I'm sorry."

Annalise smiled. "Forget about it. We're going to catch this psycho. I've no doubt you're going to help us with that. You always do."

My doorbell penetrated the discomfort I'd created. "Saved by the bell. Pizza time. Can you find the streaming channel with the marathon?" I pointed to the remote.

She maneuvered her body to enable her to shove her hand in the front pocket of her pants, pulling out two twenties. "Here, for the pizza."

I waved her away with my hand. "It's my turn. You never remember."

She shook her head and smiled. "Why fill my brain with unimportant details? I like to leave room for the critical facts." Stuffing the bills back into her pants, she asked, "Beer, cider, wine or soda? I assume you have all those choices for us."

"Cider, please."

After I'd answered the door, paid the young delivery woman, and set the pizza on the coffee table, Annalise pressed the button to start the marathon, and we began our usual commentary as the first movie played, debating everything from the ridiculousness of their superhero costumes to the disappointment that so few Marvel movies featured queer characters.

I wasn't sure what drew my eyes from the screen as we watched *The Marvels*. Perhaps it was the intensity of the light that I saw through my peripheral vision. I have excellent peripheral vision. But it wasn't something I could ignore. Once something caught my curiosity, I couldn't let go until I figured it out. I grabbed the remote and hit the pause button.

"Why did you do that? I'm still hoping Danvers and Rambeau will discover their love for one another," Annalise joked. "Screw the bone they threw us with the *Runaways* television series. I want a lead lesbian character in one of these damn movies."

I pointed to the glowing purple light barely visible through the window. "That's freaky. I'm going to check it out."

"Now?"

"You know I can't just let that thing glow without discovering what it is."

"I'm coming with. It could be radioactive or something. Then it'll zap you and turn you into some kind of freak mutant. I'm not letting you have all the fun," Annalise joked.

Before stepping outside, I rummaged around and found two sets of rubber gloves. Handing one pair to Annalise, we proceeded to my backyard and made a beeline to the soft glow. As we approached, the light began to pulsate and brighten. It appeared to originate from a small, round object about the size of an avocado pit. Donning my rubber gloves, I plucked the glowing item from the ground and placed it in my palm for inspection. It was dark out, and I could only see the pulsating light.

"What is that?" Annalise asked.

"No clue. I'm taking it back inside and examining it in my home lab. I'll put it under my microscope. I don't want to do anything to harm it."

"It sounds like you think it's a living thing. I don't think aliens are that small," Annalise joked. "Maybe it's only a body part, like an eye or something. The poor alien might be blind now."

I bumped Annalise's shoulder playfully. "Cut it out. It could be a living thing. Maybe part of a plant or something. In Idaho, this biotech firm inserted genes from this bioluminescent mushroom into a petunia to create a new glowing houseplant called the Firefly Petunia. But it has a green glow, not lavender. Maybe they're expanding."

"You're pulling my leg," Annalise argued as she leaned in for a better look at the small round object in my hand.

I mimicked crossing my heart with my free hand. "No. I swear it exists. I'll order one, but right now, I can't wait to see this specimen under my microscope."

We hurried inside and rushed to my lab. Gently placing the glowing item under my scope, I adjusted one of my objective lenses and got my first look at the strange thing. "It's some kind of pod with multiple seeds," I exclaimed excitedly. "The membrane is translucent—enough to see inside."

"Maybe we should plant one seed. Then, when it grows a huge beanstalk, I can be the one to climb it and steal the golden goose."

"Oh, I plan on growing these seeds. I'll have to experiment with different soils and plant foods to determine exactly what my babies need to flourish."

"Just don't prick your finger and start feeding it blood. Never forget *Little Shop of Horrors*." Annalise shuddered. "I refuse to capture a food source for a human Venus Fly Trap."

"Why not? It might save the taxpayers a whole lot of money. We'd only feed it serial killers, not your run-of-the-mill robber," I joked.

"Tempting, but no. Hey, are you going to tell anyone about your find?" Annalise asked.

"Nope. I'd rather wait and see if I can even get the seed to grow. I'll start with different mixtures of potting soil and compost. Boiling eggs will leave us with an empty egg carton," I mumbled distractedly.

"I'll get the potting soil and compost while you continue to examine your find," Annalise offered.

"Can you grab all my plant foods as well? I have my gardening supplies in one section of my garage."

"Of course you do," Annalise teased.

As Annalise left to retrieve the items needed to grow whatever plants would emerge, I carefully sliced open the pod, revealing the tiny seeds, and changed to a more powerful objective lens to get a better look. The viscous liquid that spilled from inside the pod piqued my curiosity further. Close enough to detect an odor, I found the smell not at all unappealing. If a person combined honey, orange, vanilla and pineapple in a blender, it might resemble the odor emanating from the liquid spreading slowly over the glass. I grabbed an eyedropper and quickly gathered my treasured finding, placing it inside a test tube for later examination.

Annalise sort of waddled into my lab, awkwardly carrying all the items I had requested. I chuckled as the various plant food and black plastic starter trays spilled onto an empty counter before she dumped the two bags of soil and compost.

"You could have made two trips you know?" I shook my head at her.

"What's the fun in that? I'm always up for a good challenge. I found these starter trays, so we won't have to eat hard-boiled eggs for the next several days. You know how I hate eating the same foods every day."

"Help me fill the trays with a variety of mixtures. We'll start with all potting soil, decrease each by twenty percent, and fill the rest with compost. That will give us alternate 80/20, 60/40, 40/60, 20/80, and 100 percent compost mixtures to compare. We can add plant food to a couple to see how the seeds react but leave the rest alone."

"Do you have enough seeds for that?" Annalise asked.

"Yes, there are plenty of seeds to use. I may even put a couple of seeds in each mixture." I noticed a tiny droplet of purple liquid on my glove and frowned. Until I performed a few tests, I wasn't about to let the foreign substance touch my skin.

"How will you remember the differences? Don't you need to label them or something?"

"Nah, I'll remember. Especially since I'm going to start a new notebook and detail my experiment for later use," I explained.

"Hey, you got some of the alien goop on your glove. You know what it looks like?" Before I had a chance to answer, Annalise powered on. "Body fluids. You know when the forensic geeks use their black lights, searching for blood and other stuff?" She reached out to touch the droplet on my glove.

I pushed her hand away. "Don't touch that. It might be toxic. And don't refer to the forensic scientists as geeks. You know I'm one of them." I pulled off my glove, pushing it into a container designed specifically for toxic waste.

"Maybe it has special healing properties," Annalise suggested.

"Or it could be corrosive. I'll need to run it through a few tests before even thinking of applying it to animals or humans."

Annalise scowled. "You mean use yourself as a guinea pig because I know you don't use rats, bunnies or other mammals in your lab experiments. It's how you got that nasty rash when developing the cream for my scars. Promise me you won't put that on your skin."

"I promise to take reasonable precautions," I answered. I was already thinking of ways to pilfer small skin samples from any fresh bodies the FBI encountered since I was always the first to be called to the scene. Skin and bone cells didn't die immediately, so I figured they'd be the perfect samples to test. As long as what I did would not compromise an investigation, what could it hurt? I quickly discarded that notion. It would be just as easy to scrape a sample of my skin onto a slide and see what happened when I added a droplet from my test tube with the viscous liquid I'd obtained from the pod.

Annalise helped me plant the strange seeds, and I put a grow light over half of the seed tray. After completing the task, we shuffled back to my living room and enjoyed a cold beverage, beer for her and cider for me. Since it was so late, Annalise decided to crash at my place. It wasn't like she was impaired with one beer; I think she just didn't enjoy spending the night alone.

ABOUT THE AUTHOR

Annette is an award-winning author, published by Affinity Rainbow Publications, who lives in the beautiful Pacific Northwest with her wife and their four furry kids. With over thirty published novels, six Lesfic Bard Awards, and one Goldie Award for her fourth novel, *Locked Inside*, she finally feels like a real author. Annette is as much a reader as a writer and is always looking for the next sapphic novel to queue up. She came up with the *One Fan at a Time* tagline, because it rolled off the tongue much better than *One Reader at a Time*. After pondering who she was at her core, she feels it was all about connecting to each reader on a personal level. Annette would be the first to admit she doesn't do well with the masses. If someone picks up her book and it touches them, she believes she has achieved what she wants with her writing by reaching each reader. It is who she is at her core. Drop her a line. She loves to hear from readers.

Email: annettemori0859@gmail.com.

Sign up for her mailing list: http://eepurl.com/cS7nr9

Annette Mori

Check out her blog: Everyday Occurrences: https://annettemori0859.wordpress.com/

Visit the Affinity Rainbow Publications website for her books and many other outstanding authors:www.affinityebooks.com

OTHER AFFINITY BOOKS

To Autumn by Katie M Hall
Sixteen-year-old Robyn Gale, along with her younger sister Anne, is sent away for the summer holidays of 1997 to stay with her grandmother at a caravan park in Devon. Robyn's had a tough few months: trying to cope with the fallout of their mother's attempted suicide, messing up her GCSEs, and finding herself attracted to girls. Perhaps getting away from her real life is just what she needs…she can focus on finding a boyfriend, watching *Neighbours,* and swimming. A solid plan, until she meets charismatic Australian lifeguard, Autumn, and her life is turned even more down under.

Fairytail Farm by Ali Spooner
Dr. Hill McCall and her wife Alice dreamed of developing a sanctuary for unwanted cats and dogs to live out their lives as a retirement project. Hill has secretly

worked on the project for months when a wealthy benefactor surprises her with a large donation, allowing Hill to be more aggressive with the project's opening. A group home operator approaches Hill about summer volunteer positions for four girls as Fairytail Farm becomes more than just a sanctuary for the animals. It creates an environment of love and kindness for the animals and all that support the project. Several love stories develop from first love to mature couples who have found their forever person. Fairytail Farm is more than a dream come true. It is a home for happily ever afters.

The Love Demand by Annette Mori

In the dazzling realm of reality television, where love and drama entwine in a complicated dance as old as time, a groundbreaking series emerges that transcends the ordinary. *The Love Demand* is not your typical reality show. Lacey Fellows isn't sure she wants to subject herself to further humiliation, however, on the off chance her girlfriend may agree to accept a second marriage proposal, Lacey reluctantly consents to participating in the new reality show. What she doesn't count on is meeting a kindred spirit—one she can't seem to shake from her thoughts. Jaimie would do almost anything for her girlfriend, including following her to the ends of the earth and participating in a conniving television show that puts her in front of a camera, which happens to be her least favorite place. Her girlfriend, Sabina, hasn't met a camera she doesn't like. They couldn't be more opposite, but Jaimie still hopes Sabina will want marriage, kids, and the whole shebang. The last thing she expects is to fall in love with someone else. Let the games begin.

Sullivan's Trace by Ali Spooner

Micah "Sully" Sullivan has settled into a solitary life at the family horse ranch after her father's death. When her long-term vet, Doc Barton, plans to retire, his granddaughter, Bryn, arrives to take over his practice. An attack on one of Sully's prized horses throws Sully and Bryn into a whirlwind as they fight to save the young animal. Just as Sully is becoming comfortable with her growing attraction to Bryn, tragedy occurs, and her brother and his wife are killed in an accident. Sully's solitary life drastically changes when a family of three is born.

Love Sins by Annette Mori

Jessica Green's life is predictable and boring. As the chief engineer for Solar Flair, her career is right on track. Her love life, not so much. The last thing she expects is a call from her estranged father's attorney. Too curious to ignore the message, she can't resist meeting with him and discovering more about specific instructions related to his estate, as well as the letter her father left for her. Rattled by what she finds at her father's home, she promptly dials 911.

Special Agent Amanda Forrester is perplexed by a call to join a homicide investigation until she arrives at the scene and learns the victim is not only a serial killer but an elite assassin the authorities have been after for years. To Amanda's increasing irritation, the daughter recognizes a picture of the last target and insinuates herself into the investigation. As the case takes a surprising turn, Amanda finds she has landed smack dab in the middle of a complicated and dangerous situation. The facts lead her to a puzzle weaving together the recent suicide of a wealthy businessman with the activities of several prominent politicians. Amanda must join forces with a mysterious organization and the persistent woman she finds increasingly hard to resist. Her instinct to protect the alluring and vulnerable Jessica Green kicks into high gear, taking the reader on a roller-coaster journey for the last book in *The Next Generation* series.

A Wild Moon Rises by Jen Silver

Successful author, Malory G Holmes, has had a rough year. Wounded by an emotional breakup and writer's block she returns home after eight months travelling to discover the startling results of a DNA test. Apparently, through her mother's side, she is related to a baronet with an estate in Briarbay, Northumberland. She decides to visit the place to find out more about this unknown side of her family.

Selene Wylde is content with life, running a bookshop in the small hamlet of Briarbay. She also looks after her father, Reginald, who is grieving over the recent death of his husband, Sir Alan Guyatt. Reginald is worrying about his claim to stay at Briarbay Hall as the Will of Sir Alan has not yet been found.

With the arrival in her shop of a very attractive, well-known writer, Selene's world begins to tilt alarmingly. Malory and Selene become entangled in a web of secrets and deceptions with the added complication of a rapidly growing attraction.

The Wolf and The Unicorn by Ali Spooner (Erotica)

Ready to explore a steamy, passionate, and tantalizing erotica romance....

Keagan and Celeste have built a solid relationship on trust and independence. A successful surgeon, Keagan understands Celeste's supercharged libido and her desire to experience a variety of sexual encounters. Everything changes when Sky, a new doctor, arrives at the hospital, and Celeste is immediately drawn to the younger woman. Keagan is surprised when she is also attracted to Sky, who shares common interests with Celeste and her. When more than a physical attraction develops, the three women discover a loving relationship beyond the bedroom.

The Blank White Page by Ali Spooner

Tatum Chastain, Corporate Officer of Chastain International, her family's real estate empire, accepts the challenge her father, Charles, has set forth. Charles has tasked Tatum and her brother, Charlie, to survive in the wilderness for six months to prove their skills in taking over the family business once he retires. Charles fails to realize that Tatum would fall in love with the southeastern Alaska cabin he has chosen for her to test her resilience and creativity. Tatum prepares for life in the bush, and shortly after she arrives, Poe, a beautiful raven, becomes her companion and guardian. When River Foster, a designated hunter for her village, crosses Tatum's path, she finds a different kind of love awaits her.

Love Hacks by Annette Mori

Joy Stiles is adrift. Having finally finished her graduate degree at the National Defense University, the only thing keeping her interest is an ongoing feud with a fellow hacker to gain access to sensitive information. Against all odds, the person snuck their way into her tech and kept leaving taunting messages. It's driving Joy crazy. She doesn't have time for this. Operation Elephant Bites isn't working as The Organization thought it would when they started down that path two years ago. Now they have a new worry. Someone is desperately trying to find out more about The Organization, believing they are behind the attacks on the mines. Whoever that person is has not only ties to the Chinese and Russian governments but also members of the US Government. Top secret files at the NSA call their unknown group The Crusaders. Joy's efforts to uncover the identity of the enemy lead The Organization to a lot more than evil plans, and it's up to The Next Generation, with support from senior members of The Organization, to thwart the inevitable trajectory, perhaps with the assistance of Joy's irritating foe.

Strength Within by Mia Barnes

Samantha Wilson is an award-winning freelance writer with a passion for being the voice of others. Despite vowing never to go back, she returns to Milwaukee, Wisconsin, for an assignment. Her return awakens memories that force her to confront her sad and lonely childhood, including the violent attack she'd rather forget. Moving away and making a quiet, successful solo life for herself, leaving the life she knew behind cannot keep Sammie from facing her past.

Fortunately, her best friend, Zoë, flies in from New Mexico to be by her side while she confronts the demons of her past. Sammie has a knack for helping others find their happy endings. Will she finally let Zoe help her become whole again and maybe discover her happy ending in the process?

Mom's Last Wish by Charlene Neil

After fifteen years away from home, Lucy Donald receives an email from her mother's personal assistant, Cameron Bishop, compelling her to return. Soon after Lucy's arrival, threatening letters start to appear, and Lucy realizes her life is in actual danger. She seeks comfort in the arms of the alluring Cameron Bishop, but can Cameron really be trusted?

Lucy's return home and the events that unfold lead to an intense and suspenseful atmosphere.

Left to uncover the mysteries by herself, she finds herself grappling with the dilemma of not knowing whom to trust.

The Next Generation by Annette Mori

Despite Toni's legendary brilliance, even she could not stop the march of time. After learning her daughter, Joy, and Joy's two best friends, Pepper and Alina, attempted to deceive the senior agents in The Organization with a bogus Spring Break cover story, she convinces her wife it's time to let the Next Generation take over.

The last thing Pepper Maggio expects after agreeing to lead a mission is literally running into the woman she's followed for years. Not only is Grace Turner beautiful, but she's a passionate crusader for the same innocents that The Organization vows to protect. Along with her two best friends, the three young women embark on an adventure to save the day. But the mission quickly gets out of hand as the human traffickers target not only Grace and her film crew, but also the young Mexican woman who managed to catch Alina's eye. Maria might be the bravest of the bunch as a survivor of one of the Mexican mines, but she's a sitting duck if they don't intervene. They might be the Next Generation, but they'll need the full support of The

Organization, including Pepper's lethal mother, Val, to get out of Mexico alive.

Affinity
Rainbow Publications

eBooks, Print, Free eBooks

Visit our website for more publications available online.

https://affinityebooks.com/

Published by Affinity Rainbow Publications
A Division of Affinity eBook Press NZ LTD
Canterbury, New Zealand

Registered Company 2517228

www.ingramcontent.com/pod-product-compliance
Lightning Source LLC
Chambersburg PA
CBHW071512260626
47170CB00002B/350